To B

Thank

Dr. Rita Makela

Daddy's Hands
Copyright 2012 Rita Makela

ISBN: 978-161306-129-9

Prepared for publication by

The Digital Knowledge Company

For details on other available titles, and how to get your book
published, visit BookbyteDigital.com or follow us on Twitter
@BookbyteDigital

CONTENTS

DADDY'S HANDS

Dr. Rita Makela

ISBN: 978-161306-129-9

Prepared for publication by

For details on other available titles, and how to get your book
published, visit BookbyteDigital.com or follow us on Twitter
@BookbyteDigital

ACKNOWLEDGMENTS

I HAVE FILLED MANY ROLES IN MY LIFE – DAUGHTER, SISTER, STU-
dent, friend, wife, psychologist, doctor, but the most important role – the most life sustaining role – has been,
and always will be Mom. There is no other role or job in life
that has been nearly as vital and important, and certainly as
rewarding, as being a good Mom. A Mom who is there with
a calming presence in the lives of her children – a consis-
tent Mom that her children know they can count on. Later
in life I received the most precious gift from God: grandchildren. They keep me grounded and inquisitive about life. I
am eternally grateful for my children and grandchildren. I
give thanks that I have them.

My husband has been the most understanding, sym-
pathetic, kind, and loving man I have ever known. My son
once told me, "Mom, he's the nicest guy I have ever met."
My husband has been there every day to help me by reading
and reading and reading chapters as I wrote them. He gave
me strength. I thank God for sending him to me.

There are many people along the way who helped
Daddy's Hands become a reality:

Dr. Rachael Reiff, an English professor from the
University of Wisconsin – Superior, did an amazing job for
me editing my manuscript not once, but twice. Her support
and work was extremely inspiring for me. She is an intelli-

gent woman who is genuine and gracious in everything that she does. Thank you, Dr. Reiff.

My daughter, Arianna Eleanor-Victoria Saint George, took several photographs for me including the one of me at the back of the book. She did such a great job, and we had a lot of fun working together. Thank you, my baby girl.

Cindi Jackson, my cousin, spent hours reading the chapters as they were produced. She provided me with honest feedback and emotional support as the manuscript turned into a book. Thank you, Cindi.

A special thank you to my brother, The Puffman, who makes me laugh nearly every day.

Thank you to Joshua Jackson, my nephew and owner of Phoenix Creations, who spent an entire weekend at my house, and hours more upon that, helping me build a website called Daddys-Hands.com. He is extremely knowledgeable and a great teacher. I would recommend him and his company to anyone seeking to build a web page or any type of work involving the computer or internet. Thank you, Joshua.

Thank you to Bookbyte Digital and Chris Fannon specifically, who helped me to publish this work. I found him to be highly professional in everything that he did. Do not hesitate to contact Bookbytedigital.com if you are seeking some help with publishing issues. You will be glad you did.

Finally, thank you to each and every one of you who purchase this book, read it, and try to gain some understanding of the horror of sexual child abuse.

CHAPTER ONE

MY NAME IS EMILY

A S I STOOD ON THE PORCH FACING OUR SINGLE WIDE TRAIL-
er, I was gripped with fear. Children down the
street were playing, and they had asked me to
come and play with them. They had no idea how much it
would cost me to be able to do so, but, oh, how I wanted
to go. Children did not usually ask me to play with them
because I was too shy and quiet, and I never asked other children to come to my house to play. It was not safe
there. I had to protect them.

I stared at the door; my senses became acute, as
they had learned to do long before I could remember. I
could feel the touch of the breeze on my face; I could smell
the tulips freshly in bloom. I also imagined I could hear
Daddy breathing on the other side of the screen door.

I debated for what seemed like a long time, but
in reality it was only a couple of minutes as I stood there
wondering if it would really be worth it. I thought, "Should
I go in? How bad will it be? I am safe outside as long as
Daddy is doing other things. I want to go and play with
the other children. I can hear them laughing and playing

Red Light/Green Light. It is one of my favorite games next to Simon Says."

I gathered up the small amount of courage I had and told myself it does not matter. It was going to happen to me anyway, regardless of what I did, but at least this way I might get something in return for my pain.

Quietly, I opened the trailer screen door and stood inside pinned against it. I was wearing a red skirt with a tear in the bottom and a white sweater with ruffles around the sleeves that was already dingy looking when Mama bought it second-hand. I loved the sweater, but I hated skirts. Mama would not allow me to wear pants. She said girls were supposed to wear skirts or dresses. Pant wearing was strictly for boys. Other girls in the neighborhood wore pants, and they did not look like boys to me. Sometimes I thought Mama had strange ideas.

The trailer was small; there was nothing fancy about it, although it was brand new. The kitchen was in the front with a beat up dining table and two chairs. The table was the kind where the sides could fold down when you did not need it to be so big. I thought that was rather clever. Mama would eat at the table with my older brother, Charlie. I ate in the living room with Daddy. Daddy would lie on the couch, and Mama would deliver and pick up his meal for him. He ate lying down with his plate sitting on his chest. I tried it once and could not do it. Food would get stuck in my throat and my stomach would hurt.

Daddy never came to the dinner table, not even for the holiday meals when Mama would fix things so that all of us could eat together. This seemed to be important to her at least three times a year. My parents would fight on every holiday because Daddy would refuse to eat with the family. Mama would eventually give in and deliver his meal to him. She seemed more like a servant than his wife.

Next to the kitchen was the living room with a broken down couch that had a sheet thrown over it. I suppose

Mama thought that made it look better. We had to be careful how we sat on it because there were spots that sank down pretty far. The chance of anyone besides Daddy being able to use the couch, at least when he was home, was slim to none. The couch was the only place Daddy liked to be in the living room; he could always be found lying there. He was never concerned that he took up the space of three or four people.

There was one recliner that was broken so the foot rest would not pop up. The seat and arms of it were in tatters, but Mama said it should still last a long time because it was made out of "high quality vinyl." She had draped old kitchen towels across each arm and a braided rug folded in half over the seat part of the chair. My legs would get weird imprints from sitting on it with them folded under me. I tried to remember not to sit on the recliner like that on the mornings that I had to go to school; otherwise, the other children waiting at the bus stop would tease me because my legs looked funny. I did not want to tell them it was because Mama made us sit on old rugs folded on a broken down recliner. I would've been teased beyond tolerance if they knew that was the case.

There was little decoration in the living room except for a large mirror hanging above the recliner. There was a small coffee table in front of the couch. It belonged to Daddy. He had it strewn with paperback books, TV guides, his Pall Mall unfiltered cigarettes, overfilled ashtrays, and a cup of coffee that he never went to fill himself. He was the central and dominate figure in the house. Charlie and I were afraid of him.

"Just wait until your Daddy gets home!" Mama would regularly say, using him as a threat against us.

We were seriously afraid of Daddy, and Mama's promise to tattle on us for the smallest of things was always effective in getting us to do what she wanted; but this was never a guarantee that she would not complain to Daddy anyway. Mama would sell us out immediately when he walked through the door. We never wondered why she did this because we knew: she enjoyed it.

The living room led to a hallway with three bedrooms and a bathroom. My parents' bedroom was located at the end of the hallway. My room was the middle bedroom. I had one window and a bed, no dresser or toys. They would not fit. There was barely enough room to get into my bed. I did not mind that, but what did bother me was that my room was the one closest to my parents' room. It was separated by only the bathroom. I guess, though, it really didn't matter where I slept. Daddy made sure he knew what room I was in, and he could always get to me.

We were poor, and I knew it. Mama was a housewife. She said that ladies had no business getting work outside the home, unless they absolutely had to in order to feed their families. I think Mama said that just in case she changed her mind and wanted to go to work.

"It might be 1969, but a woman should still do a woman's job," Mama insisted.

I guess that meant staying at home, cooking, cleaning, and taking care of Daddy and Charlie and me.

Mama loved to cook, and she spent a good deal of time doing it. She thought we could eat more than we really could because there were usually a lot of leftovers. She would explain that her "eyes were bigger than her belly." It took me a while to figure out what that saying meant.

Mama told everyone she was a great cook. We could tell she liked her cooking by the amount she ate, but Charlie and I didn't care much for it, although we would never have told her.

Mama hated to waste food, so if we left any on our plates, she would eat it. She always gave us much more food than we could possibly eat. I think she did that on purpose so she had a good excuse to eat our leftovers.

Mama would also eat our leftovers when she took us

out. One day she decided to take us to a restaurant for a treat. Charlie and I were excited to go, especially because Mama was in a good mood. When we got there, she ordered the biggest ice cream treat they had on the menu for us. It was called The Lollapalooza! It sure sounded big to me. Mama got one for herself, too. It was the largest dish of ice cream I had ever seen. The waitress tried to warn Mama that it was too big for little kids to eat, but she ordered it anyway, and called the waitress a name under her breath as she walked away.

Just as the waitress had warned, we couldn't eat all of it. In fact, it didn't look like we had eaten any of it because it was so large. I was afraid Mama was going to be mad; I did not want anything to ruin the happy mood she seemed to be in.

Mama finished her ice cream and looked up at us. Smiling, she said, "See, when you get to the bottom of the dish there is a slice of pineapple. This is the best part for you."

Mama sucked the circular slice of pineapple into her mouth in one big bite. Then she drank the syrupy ice cream that had melted in the bottom of the dish. She told Charlie and me to hand her our leftovers. We sat there and watched Mama greedily eat all 3 ice creams. Each time she got to the pineapple slice, she triumphantly held it up in the air with her fingers and waved it, as though she had just won some sort of award. Mama was short, but quite big around.

Daddy, on the other hand, was tall and thin. Mama said Daddy was in the United States Air Force. Certainly, that sounds impressive, and he looked impressive all dressed up in his blue uniform that he wore to work. I thought of his uniform as a disguise. It hid what he was in his private life: a monster. The uniform never fooled me. I could see the monster beneath the clothing; however, I knew other people could not, and I did not blame them. It wasn't their fault. Daddy was good at hiding his terrible secret and looking like he was a highly respectable family man.

Daddy had been in the USAF for a couple of years. Mama said Daddy was "just an enlisted man," which was why we were poor. Sometimes when they fought, Mama would tell Daddy that she should have married an officer. Daddy would remind her that she still had time.

As I leaned against the inside of the screen door feeling the warmth of the sun on my back, I could see Daddy wasn't wearing his disguise because it was the weekend. He was the only person home; Mama had taken Charlie to the grocery store with her, and, once again, even though I had begged her not to, she left me home alone with Daddy. This happened a lot, and I began to believe that she did it on purpose.

"Please Mama!" I would beg with tears clouding my vision. "Please don't leave me here with Daddy!"

She left me.

Daddy was across the room, lying on the couch reading a paperback book and watching television at the same time. He was dressed in a shabby t-shirt and old blue jeans. On his feet were black socks. He always wore black dress socks; it seemed he never changed them, nor did he bathe or shower much. Daddy's feet would smell up the entire house at times. I thought they smelled like popcorn coated with rancid butter. Charlie thought I was crazy.

Daddy was aware that I was standing there, and I waited for my instructions. There was no doubt in my mind what I was going to have to endure. I knew what was expected of me, but I don't know how I knew it or for how long I had known it. It had always been like this: I would never get used to it, and it would always hurt.

I continued to stand quietly against the door. I wished he would get this over with because I hated the waiting. The anticipation of what he would do to me made it worse. I thought, "I can't leave...it's too late...I will be quiet... I'll pretend I'm outside playing with the other children." I was hoping this time it wouldn't take too long; otherwise, I might miss out, and the children would all go home.

After a few moments, without even moving his face from his book, Daddy said, "Come here, Emmy."

My legs felt heavy and frozen. I could not move them. They did not want to deliver me to Daddy. They were trying to protect me, but, I had to find the strength and courage to move.

"Emily!" he shouted. "I said come here!"

How could I explain to him that my legs were protecting me by not allowing me to move? Daddy did not view himself as a monster; therefore, he would never understand my longing for protection.

Finally, my legs moved. I reasoned with myself that it would be worse for me if I continued to stand by the door, and, besides, I was the one who had made the choice to come inside. I had learned the art of taking the blame, and I was very good at it. Daddy had taught me well.

I walked over slowly, keeping my head down so that I wouldn't have to see his eyes. Daddy had the darkest eyes I had ever seen; they looked black to me. Mama said I had the same color eyes, but I couldn't see it. As I got closer to him, I wished I could hold my breath so I would not have to smell his stinky feet as I waited to suffer through what he was about to do to me. I stood near the sofa but still out of his reach.

"Emily, move closer to Daddy," he said, as he patted the side of the sofa. He tried to sound kind and friendly, but I didn't fall for that trick anymore.

I inched in closer, quietly and fearfully. It was too late now.

There was no turning back.

"What is it you want?" Daddy asked, as though that was what was really on his mind.

"I want to go and play with the children down the

street," I said so softly that I was surprised he heard me.

"Let me think about it for a few moments," he stalled.

I waited and thought, "How bad is it going to be? It's going to start any minute now. I have to think about something else, anything! Think about the children wanting me to play with them...oh, how much fun that will be...I want to run back outside...I have to run — no, I can't run now because Daddy will just chase me...think about the other children playing...think...think...think...why did I come in! I want to run...I can't run!"

Within a blink of an eye, Daddy put his hand under my skirt and found the top of my panties. He stretched them out to fit his large hand in. Mama would yell at me and punish me for ruining them.

"Do you realize that panties are very expensive? Why do you keep stretching them out? They do not grow on trees, you know," Mama would reprimand.

I would picture panties growing on trees in my mind to escape from her anger. She would never believe me if I told her how they really kept getting stretched out. It was much safer to accept my punishment, which was usually standing in the corner and getting my face slapped. I did not trust Mama to protect me if I told her the truth. She would blame me, and, besides, I had the distinct feeling that she already knew how Daddy was hurting me. Horrifically, the knot in my stomach kept trying to warn me that Mama was helping Daddy to hurt me.

As I stood there, with Daddy's hand covering my entire bottom, I began to chant silently, "I don't feel it...I don't feel it...I don't feel it..."

Daddy squeezed me and felt me and pushed his fingers into places that made no sense to me. It hurt when he put things inside of me, and I prayed, begging God to make him stop every single day and night. I was terrified. I grew to hate his hands. Daddy's hands were never kind to me.

At least he did not talk to me. He kept reading. There were times when he would talk, which was worse because he expected me to be listening to him. Sometimes he would ask me questions that required me to answer. When I had to pay attention to Daddy's questions, it was impossible, no matter how hard I tried, to escape in my head.

While Daddy continued to hurt me, I tried to think about good things, but, instead, all I could think about was bath time the other night when Daddy told Mama he would help her by washing my hair. It was going to be a bath I would much rather never have to take, but I had no way out of it. If I whined about it or said I did not want to take a bath, Mama would smack me hard across the face, hitting my mouth, because that's where she said what she called "back-talk" came from, and Mama hated back-talk.

I tried to put my bath off for as long as I could. I hoped Mama would forget about it, but she didn't. She never forgot about things that caused Charlie and me some kind of pain. Mama could be really mean.

After Mama ran my bath water, she told me to get in the tub and wait for Daddy to wash my hair. Daddy would get soap in my eyes because he would try to wash my hair very fast. He was saving time for other things – things that hurt. I didn't care about the soap in my eyes; no, I didn't care about that so much. Soap in my eyes was just a little sting that I could wash away.

Mama said I was pretty good at washing my body, although Daddy would wash it anyway, but she said I had to have help with my hair. I thought I could wash my own hair too, but Mama and Daddy would not let me. Mama said I didn't do it right, and that I used too much soap when I tried, which, she explained, cost a lot of money.

I was in the bathtub when Daddy came in the bathroom. I wished I had some bubbles that I could have put in the water. At least that way, Daddy wouldn't be able to see all of me. I could hide under the bubbles. He could still touch me, but I wouldn't have to see him doing it. It seemed to hurt more if I saw what he was doing to me.

He knelt down by the bathtub and smiled at me. He was trying to look cheerful and nice like he was a regular Daddy, but I could see the evil in his black eyes. I was petrified. He spoke very loudly when he washed me; I think he wanted Mama to hear. My fear of Daddy was always there; I never knew what he might do next.

I sat in the water with my legs curled under me, staring at the bar of soap I was holding. Any minute now Daddy would take it away and pretend to drop it in the water. He would use his hands to search all over my body for it – inside and out.

Daddy touched my bottom and put his fingers down there, and asked me, "Are you sitting on the soap, Emily?" Then, he belted out a piercing laugh as though he were having fun.

I felt terrorized.

Daddy put the soap on my hair and lathered it up. He scrubbed my head hard and then rinsed it spraying water in my face. I didn't cry or try to wipe it away. I waited for him to finish. When he was done with my hair, he started to wash my body saying that I didn't do a good enough job.

"Emily, you never seem to get all the dirt off of your filthy little body, now do you?" said Daddy.

I stared down at the water trying to think of anything except Daddy and the bathtub, but it wasn't working because Daddy wouldn't stop talking. He rubbed the bar of soap over my nipples and used his other hand to scrub the soap into my skin. He pinched my nipples hard as he rubbed the soap around them. It made me jump because it stung. He did it so quickly that I didn't see it coming. I would have to learn to pay better attention.

"What did you do today while Daddy was at work?" he asked as he rubbed the bar of soap on my back.

"Nothing, Daddy," I automatically responded.

"Well, you must have done something. You didn't sit around all day with your finger up your butt – did you?" he said. "Stand up so Daddy can wash your butt."

"I don't want to stand up, Daddy. I am going to fall. It's too slippery," I complained.

I wanted to avoid standing up naked in front of him, while he searched my body for all the little nooks and crannies that his hands seemed to enjoy so well.

"Stand up now. I don't have all f'n night to sit here and wash you!" he ordered, sounding more like the Daddy I knew him to be.

Wet and naked, I stood there, shivering in my shame, wanting more than anything in the whole world to disappear. I thought, "Why can't I be like Casper the Ghost? It would be wonderful to be like Casper and be invisible. Mama said you have to die to become a ghost. I wished I could die right now, right at this moment – then I wouldn't have to feel Daddy's hands all over my body."

Daddy washed my bottom, and then he forced his hands between my legs.

"Spread your legs out further, Emily. How do you expect me to get you clean if I can't reach all of your filth? Someone has to teach you how to keep this nasty area clean. Your mother sure doesn't have a clue as to how to do it. She smells like a rotten, old, dead fish. Do you want to smell like that, Emily?" he asked me.

"No, Daddy," I muttered.

He rubbed his hand on the place where I go potty. It was one of Daddy's favorite spots to touch me. I wished I understood why.

"So, you did nothing all day then?" he continued with his meaningless questions, as he thrust his finger inside me.

I jumped and then slipped, falling backwards. My

arms and legs went flying up in the air as I tried desperately to catch myself before the fall, but there was nothing for me to grab hold of, and Daddy did not offer to help me. He had moved away quickly trying to avoid the water I was splashing.

My back hit the wall on the way down, and my butt landed hard against the bottom of the bathtub. It didn't hurt right away. It took a couple of days before a bruise appeared on my back. Mama asked me how I got it, and I wondered how she could not have known because when I fell it made a lot of noise and Daddy yelled at me.

"Jesus H. Christ!" he bellowed.

Once I asked him what the 'H' stood for in Jesus H. Christ, and he slapped my mouth so I never asked again. I still do not know.

"I'm sorry, Daddy," I said as I was scrambling to steady myself.

"You damn well better be. You got me soaking wet! Now, get your ass back up here so we can get done," he demanded.

I stood back up shaking. I felt so afraid – afraid of everything: Daddy's hands, Daddy, Mama coming in and seeing what Daddy was doing to me, Charlie coming in and seeing what Daddy was doing to me, as well as falling down again in the bathtub. I felt dizzy, and the room looked like it was getting dark around the edges. I was afraid I would throw up.

Daddy became very upset with me, so he had stopped talking. He grabbed a wash cloth and started scrubbing my body harshly. Before long, he threw it at my face. He told me to finish washing myself because he was done helping me. To my relief, he left.

I could hardly wait to feel that same sense of relief again, as I waited for Daddy's answer. My legs started to tremble from standing by the couch so straight and still. Although I could hear the children laughing and giggling and cheering and shouting, I no longer cared if Daddy was going to let me play with them. I thought, "He is probably still mad at me for splashing water on him the other night. He is never going to let me go! Please answer me so I can leave...I should run out the door...no, stand still...he is hurting me. I shouldn't have splashed the water on him...I didn't do it on purpose...he is hurting me...don't cry...think about playing with the other children...I want to run...I can hear them down the street laughing and laughing and laughing."

I did not hear my heart beating faster and faster and faster.

"Please let this stop...please let this stop," I repeated to myself. Many times I would cry silently, although I always tried to keep from doing so. This time I was successful. I did not want the other children to think I had been crying. Tears never changed a thing anyway.

He stopped.

I felt myself breathe again.

Daddy ripped his finger out of me, as violently as he had thrust it in and put his hand back on his book. Without ever looking at me, he said, "You can go and play, Emmy."

I scurried out of there as fast as my legs could carry me. As I heard the screen door slam behind me, I was already halfway to putting that memory in its own little box and closing the lid.

I was five years old.

CHAPTER TWO

ALL IS CALM, ALL IS BRIGHT

MAMA SAID IT WAS TIME TO GO AND GET A CHRISTMAS TREE, although we hadn't even had Thanksgiving yet. Mama liked to have the Christmas tree up in the house as long as possible. She was happy on this day because she loved this time of the year. I hated this time of year. Christmas time always gave Daddy more chances to be with me alone, and that was never a good thing.

I didn't like Mama's birthday or Mama and Daddy's anniversary or Valentine's Day or any holiday that Daddy thought he needed to buy a gift for Mama. Whenever Daddy had to buy a present for Mama, he would tell her that he wanted to take me with him to help him pick things out. He explained to her that since I was a girl, I would have a good idea as to what Mama might like as a present. I had no idea. I knew I liked the dolls that I saw during the Saturday morning cartoon commercials – the ones that actually cried, moved their eyes, wet their diapers, and even said "Mama" when you picked them up. I really doubted, though, that Mama would want the same thing. Mama didn't play with toys, which was too bad really, because maybe she would have more fun and be happy more often if she played with toys.

I dreaded Christmas time because it was going to be just like it was a couple of months ago when it was Mama's birthday. Daddy said I had to go shopping with him, so when it was time to leave I ran out to the car ahead of him and got in the backseat. I wanted to be as far away from Daddy as I could get.

"Get your little ass up here in the front seat, Emily. I am not your chauffeur," Daddy commanded.

"What's a chauffeur?" I asked.

"Shut your smart mouth and do as you are told now! You are holding us up. The stores don't stay open forever just for Emily, you know," Daddy reprimanded.

I had little choice. I moved to the front seat and sat as close to the door as possible. I never locked the door because I was afraid that somehow I would get locked in there forever with Daddy, and since I sat leaning up tightly against the door, I was also afraid that the door would fly open and I would fall out. This seemed to be a better option than being locked up in the car forever with Daddy though.

Before we left, Daddy had been acting very happy around Mama. Mama was happy, too, because she thought Daddy was in good mood because he wanted to go and buy presents for her. Mama thought Daddy was thinking only about her and how much he loved her, but I knew better. I knew why Daddy was really in a good mood, and it had nothing to do with Mama or buying presents for her. Daddy was looking forward to getting me trapped in the car alone with him.

Daddy drove us to the five and dime store. I was surprised that he had allowed me to sit by the door the entire way, and I wondered what he had planned. When he got there, Daddy drove the car around to the back of the store. There were a couple of cars parked back there, but not a person in sight. Daddy shut off the car.

"Move over here now, Emily," Daddy said.

I could not do it. He was going to have to drag me away from the door, which would make everything worse for me, but I simply could not move toward him.

Daddy grabbed me and pulled me over to him. He had his right arm around my shoulder holding me tightly against him.

"So, what do you think we should get Mama for her birthday?" he questioned as he touched my leg with his left hand.

I squirmed and tried to get away, but he had me pinned so tightly that I could not move.

"How about if Daddy turns on the radio while we think about what to get her for a few minutes. Maybe that will help us get some ideas," he suggested.

Daddy stopped touching my leg and started fiddling with the radio until he found the country station he had been looking for. He then put his hand back on my leg and continued talking as he hurt me.

"So, the cat got your tongue, young lady?" he asked me.

I sat quietly with my head down and my eyes closed trying so hard to be anywhere but there with him. The radio started playing a song I had never heard before, so I concentrated on the words as hard as I could, but as the song kept going it reminded me of what my Daddy was doing to me.

The man sang, "Oh, there's gonna be, there's gonna be a whole lot of trouble in your life. Oh, so listen to me; get up off your knees 'cause only the strong survive. That's what she said, only the strong survive. Oh, you've got to be strong, you'd better hold on. Don't go all around with your head hung down." The man on the radio said the song was by Jerry Butler. I wondered if his daddy had hurt him too

27

and that was why he wrote the song.

Daddy started humming along to the music as he put his hand up between my legs. I closed my eyes even tighter, and I felt a tear squeeze out of one eye as I squished my face up to help hold my eyes shut. Daddy told me to "lift up." He grabbed my panties and yanked them down by my knees. He began to roughly rub the spot where I went pee-pee. It kind of made me feel like I had to go to the bathroom, but I ignored it. Daddy was pinching my nipple with the hand that he had wrapped around me. He pinched me so hard. It really hurt a lot. How I hated Daddy's hands.

I felt Daddy trying to put his finger inside me. He got it in me just a very little bit, but oh, how that hurt! I squirmed even more, and Daddy held me even tighter. I opened my eyes for just a second, and I saw Daddy staring out toward my window, but it looked like he was not really seeing anything at all. He almost looked like he was dreaming. I shut my eyes again quickly.

Daddy pulled his finger back out of me, smelled it, put it in his mouth, sucked on it, and then let me go. Just like that, it was over for the moment. I moved away as fast as I could go.

"Fix your panties, Emily," Daddy ordered, "Let's get in the store and get this shopping done."

We got inside the store, and Daddy asked me again if I knew what Mama wanted for a present. I could not bring myself to look at Daddy after what he had done to me just moments before. Daddy stopped in the middle of an aisle and grabbed my face, turning it up towards him, and asked me again.

"What would your Mother like for a present," he said with gritted teeth.

"Last week she said she needed a heating pad," I said, wanting to disappear into the floor.

Daddy went through the store with lightning speed.

He got Mama a heating pad, a massager for her back, a foot bath massager, a neck massager, a hot water bottle, and some Ben-Gay ointment. He also bought wrapping paper and tape.

When we got back out to the car, Daddy started it right away, and I was hoping that we would be going straight home, but that was not to be. I sat by the door, as usual, but Daddy pulled me over next to him right away.

I could hear Daddy unzip his pants, so I held my eyes tightly shut again. He then took my hand and tried to wrap it around his pee-pee. I held my fingers out straight as hard as I could because I hated having to touch it, but Daddy was a lot stronger than I was, so my fingers were forced around it. He wrapped his hand around my hand and made it go up and down very fast. He was making the same moaning sounds I had heard him make many times before. It almost sounded like he was hurting, but I do not think it was hurting him. He always smiled afterwards.

Daddy had the radio on, so it did not take long for him to start moving my hand up and down to the beat of the song. Long before the song was over, Daddy shuttered and something warm and wet came out of his pee-pee and dribbled all over my hand. It didn't seem like regular pee that I had when I had to go to the bathroom. Maybe Daddy was sick.

Daddy released his grip on my hand and my body. I grabbed my hand back fast and moved over to my door. I heard Daddy zipping up his pants as I lay my head against the window staring out at nothingness. My eyes were open, yet I could see nothing...nothing. There was this vast open space of blinding whiteness. I was numb.

When we got home, Mama wanted to know why we were gone so long, and Daddy lied and told her we had gone to three stores looking for gifts for her. She seemed pleased about that until she opened her presents. She hated them.

"What in the hell did you get me all this shit for? Do

you think I am an old woman! That's how you see me, isn't it?" Mama yelled.

"It wasn't my idea to get you all this stuff," Daddy explained. "Emily said you wanted it."

I stood there horror stricken. The only thing I had said was that Mama wanted a heating pad a few days ago. Daddy was the one who picked out everything else as fast as he could so he could get back in the car to hurt me. I didn't dare say a word though; it would just make matters worse for me if I did.

"Is that right, Emily? You told Daddy to get me all this shit? Well, aren't you a selfish little brat. Just wait until it's your birthday. I am going to make sure you get some crappy presents, too, and then we can see if you like it!" she screamed at me as she slammed the foot bath down on the table.

I hoped this meant that I would not be allowed to ever go shopping with Daddy again, but somehow I knew that was too great of a wish to come true.

I could not share in the happiness that Mama was feeling because it was Christmas time. I wanted it to get over with as quickly as possible. Going to get the Christmas tree was just a reminder for me that it would not be long before Daddy would be able to hurt me in the car again.

Mama told Charlie and me to get our coats on so we could go and pick out a Christmas tree in the parking lot of a department store. I watched carefully to see if Daddy was also getting ready to go. He was lying on the couch, as usual, and, for a moment, I happily thought he was not going with us, but then he moved. He got up, stretched, and went to get his coat that he had left on the back of the chair in the kitchen. My heart sank. This was going to be another horrific trip.

I went back to my bedroom and took off my winter coat so I could put on my snow pants. I loved my snow pants. They were pink, my favorite color. They were so warm and snuggly, and most important of all, they kept me safe. As long as I had my snow pants on, Daddy could not easily reach the parts of me that he seemed to like so well.

I walked out to the living room all snug and secure in my snow pants and winter coat. I was getting quite warm, so I was hoping we would leave soon. I would feel more comfortable in our big car because the heater did not work that well, and I usually was cold in the back seat.

Daddy glared at me as I walked into the room. It was as if he could read my mind and knew why I had put on the snow pants.

"Go get those snow pants off, Emily. You look ridiculous. It's not that cold outside," Daddy ordered.

Mama looked at me and nodded in agreement.

I returned to my room to remove the safety and security that I felt with the snow pants. As I peeled them off, I was trying hard not to cry. I did not like going out with the entire family. Daddy always found some way to touch me even with everyone around. It was so hard not to let it show. It was so hard not to cry from the pain. The fear that I felt about this trip was consuming. I was so afraid Mama and Charlie would see what Daddy did to me. I never imagined they would save me, in fact, just the opposite. Maybe that is what I was afraid of most of all: they would never save me.

I slowly walked back to the living room with my head down, feeling exposed and vulnerable. Everybody was standing there waiting for me.

"Good girl, Emily," Daddy said.

I didn't feel that good.

We all got in the car to go to the tree lot. Daddy owned a big, blue car that he called his caddy. I wasn't certain as to what that referred to, but the car was huge and looked as beat up as the furniture in our house. The car was loud when it was running, and I was grateful. This meant that no one could easily talk to me over the noise.

I sat in the back seat as quietly as possible, staring out the window and wishing I was anywhere else. My legs were freezing since I hadn't been allowed to wear my snow pants. My skirt and tights did not provide much warmth for me. I knew I was supposed to act happy because Mama was happy, but it was nearly impossible. I dreaded Christmas time.

"Emily, you had best get that scowl off your face," Mama said as she turned around to face me from the front seat.

I didn't know what a scowl was or how to get it off my face, so I just smiled at her. It seemed to work.

"You know, Emily, Santa Claus sends out all of his elves to watch all the little boys and girls. He knows if you have been bad or good. You want to get presents on Christmas morning, don't you?" Mama warned.

I was in shock. They were watching me! I meekly answered Mama that, yes, I wanted presents. I couldn't believe the elves could see me all the time. This was a disaster. If they saw me, then they also saw Daddy and me.

At the Christmas tree lot I walked around with my family feeling dazed and overwhelmed by the news of the elves. I always tried to be a good girl, but I was sure the elves would blame me for what Daddy did to me.

I figured it was probably girl elves that watched me since I was a girl. I pictured them just like the go-go girls I had seen on the television show "Banana Splits." They had tall white boots and pretty short skirts, but unlike go-go girls, the girl elves had pointed ears and elf hats. I wondered what they would have thought of me had it not been for Daddy.

Mama was prancing around the Christmas tree lot with no awareness that she had shattered my world. Daddy told her he would keep an eye on me as she focused on the trees. Mama was standing next to Charlie holding his hand. Daddy guided me away from Mama and Charlie explaining that he wanted to look at the trees on the back side of the lot.

"I don't want to go there!" I shrieked. "I want to stay with Mama!"

Mama looked at me and shook her head and told me to stop yelling and to mind Daddy.

He took me to an area in the far back corner of the lot where we were alone and hidden by the Christmas trees.

"You want to be a good girl, don't you, Emmy?" he asked.

"Yes," I whispered.

"Then you must always do what your Daddy tells you to do, Emmy, or Santa Claus will never bring you any presents," he explained.

I didn't care about the presents. For Christmas, all I wanted was for Daddy to stop touching me. I doubted I was going to find that wrapped up under the tree.

I thought, "If being good means doing everything Daddy tells me to do, then why does it feel so bad, and why does Daddy always blame me for it, and why is it a secret, and why would Mama be mad at me if she found out? Maybe the elves will think I am being good after all, since I am doing what Daddy tells me to do. I just don't know."

Daddy held my hand, and kept me close to him. He pointed up to one of the tallest trees and said, "Look at that one, Emmy. Do you like that one?"

As I looked up at the tree, Daddy pulled me in front of him. I felt his hand go under my skirt and into my panties. He put his other arm securely around me and under my coat where he pinched my tiny nipple. I could hear the Christmas music playing "Silent Night" in the background. It was one of my favorite Christmas songs, and I focused on it trying to lose myself in it.

"Silent Night, holy night, all is calm, all is bright. Round yon virgin Mother and Child. Holy infant, so tender and mild,..." I sang to myself.

It was lightly snowing, so I stuck my tongue out to catch some of the snow. I wanted any sensation that would take me away from what was really happening. The snow-flakes were light on my tongue and melted quickly. They tasted clean and cold. Daddy had picked me up and put my butt by his pee-pee area, and he was rubbing against me hard. Suddenly, he turned me around and told me to look at his pee-pee. It was big and ugly and it scared me. I closed my eyes tightly. I did not want to see Daddy's angry looking pee-pee.

"Open your eyes! You did that to me, Emmy," Daddy hoarsely whispered, as an evil grin spread across his face.

I didn't say a word and looked away. He turned me back around and started rubbing against my butt again. I thought I had done something wrong. I thought, "How had I made his pee-pee look so angry? What had I done? Was this a good thing or a bad thing? Oh, dear God, please help me figure this out!"

He grabbed at my panties and tights and pulled them down. I kept singing the Christmas music to myself. I felt his hard pee-pee against me, and I was afraid. All of a sudden I felt him trying to push it inside of me! It hurt so badly. I tried to keep singing, but I could not. I screamed because of the pain, but Daddy had clamped his hand over my mouth so no one could hear me. He must've known that what he was going to do to me was going to hurt bad enough to make me cry out. He started rubbing his pee-pee between my legs and did not try to push it inside me again. I did not think it would ever end. I hated Christmas. I hated Christmas trees. Finally, Daddy's body shook next to me, and he put some-thing wet all over my panties. He dropped me back down on the ground and told me to pull my panties and tights up. So, I did.

"Let's go see if Mama found a tree," he said cheer-fully.

34

"Okay," I muttered.

"Emmy, you remember the talk we had about you being a good girl?" he asked.

"Yes," I responded.

"Well, part of being a good girl means that you never tell Mama about what you just made me do because it would make her very angry at you," he explained. "You should never tell anyone."

"Okay," I muttered again.

We found Mama and discovered that she and Charlie had picked out a tree. Charlie was smiling from ear to ear because Mama had allowed him to choose the tree. I was happy for him.

Daddy gave the man in the lot some money, and then he started to tie the tree on top of our big car. I got in the back seat and sat quietly. I felt lonely and rejected and my butt hurt. My parents looked happy tying the tree on the car together. They were laughing and talking about Christmas.

Mama got back into the car, turned around and asked me, "Now, wasn't that fun, Emmy?"

"Yes, Mama," I replied. I could still hear the Christmas music as we drove away from the lot. They were playing "Silent Night" again. "...Sleep in heavenly peace. Sleep in heavenly peace."

It used to be my favorite Christmas song.

CHAPTER THREE

THE TRANSFER

I T WAS SNOWING WHERE WE LIVED ON THE EAST COAST IN THE state of New York. It wasn't a lot of snow but enough for Charlie and me to go outside and have fun. We tried to make a snowman, but there was not enough snow, so we made snow angels instead. I never wanted to go back in the house. I was so happy outside with Charlie. He made me laugh and feel safe. Charlie was a year and half older than me, and I often wondered if he knew what Daddy did to me, and then I wondered if Daddy did the same thing to him, but I could never bring myself to ask him.

It was dark, but we were still outside playing. Christmas had come and gone, yet the yard was lit up from the Christmas tree lights that Mama had hung on our trailer. They were pretty, and I liked them. They made the trailer look happy, but it was a lie. The lights were just another disguise masking the truth of the sadness that lived within.

We made Mama yell for us three times before we acted as though we actually had heard her. We were savoring every moment of the freedom in the snow that we could possibly get. Finally, we started to go in, the crunch of the snow below our feet our final good-bye to the night.

The Christmas tree was still up in the living room, although it was almost the end of January. Mama said she wanted to enjoy it as long as she could. It looked rather brown and thin to me. I had stopped enjoying that tree long before it ever came into the house. I wished she would just throw it away.

Mama said we had to get ready for bed quickly because she had something she needed to tell us. I was very curious. Mama and Daddy never included us in any type of news. I went to my bedroom and put on my pajamas with the feet in them. I had the mistaken belief that since they were one piece they would keep me safer than a night gown. I had found out differently the first night I had worn a pair of them and Daddy tore the zipper apart.

I met Charlie back in the living room. Daddy wasn't at home. It was beautiful. I had no idea where he was and really did not care.

Mama looked at both of us and said, "Do you remember when Grandma came here to visit us?"

We responded in the affirmative.

Grandma, my Mama's mama, had come to visit us during the summer, and she had spent a month with us. I had never felt so loved and cherished in my life. She was the kindest person I had ever met, but I did not feel safe telling her about Daddy. I was so afraid she would blame me and be mad at me like Daddy always warned me about, and I simply could not risk losing her love and attention.

Grandma had slept in my bed with me for the entire time she was visiting. I worried every night that Daddy would still try to come into my bedroom and hurt me. There was not much of anything that seemed to stop him, but he never did. Although he found other ways to hurt me and touch me, my bedroom had become a sanctuary. Oh, how I loved Grandma.

When she was ready to go home, I begged with all my might to be allowed to go with her, but, of course, Daddy would not relinquish his hold on me. I thought I would never stop crying after Grandma left. Once she did leave, Daddy started to visit my room at night again. When he was done with me and would leave my room, I would bunch up the corner of my blanket and stuff it into my mouth to stifle my cries for Grandma. As I lay crouched on my side with my knees pulled tightly to my chest, I would sob out her name repeatedly, until, finally, I would fall asleep. The thought of being able to see Grandma again filled me with unimaginable joy.

"We are going to see Grandma and Grandpa again very soon," announced Mama.

My heart soared. I was so excited that I felt giddy.

"When will we see her? Is she coming here again?" I asked quickly.

"No, she isn't coming here. We are going there," Mama responded.

We both looked at her quizzically. She explained that Daddy had been transferred, which she said meant that we were going to move our trailer to Grandma's house and put it right in her yard.

"Is Grandma going to stay in my bedroom with me?" I asked hopefully.

"No, Grandma will stay in her own house, and we will stay in ours," she explained.

My heart sank. But, still, it was better than nothing. Grandma would be close during the day, but at nighttime she might as well have been a world away.

Mama wasn't kidding about moving soon. Men showed up the next day and started packing up all of our things. I managed to grab my Raggedy Ann doll which Mama had said I could take in the car with me.

My parents got the car all packed up to move, and we left the next day. Daddy said it would take us three to four days to get to Grandma's house. I was really worried about the trip, and I wondered how Daddy would try to get to me. I was safe as long I was in the backseat of the car and we were moving. It was the times when we stopped that worried me.

I was told that Grandma lived in a place called Minnesota where there was a lot of snow. Charlie and I were excited to see it. We couldn't imagine the snow the way Mama described it. She said there was snow as deep as we were tall. Imagine that!

The trip during the day was rather uneventful and downright tiresome. Once in awhile, Charlie and I would get into a fight mainly because we were bored. The fights never lasted very long, though, because Daddy would yell and threaten to beat us with his belt if we said one more word. He had beaten us with his belt several times before, and we knew how that left welts on our legs and made it hurt to sit down. Usually whenever Daddy got ready to use his belt on one us, he would fold the belt in half and snap it very loudly to frighten us even more. He could have skipped that part; we were already scared.

We stopped at fast food places during the day, but we never ate inside a restaurant. Mama preferred to eat in the car. The backseat quickly filled with the garbage from eating, as well as chip and cookie bags that Mama would throw back on us when she was done with them. Mama seemed to have this need to always have food with her. It was like she was afraid we were going to run out of food or not be able to find any.

Mama loved to shop for food, too. Daddy would give her money to buy groceries when he got paid, and every two weeks she said the same thing when she came home with the food, "At least we have food and a roof over our heads," as though these were the only two things that mattered. I never worried about going hungry, but I sure worried about a lot of other things.

Mama was a very large woman. She was much shorter than Daddy, but she was much, much wider. She had short blonde hair that she made look real big on her head. She told me she got it that way by back teasing it with her comb. I tried it once on my hair because I thought Mama might like me better if I looked more like her, but all I got was a head full of snarls that Mama had to rip out with the comb.

During our trip to Grandma's house, we were allowed to use the bathroom in the morning before we left our motel room and once in the afternoon; otherwise, we were told to hold it. On one occasion I just couldn't hold it, and I begged Daddy to stop so I could go. There was no doubt I would wet my pants if I did not get to go to the bathroom. Finally, he stopped the car on the side of the road.

"Get out and pee right there on the road. You had best hurry or I will drive off and leave your sorry ass," he shouted at me.

By the time I got outside of the car, I was quietly crying. Daddy called me a baby. I was so upset and truly concerned that he would drive off and leave me that I had a hard time going to the bathroom. The threat of him leaving me there was rather exciting, but I was more afraid of being on the side of the road alone than I was of the evil I already knew so well in the car. When I was able to start going, I hurried so fast that I started pulling my panties up too soon and ended up wetting myself anyway.

All of the motels that we stayed in seemed as run down as the inside of our trailer. They all smelled very musty, and looked old, dirty, and depressing. The second night of our trip, I was dismayed to discover the motel room my parents rented had only one bed in it. It was a very big bed but still only one. I was afraid of what this might mean.

"Where do we sleep?" I asked Mama. I didn't want an answer from Daddy.

"It was the only room we could get, and it was the

cheapest, so we will have to make do. We can all fit on the bed and get some rest. You like sleeping with Mama and Daddy, anyway don't you, Emily?" Mama asked.

I just looked at her and said absolutely nothing. All I could hope for was that I would get to sleep on the outside of the bed next to Mama. But, that was not meant to be.

Daddy said Charlie could sleep in the middle, and I was to sleep on the outside of the bed next to him. What a living nightmare. I felt suffocated, as though the room was crashing in on me. I began to wish that Daddy had left me on the side of the road.

That night I put on my pajamas with the feet in them. I called them my feetsie pajamas. It was all I could think of to provide me with some sort of barrier from Daddy. Daddy watched me coming out of the bathroom in my pajamas, and he immediately told me to put on my nightgown.

"Emily, it is going to be much too hot in that bed with all of us sleeping in it for you to be wearing heavy pajamas like that. Go and get your nightgown on," he demanded.

"I like it really warm at night when I sleep," I said weakly.

"I don't care what you like, Emmy. I am not sleeping in a bed full of sweaty ass people. Now, go and change," he responded.

I looked to Mama for some help, but, as usual, she simply agreed with Daddy.

I was desperate, so against my better judgment I tried again.

"But, I am going to be cold! I have to wear these pajamas!" I stressed.

Daddy jumped up off the bed, grabbed his belt off the floor, and quickly smacked me twice on the legs with it. I didn't ask again. I went to the bathroom, changed, and came back out wearing my nightgown.

"Now, that is a good girl, Emmy," Daddy gushed.

It was always so strange the way he could hurt me one moment and in the next act like nothing had ever happened.

Everyone was already in bed when I came back out of the bathroom, so I had no choice but to go and lie down beside Daddy. I had no doubt that he would touch me, especially since he hadn't been able to the day before. He usually hurt me every single day – only the when, where, and how changed.

Daddy held the blanket up for me to get under, and as I lay down, he scooped me up is his arm. Oh, how I wish that had been a comforting feeling and not one of complete horror. I thought he would at least wait until everyone had fallen asleep before he would start in on me, but, once again, I was wrong.

He put his hand under my nightgown and rubbed my chest area. He had me pinned tightly against him, and I could feel his breath on my face. It stunk of cigarettes, onions from his hamburger, and coffee. I felt like throwing up.

He stopped rubbing my chest and put his hand over my mouth. I thought he might kill me. It was so hard to breathe, and I was petrified beyond comprehension. I felt a finger from his other hand pushing inside me; it felt like I was being ripped open.

He took his finger out, clamped his hand tighter on my mouth, and put my legs between his, holding them tight. I could hear him sucking on his finger, and I wondered why no one else could hear him. Suddenly, I felt an extreme pain in my butt: a searing, hot, excruciating pain. It shot through me with the speed of a bullet, and it felt like someone had stabbed me down there. Now I understood why my mouth was covered, and I was pinned down so tightly. My face felt puffy and sweaty. I realized I had been holding my breath. I thought I might faint.

I tried so hard to go away in my head. I tried thinking about Grandma, but the pain was too intense, and it kept bringing me back to what Daddy was doing to me. He had been moving his finger in and out of my butt for a minute or two, and the more he did it, the worse it hurt. He took his finger out, and I felt relief, but it still hurt, and it would for days.

I felt his pee-pee next to me. It was big and hard, and it was my fault it was like that. I wished I knew what I did to make that happen so I could stop doing it. Daddy started to rub his pee-pee against my butt with his hand still covering my mouth. The bed moved rhythmically each time he rubbed against me. He pushed his pee-pee against my butt the way he had put his finger in there. He grunted, and then stopped trying to put it in there. Instead, he kept rubbing until I felt wet stuff all over my back. I was so sick to my stomach, so horrified, and so exhausted from the pain that all I wanted was to escape it somehow.

Daddy fell asleep quickly after that, but he never took his arm from around me. I lay there crying silent tears until I finally fell asleep.

The next morning I got up as soon as I woke. My nightgown was bunched up and pasted on my back, and I smelled bad. The memories from the night came flooding back, and I felt pain in my butt as I moved toward the bathroom. I was filled with such intense shame that I could not lift my head to look at anyone.

As I headed to the bathroom, I heard Mama say to Daddy, "I see she sweated a lot even without the warmer pajamas. Her nightgown is stuck to her."

I had to go to the bathroom, and it hurt as I tried. I saw blood in the toilet, and I thought I was dying even though I was only six years old. I was relieved that it would all be over soon. I wondered if Jesus would let me go to heaven or if I would be sent to the bad place for causing Daddy to do things to me that would make Mama upset.

Daddy was in a very good mood as everyone was getting ready to get back into the car and continue traveling. He was even singing one of his favorite Johnny Cash songs. Mama and Charlie started singing with him, and he told me to join in.

I mumbled along singing, "I fell into a burning ring of fire – I went down, down, down, and the flames went higher, and it burned, burned, burned, the ring of fire, the ring of fire."

CHAPTER FOUR

TO GRANDMA'S HOUSE I GO

B Y THE TIME WE ARRIVED AT MY GRANDPARENT'S HOME, I WAS sufficiently traumatized by the trip and praying to God to help me make it to Grandma. I wondered if there was something wrong with me because it was obvious that God did not love me, nor did he protect me, but I kept praying to him, asking for help and apologizing for being so bad.

It was very cold outside, and there was a lot of snow on the ground, more snow than I had ever seen before in my life. Mama explained that Grandma got a lot of snow where she lived because it was northern Minnesota, and it was really cold because it was January. I had no real conception of what northern Minnesota meant, but I certainly understood it was cold.

My grandparents lived on a dirt road in the country. Their house looked small, but the land around the house seemed endless. I learned later that my grandparents owned 50 acres around their home. The driveway was very long, but we had to park on the road because it was so full of snow that Daddy could not drive his caddy up it. He was less than happy about leaving his car on a dirt road. I could hardly see how leaving it on the road could cause it to look any worse than it already did.

As usual, I had on a skirt with no boots and no coat. I had forgotten to grab my winter coat before the movers packed it, so instead I was wearing a light pink sweater that was missing most of its buttons. When Mama gave me the sweater, she explained that it was a hand-me-down from a friend of hers. She promised to fix the buttons as soon as she could. I had nearly grown out of the sweater, and still Mama had not been able to fix the buttons. I figured buttons must be very expensive.

I saw Grandpa coming down the driveway to greet us, and I became very excited. I jumped out of the car as fast as I could, to put distance between me and the wickedness that Daddy's Caddy held. I started to run towards Grandpa. My heart was bursting with joy and love. I thought there was finally someone to love and protect me. The snow looked so white and fluffy and beautiful that I decided to take a short-cut across the huge yard through the pine trees dripping heavily with snow to get to Grandpa. It all looked so magical to me, especially those giant trees with the snow on them. I had no concept of the depth of snow, and I had expected to walk right on the top of it, but, of course, I sank into the snow up to the top of my thighs. It was so cold and I was in so deep that I could not pull myself out of the hole I had gotten into. I could see my parents using the path that had been shoveled down the driveway that led to house.

"Mama, I am stuck! My legs are freezing!" I whimpered.

"Leave her there. It will teach her a lesson about snow. She will either freeze or find her way out," snapped Daddy.

Thank goodness Grandpa did not agree with Daddy; however, he was not very kind about it either. He took his time getting to me, beating down a path with his big galoshes so that the return trip would be easier. Up close he looked like a giant of a man. He was wearing dirty bib overalls, a fur lined hat, and big rubber boots. He had a frown on his face, didn't say a word to me, and grunted hard as he ripped me out of the snow. My feet were so buried that as he lifted me up, my shoes came off my feet and remained hidden there in the deep snow. I never saw those shoes again. He carried me under his arm like a football all the way to the house. I was grateful to be out of the snow regardless of how I was taken out.

Grandma was waiting with her arms open for me. Grandpa put me down and I ran to her, jumping up into her warm, safe arms. Grandma was a short, plump German woman with sparkling blue eyes and gray hair rolled up in a bun on top of her head. She wore a housedress with a large homemade apron tied around her that covered most of the front of her. She smelled so good – like sugar cookies and love. She put me on the ground and stood back to look at me. She was quite upset that my legs were cherry red in color. I hadn't even noticed; however, I could feel that they were smartly tingling as they started to warm up in the house.

"This child needs some warm clothes wrapped around her legs right now," she commanded Mama.

Mama actually got up from the sofa (Grandma called it a divan) and went to get warm clothes for me. I was so impressed with Grandma, and I smiled to myself as I watched how Mama had to do what her Mama told her to do. It was an unexpected joy.

Our trailer had not arrived yet, so we had to sleep in Grandma's house. I was worried about that because I didn't know what Daddy would do to try and get to me with my grandparents around. Above all, I didn't want to lose the love of Grandma if she thought I was the one being bad.

I learned that the house my grandparents lived in was actually a converted garage. The house they had been living in had burned to the ground, and they had no money to rebuild, so they made the garage into a house. It was a bit different than I was accustomed to, and I was surprised to learn there was no bathroom in the house. Grandma explained that there was an outhouse, but, because it was too cold to go outside, she had put a bucket in a small room off the kitchen with a toilet seat on it. She said we could all go to the bathroom in there. The smell in that room was overwhelming, so I never dilly-dallied in there.

Like no toilet, there was no place to take a shower or bath. Grandma said we could wash up in the kitchen sink if we needed, or she would bring in huge square metal tubs on legs that she would fill with water for me. She would cover the stove with pans of water to heat for my bath because she said she had no hot water that came out of the faucet. I felt kind of bad for Grandma, but she never complained.

At first I was happy that there was no bathtub or shower because taking a bath had always been a treacherous thing for me to do. I was never able to relax or play while taking a bath because I never knew when Daddy was going to come in and hurt me. However, my relief at not having to take a bath where Daddy could get me was soon replaced by dread when Grandma wanted me to take all my clothes off and get in the metal tub so she could wash me.

I was embarrassed and very afraid to take off my clothes, so Grandma began to gently help me. I felt completely exposed being naked in the kitchen. Although no one else was in there, someone could come in at any minute. Most of all, I was afraid that Grandma would notice something strange about my body. I was certain there must be something wrong or different about me because Daddy kept telling me it was my fault that he touched me. If she did notice anything, she never said a word. I loved her even more.

The first week went by happily. I thought, "I must be living someone else's life." Daddy pretended to be someone he was not, which was fine by me, but if he thought I forgot the truth about him for one minute, he was very, very wrong. He went around being helpful and cheerful, and was always extra nice to Charlie and me when my grandparents were around. If only this phony Daddy could have lasted forever. He became the Daddy I had dreamed of all my life while we were staying at Grandma's house, yet I was always on edge because I trusted this version of Daddy much less than the real person. I knew his mask could come off at any time.

Daddy hadn't attempted to touch me during that first week, and the stress of living at my grandparent's house was beginning to wear on him. He had started going to work again during the day, which left me free to play and be with Grandma. It was like being on vacation.

Grandma's house had flooring throughout most of it, except for the back quarter of the left hand side of the house and the room off the kitchen. Both of those floors were dirt. I thought that was grand – dirt floors inside to play in! Grandma's house was amazing – cold but amazing. The moles that would crawl in under the wall by digging holes in the dirt didn't bother me at all. I thought they were rather cute, and I imagined they had come to play with me. I felt bad for them because Grandma said they were pretty blind. She said she didn't like them because they were pests.

Grandma used the back room as a pantry. Three of the walls had shelves from the top to the bottom, and Grandma had hundreds of mason jars on them with all kinds of different foods pickled and "put up," as she called it. There was also a ragged old bed in the corner of the room. My parents had been sleeping on it. It sagged almost to the floor in the middle, and the mattress was very thin. The blanket on top of it was very pretty though; it was a patchwork blanket that Grandma had made using scraps of old clothes. I asked her if she could make me one, and she said she would "one of these days."

The room had a funny smell like musty dirt. There were cobwebs draped in every corner. I loved playing in the pantry when no one was in there and Daddy was at work. I had no toys besides my Raggedy Ann doll, so I used some of the mason jars filled with different types of food and imagined they were all kinds of different people. Grandma saw me doing this and said I was cute. She gave me a marker and told me I could draw faces on the jars if I wanted to, but I could not bring myself to ruin Grandma's jars. I could spend hours playing there enjoying the tranquility of being alone, safely tucked away in Grandma's house. I never wanted to leave. I thought for sure God had finally answered my prayers.

One morning after waking from sleeping on the floor in the living room with my brother Charlie, Grandma called us into the kitchen. She had made us a breakfast of eggs and fried potatoes with toast. She also gave us each a tall glass of ice cold milk that she said had come fresh from the cow yesterday morning. Grandma had one milking cow that she milked every day. She would put the milk in a glass pitcher in the refrigerator, and by the next morning the thickest part of the cream had separated from the milk. Sometimes Grandma would skim off the heavy cream and use it for other things, but most of the time she simply mixed the milk well with a whisk before giving it to us. The cold milk was deliciously creamy. Charlie climbed up in a chair opposite of Grandma at the table. As I went to sit down in the other chair, Grandma patted her lap, indicating she wanted me to come and sit with her. I didn't hesitate a moment.

I snuggled as deeply into her as I could and relished the feeling of her one arm wrapped tightly around me while she used the other one to feed me. Normally, I wouldn't have liked being fed, that was for babies, but it was Grandma after all, and it was perfect.

As we ate, she told Charlie and me stories from when she was a little girl. The stories sounded so old and far away to us. We could not imagine growing up without a television or a telephone. When our plates were empty, she squeezed me tight and gave Charlie a loving look. I sensed immediately that something was amiss.

"Grandma is going to miss having you living with her so much," she said, as I saw a tear coming down one of her cheeks.

"What?" I asked.

"Oh, sweetie, your Mama and Daddy's trailer arrived this morning, so it means you have to go back to living in it. Grandma will still be right here only a few steps away, but I will miss having you in the house with me all the time."

My heart stopped. The breakfast that Grandma had so lovingly made turned to stone in my stomach. The weight of it seemed to drag me down as I quickly left her lap and ran to the front window. I had to verify the tragic turn of events for myself, and there it sat, the trailer, in the middle of the front yard looking out of place, sad and surrounded by all the snow that had been dug out in order to place it in the yard. My heart was beating wildly in my chest; a sudden clammy sweat covered my face. I needed to throw up. I had known this day was coming, but with each passing day that I remained at Grandma's house, I had allowed myself to feel some hope that maybe, just maybe, I would get to stay with her forever. I should have known better.

"Grandma, I want to stay with you," I said as I started to cry hysterically.

"It's okay, baby girl. Grandma will be right here. Look at how close your trailer is to my house. You can come and see me every day."

"Can't you ask Mama if I can stay with you, please, please, please, Grandma," I choked out through my sobs and tears.

"I already asked your Mama, Emily, and she said no because your Daddy wants you to stay with the family," she explained.

I felt so hopeless and so fearful and so very alone. It had been a week and a half since I had been touched and hurt by Daddy, and now it was going to start all over again. The thought of going back to live in the trailer with Daddy was nearly more than I could bear. I felt like my soul had dried up and blown away leaving me empty and hollow.

I stood there looking into Grandma's beautiful blue eyes that were framed by her soft, gray hair, and I could see the love and care she had for me. I strongly debated in my head if I should tell Grandma what Daddy did to me. If only I had some idea as to what would happen to me if I told her. I finally decided that I couldn't risk it, and I was fairly certain that nothing good would come from me telling her anyway.

I watched as Mama came out of the door of the trailer and headed toward us. She came into Grandma's house cheerfully and told us to get our things because she had finished setting up the trailer so that we could move back into it.

I moved as slowly as possible, but I was afraid of making Mama angry, so I watched her mood carefully as I found my things throughout the house. At the last moment, and out of desperation, I begged Mama to let me stay with Grandma.

"You belong with your Daddy and me, Emmy," she said happily with a scrunched up look up on her face.

I could see her eyes flashing with anger, so I stopped asking immediately. I gave Grandma a big hug, as though I would never see her again, and I told her I loved her. We half ran to the trailer because it was too cold to stay outside for any length of time. The crunching of the snow under our feet seemed very loud in the stillness of the white, blanketed yard and watchful pine trees. We sounded like intruders shattering the peacefulness of a cold winter's day.

I had thought Daddy was at work, but I had forgotten that it was Saturday. I was the first to the door, opening it quickly to escape from the cold, and to my horror, there sat Daddy.

His mask was off.

CHAPTER FIVE

MY SECRET PLACE

SPRING HAD FINALLY COME, AND IT WAS BEAUTIFUL OUTSIDE. THE winter had been a nightmare being cooped up in the house all the time. I had been right about Daddy being worse to me once we all moved back into the trailer from Grandma's house. His meanness was only topped by the amount of pain he could inflict upon me.

The first night I had been back in the trailer in my own bedroom crying myself to sleep, Daddy came in. He approached me slowly and lay down on the bed. Everyone in the house had gone to bed hours ago, but, I thought, "How come Mama doesn't know that Daddy isn't in bed with her? Doesn't she know when he leaves their bedroom? Can't she feel him and hear him when he moves? I sure can. Doesn't she wonder where he is and what he is doing if she wakes up? Or does she already know...Oh, dear God, please send Mama to save me – please God, please, please, please, let Mama save me!"

I was lying on my side facing the wall as I felt Daddy's hand come under my neck. I wanted to die. Everything seemed so hopeless. I had lost the one person in the world who could protect me and love me. I felt doomed. I started to cry even harder – it was just too much.

"Be quiet, Emily, right now. Daddy isn't going to hurt you," he lied. "I'm your Daddy. I love you."

I shoved my face deep into my pillow to muffle my tears, but I couldn't stop my body from trembling, but this didn't seem to bother him.

He moved my blankets off me and turned me on my stomach. I was frozen with fear. He pushed up my night-gown and took off my panties. My crying increased in my pillow.

"Quit your crying, Emmy. This is your fault anyway," he said. "Do you feel that? Do you feel Daddy's pee-pee rubbing against your butt? That's your fault, and I will have to take care of it now."

I felt him rubbing his pee-pee hard against me. It was very slippery as though it had some sort of grease on it. He slowly lay down on top of my body, his weight crushing the air out of me, while his body completely hid me under him. He reached up with one hand and covered my mouth tightly. At that moment, whatever he had planned, I knew it was going to be bad, really bad.

I could feel his free hand moving up and down on his pee-pee quickly. Then suddenly, without warning, he shoved his pee-pee into my butt. The instant pain was nearly unbearable. I thought I would pass out from a combination of the pain, the fear, and the lack of oxygen from his body crushing me.

"Don't worry, Emmy," he muttered, "I am only putting the head in."

In my mind, I screamed, "The head of what? I don't understand!" My eyes felt wild with fever, and my heart was beating to a rhythm of agony. It felt as though he had torn me in half. I thought, "I want to die. I want to die. Please, God, let me die!"

The pain was so intense that I found it impossible to go away in my head. As his pee-pee was in my butt, I could feel him still moving his hand up and down part of it, his hand striking my butt as he got to the bottom. Finally, I felt him shutter, and a warm substance was dribbling down the middle of me. It made me itch. He took his pee-pee out of me quickly, which hurt incredibly. He got off me and stood by the side of my bed. I was still lying on my stomach. I felt like I was not even human anymore. Without saying a word, Daddy left my bedroom. I could hear him walking down the hallway to his bedroom. I remained on my stomach for the rest of the night unable to move a muscle.

The next morning it was once again as though nothing had happened the night before. When I finally got out of bed, I found my parents sitting at the table in the kitchen. Daddy was reading a newspaper and slurping a cup of coffee. Mama was yelling at him, telling him to stop slurping his coffee.

"Good morning, Emily," Daddy said with a smile on his face. "It's going to be another beautiful day outside."

Nothing was beautiful to me. I didn't go over to Grandma's house for several days. My bottom hurt so bad that I found it difficult to walk and sit. I was afraid Grandma would notice the difference, and I was afraid she would be able to read the intense shame on my face; I could see it staring back at me every time I dared to look into the mirror.

Spring moved on and summer arrived in all its glory. The days became increasingly hot and seemed to last forever. I spent as much time outside as I possibly could, and I was thrilled to discover two rows of beautiful pine trees that had been planted side by side so closely that the branches of the larger ones were growing together. There were seven pine trees in each row starting with medium size trees and going up to very large trees. At the end of the two rows there were five very large pine trees grouped together in a tight circle. I was small enough to walk through the middle of the rows; however, it was better to crawl because I got scratched less that way.

I loved being with the pine trees. I would often crawl along the path between the two rows that were littered with brown, dry pine needles creating a crunchy carpet, rich with fragrance in order to reach the small opening where the trees sat in their circle like they were waiting for me with open arms. It smelled so good in there, and in the heat of the day, it was always cooler.

The trees protected me, or at least it seemed as if they did. I felt like a princess entering my kingdom when I was with them. No one could see me in there, and it quickly became my favorite play area. I brought my doll, wrapped in her blanket, with me and left her in the safety of the circle of trees. I would think about my babydoll when I was back home wishing I could change places with her and knowing that at least I had kept her safe. I never shared this area with anyone. I never talked about it, and I never took anyone there with me, not even Charlie. This was my place, and I would keep it secret.

Grandpa said it was perfect weather for planting vegetables, and he used a good portion of his land to do so. He allowed me to help him out as much as I could. I enjoyed being in the garden pulling weeds or planting seeds. I felt so proud when things I had helped plant started to grow. There was something about working in the dirt, planting seeds, and then watching them grow that made me feel at peace and connected to something. I loved it.

Mama's family was from Minnesota, and I soon discovered that I had a lot of cousins around my age. This particular summer my cousin Mary came to spend a few weeks to help Grandpa in the garden. Her daddy was Mama's older brother. His name was Melvin. Mama said he drank too much. I didn't know that drinking too much could be a bad thing, so I started paying attention to how much water I was drinking, although I had no idea as to how much was too much.

Mary said she was two and a half years older than me, and eight and a half years old seemed very grown up to me. I worshiped her. She seemed to know everything, and she was willing to explain things to me. She had short, blonde hair and pretty blue eyes. Mama said her hair looked ratty, but she was just being mean. Mary was taller than me, of course, and "thin as a rail," as Grandma said. When she first arrived, she had lots of bruises all over her legs, arms, and back that she showed me. She said her mama would beat her when she would pick the lock to get into the refrigerator. I told her that I did not know that refrigerators had locks on them, and she explained to me that her mama had put a padlock on their refrigerator so that neither she nor any of her brothers and sisters could get the food stored in it. I felt so bad for her. She said she was happy to be spending the summer with us, and I prayed that it could stay that way for her. I wanted to do everything in my power to make sure she was not hurt.

Mary and I worked in the garden almost every morning. She loved being there as much as I did. She said she liked being with plants more than with people because plants couldn't hurt you. I had to agree. In the afternoon, after lunch, which Mary ate like she was starving, we would play together until we were called inside by Mama for supper. We ate fast and hurried back out the door to play and talk until the sun went down and Mama made us come in.

Mary brought so much joy to my life, and I smiled a lot when I was with her. She stayed at Grandma's house, thank goodness; Daddy could not reach her at night as long as she was there. I did not know if Daddy would hurt her the way he hurt me, but I did not want to take any chances. The thought of Daddy hurting Mary made my stomach sick, and my heart beat faster. In the morning, when I would leave our trailer, I put all my bad memories and fears tightly away in a sealed box in my head; otherwise, I wouldn't be able to genuinely laugh and smile with Mary.

One afternoon we were playing with her dolls that

she had brought with her. The dolls were pretty beat up, and the hair on them was cut off in patches. She had no clothes for them, so we had to pretend they were dressed. I asked Mama if we could borrow two pieces of clothing that she had from when my brother and I were first born, but I was soundly told no. I told Mary she should have asked instead of me because she would have had a better chance of success. Mama always seemed to say no to me even before I had finished asking the question.

Mary said we should go out in the field to play. The field was a wonderful place to be. It was five acres of land that Grandpa had allowed to grow wild. It had a few scattered trees on it, but mainly it had lots of big boulders. The grass and weeds grew so tall that they almost went over my head. Lying down in the middle of the field, I felt so safe and secluded, but it was not safe; there was no safe place. I allowed myself to pretend the field was safe anyway, and that magically no harm could come to me while I was there.

As Mary and I walked through the tall grass, we would both pull weeds and chew on the sweet bottom part of them. I didn't know what kind of weed they were, but they were good to chew on. The sun kept hiding behind clouds against a bright blue sky, and the temperature was perfect.

The smell in the field filled me with hope and peace. It smelled like earth and fresh grass. We would both stand still and breathe in very deeply so we could get every bit of scent that was there. We tried skipping through the tall grass, but it was impossible, and we tumbled, rolling on to each other on the ground. We lay there giggling, and then Mary spotted a huge boulder.

"Let's go pretend that is a table and we can feed our babies," she suggested.

I agreed as usual with whatever Mary wanted to do. We made our pretend supper and fed our naked babies, and then Mary said we should lay them down for a nap because babies take naps after they eat. She knew so much.

"We should lie down, too. Mamas need their rest while the babies are sleeping," she explained.

I certainly didn't feel tired, but Mary said we should rest, and that it was what Mamas did, so I lay down in the grass with her. As we lay there, we stared at the clouds in the sky and whispered to each other so as not to wake the babies. Mary told me what she could see in the clouds, and I thought I was so lucky to be with someone so talented and smart.

Mary started to talk about babies. She was the oldest of five children, so she had a lot of experience with babies.

"Do you know how a girl gets a baby in her belly?" she asked me.

I had no idea. I had not even thought about it, although my Mama had a friend who had gone to the hospital with her belly looking very big, and when she came out, she had a baby with her, and her belly looked like a deflated balloon. Yet, I did not question these things. For me they were what they were, and it mattered little to me how they got that way. I had more pressing things occupying my mind on a daily basis.

"I don't know how a baby gets in a Mama's belly," I said rather shyly.

"I will explain it to you, Emily. Don't worry," she assured me.

I was anxious to find out the information now that she had brought the subject up, and I knew she knew what she was talking about because she knew everything. She was older than me, after all.

We were both lying on our backs, and Mary turned over on her side toward me. Her face looked very serious, so I knew this was important information and that I should pay close attention.

"Well, see it takes a Daddy to help the Mama get a baby in her tummy," she began.

"How does he help?" I asked.

She moved her hand down and lightly touched me between my legs. She said, "When a Daddy touches you with his finger right here it makes a baby in your tummy."

I stared at her wide eyed for a few minutes in utter disbelief. I had had no idea how babies were made. The only instructional show besides cartoons that I was allowed to watch was Captain Kangaroo, and he never said anything about this. I had no idea what I was going to do now. This must mean that I had had a baby in me for a long time. I wondered how long it would stay in there and how I was going to get it out. I was scared to death. Mama was going to be very mad at me.

I really wanted to tell Mary that I thought I must have a baby in my belly because Daddy touched me down there all the time, but I couldn't do it. It was so hard for me to trust people, and I didn't have any idea as to how she would act if I told her. Strangely enough, I always had a feeling that her Daddy did the same thing to her, but I never asked.

We woke up our babies and started walking back towards the house. I told Mary that I needed to use the outhouse, so we stopped at it on our way back. Mary waited outside for me. No one ever wanted to be inside the outhouse unless they absolutely had to be. As I sat in there, trying to hold my breath while I went to the bathroom, I looked at my stomach and then touched it and caressed it. I whispered to the baby that I suspected was in my tummy that I loved it and I would always take care of it. I had no idea how I was going to do anything to take care of my baby, much less how I was going to get the baby out of my tummy, but I was determined that I could do it.

Finally, I came out of the outhouse. I had needed the time alone. We headed toward the house, and as we got close to it we could see Uncle Melvin's old, rusty red, beat-up Ford truck. Daddy said Ford stood for "fix or repair daily." For some reason, my uncle did not like my Daddy. Mary stopped dead in her tracks.

"We should run away," she said.

I never knew that was an option before. I immediately said I would go anywhere with her. Then her daddy spotted us and yelled out to Mary, telling her to get up to the house. We had no choice but to go. I had never seen Mary quite so sad before.

"I thought I got to stay for three more weeks," she hesitantly questioned her daddy as she got closer to him.

"Well, what you thought and what happens appear to be two different things, now doesn't it," he snapped back at her.

"But why do I have to go home already? Grandpa still needs me, don't you, Grandpa?" she asked.

Grandpa stood there next to his son Melvin and said it was okay if Mary went home and that he could manage just fine without her. Grandpa could be just as mean and thoughtless as Uncle Melvin.

In desperation, Mary pleaded once more to her daddy, "Please, please, please, let me stay."

She was risking it by asking again, and I was afraid for her. Uncle Melvin slapped Mary so hard across the face that it made her whole body move to the side.

"Children are to be seen and not heard. You will do as you are told and you will like it," he growled at her.

I felt so bad for Mary that I started to cry silently. I knew she was embarrassed to be treated so meanly in front of me, so I kept my eyes on the ground. She ran into the house, gathered her things, said good-bye to Grandma and came back out to stand next to her daddy.

"Tell your cousin good-bye, Mary," Uncle Melvin instructed her.

Mary looked at me with total fear in her eyes. Her face was stinging red and already swollen from the hard slap her daddy had given her. She mouthed good-bye to me, and I grabbed her and hugged her as hard as I could. I wanted her to feel the love I had for her. And just like that, she was gone.

CHAPTER SIX

MAMA, DADDY TOUCHES ME

B Y MY SEVENTH BIRTHDAY, MY PARENTS HAD MADE AN ART FORM out of fighting with each other. Charlie and I did our best to stay out of their way when they fought, but sometimes they brought us into their fights anyway. We were supposed to take sides, and there was never a good choice for either one of us.

Within weeks of Mary leaving, Grandpa announced that he and Grandma were going to move 250 miles away and live by Uncle Melvin. I was devastated and felt as though my life was over. Grandpa told Mama and Daddy that he would trade his house and land for their trailer. They agreed.

By Halloween, we had moved into Grandma and Grandpa's old house. It was not as amazing as it once was to me, and I realized that what had made it truly amazing was Grandma. I tried so hard to feel her in the house or smell her, but there was nothing left. She had taken her essence with her.

The house still had no bathroom and no shower or bathtub. There was no hot water, but we did have dirt floors in part of the house. In other words, nothing had changed. At first Mama seemed happy about the move. She told us how Daddy was going to fix everything up in the house, and it would be grand. He promised, she said.

Daddy let a month go by without fixing a thing in the house. This is what my parents fought about the most. When Daddy came home from work, he would change out of his uniform and put on his dirty clothes. He would head for the couch and stretch out on it, stinking up the whole room, reading and watching television until Mama served him his meal. He would eat and then go right back to doing what he was doing. Mama said she was frustrated. The more she fought with Daddy, though, the kinder she seemed to Charlie and me. I think she wanted us on her side.

The house only had one bedroom, and it was constructed by hanging a curtain between it and the living room. The back room with the dirt floor was converted into a makeshift bedroom for Charlie, while I had to sleep in the living room on the couch. Some nights I did not get to go to sleep until very late because Daddy would not stop reading and watching television, and then, of course, he rarely went to bed without touching me and hurting me first.

I would sit in the broken recliner and wait for him to show some sign of movement. I figured he stayed up so late because he was waiting for everyone else to go to sleep so he could touch me. He wanted me awake. I was often tired and sleepy at school.

The layout of the house did not impede Daddy from touching me. If anything, he seemed to be doing more of it. The living room was right next to his bedroom, so he did not have to go too far to get to me at night. I could hear every sound they made in their room, and I knew when he was coming. It was like waiting for the devil to arrive every night.

Daddy touched me every chance he got regardless of the time of day. One of his favorite times to touch me was when I was washing the dishes after supper. Mama said I was old enough now to take care of that chore, and because Charlie was a boy, I was the one who had to do it. The minute I was left alone in the kitchen at the sink washing the dishes, Daddy would come in there and stand close behind me. He would put his hands under the top of my blouse and touch my nipples. Every night I would try to get him to stop by pushing him away as best I could, but I was not strong enough. He never stayed there very long, but it felt like an entirety to me. I could hear Mama in the next room sitting down to watch television. She was only a few footsteps away! My fear of her walking in and seeing Daddy touching me would become overwhelming when I could not hear what she was doing in the other room. Daddy never seemed troubled by the thought that Mama might see what he was doing to me. I could not understand this. I thought, "Why isn't he worried? Maybe he is right, and Mama will blame only me and not be mad at him at all." There was rarely a day gone by without Daddy finding a way to touch me and reminding me that what he did was my fault. My only escape was school.

One afternoon when I came home from school, my parents were fighting once again. Mama was yelling at Daddy, who was lying on the couch calmly reading his book. She was hysterically crying and screaming. She sounded especially mad and angry. She sobbed that Daddy never took her out anymore, and then she screamed at him, saying he was lazy and nothing more than a big time loser. She called him lots of names, some I had never heard before, but they certainly did not sound nice.

Without looking away from his book, Daddy said to Mama, "If you don't like it here, you can leave. Don't let the door hit you in the ass on the way out."

Mama became intensely angry. She looked at Charlie and me and told us to decide what we wanted to take with us because we were all leaving. Charlie and I stared at each other and knew without saying a word that we both needed to get out of the house. The bullets flying around in there were getting too big, and we were afraid that one of us would get hurt in their aftermath.

We rushed outside as soon as Mama was distracted from us and had moved on to yet another tirade against Daddy. I went down the path in the yard that Mary and I had used so many times, and I found a quiet spot to sit and think alone. There was a slight chill in the air; winter was near. The trees had already lost their beautiful colors of red, yellow, and orange. Now, everything looked brown and dead.

I was overjoyed by the idea of Mama taking Charlie and me away from Daddy and living somewhere else out of his reach. I had prayed for this so many times that it seemed somehow unreal to me. She had made this threat to Daddy before, but this time she sounded very serious.

I sat in the field thinking about what it would be like to live without Daddy. I imagined the three of us living in a big, beautiful apartment like what I had seen on television. We would have beautiful furniture and nice clothes. Mama would be extra nice because she no longer had to fight with Daddy. We would actually have a bathroom with a regular toilet and a working bathtub. How wonderful that would be. We would have a beautiful kitchen equipped with all the latest gadgets, but, best of all, it would have hot and cold running water all year long.

I just knew my world would be wonderful, beautiful, carefree, and stress free, as long as Daddy was not in it. I tried to think of what it might be like from day to day to not have Daddy there constantly hurting me. It was too much for me. I could not grasp the idea of it. I was certain it would be unbelievable though.

I began to wonder if now would be a good time to side with Mama against Daddy and tell her that he touched me down there and that I did not like it. I still had this feeling that Mama had known all along what Daddy was doing to me – some things seemed too coincidental. My hope was, though, that I could make her understand that I did not like

Daddy touching me and that what he was doing to me hurt. Maybe then she would not be angry with me like Daddy had warned me about countless times. I could hear Daddy's voice in my ears telling me that it was my fault and that if Mama found out she would hate me, yet there was something about this particular moment in time that seemed right to me. I decided it was worth the risk telling Mama. Surely she would listen to me and side with me against Daddy, especially since she was already angry enough to want to leave him.

I turned around on the path and headed slowly back toward the house. I was filled with trepidation but also determination. When I got back inside the house, Mama was standing with her hands on her hips, yelling at the top of her voice, with her face all puffy and red from crying. Daddy was lying on the couch ignoring her by keeping his book in his face.

My senses became acute, as they had so many times before in stressful, anxious circumstances. Mama's breathing sounded loud and labored to me, while Daddy was breathing calmly and normally. There was a haze of smoke hanging in the air in the living room from Daddy's cigarettes. It looked like a floating, thin cloud in the middle of the room. I saw Daddy smashing his cigarette out in the ash tray that was spilling over from all the cigarettes he had smoked during the day. Then he took another one out of the pack and lit it. When he blew his smoke out into the room, it disturbed the cloud of smoke that was already there, making it curl and fly in all different shapes.

Mama had a wild look in her eye, so much so that it frightened me, and I almost changed my mind about telling her. I had to remind myself that she had that look because of her anger toward Daddy, not me.

Neither one of them appeared to notice me when I came through the door. I couldn't see Daddy's face hidden behind his paperback book. The cover was ripped off it, and the top of the pages looked frayed. His books always had that look to them as though he pulled them out of a trash can somewhere.

I slowly shuffled across the room to stand next to Mama. She still had not noticed me. Over the years I had learned how to be extremely quiet when I needed to be, especially when I wanted to hide. I moved closer to her until my arm rubbed against her skirt. She must have felt my presence then because she stopped yelling for a moment and looked down at me.

She had tears in her eyes, and I felt sad for her. Behind the tears I thought I had seen tenderness and love for me, or maybe I was just fooling myself. Mama reached out her arm and put it around me, pulling me closer to the side of her. As she continued to look at me she said, "You still love Mama, don't you, Emily?"

"Yes," I answered. I was filled with hope that now was the time. She wanted my love. She would protect me. It would finally be over.

"I love you too, Emily," she cooed.

I couldn't bring myself to tell her when she was looking directly at me, so I waited until she looked up again and towards Daddy. However, the minute she did look at him she started yelling again, and there was no way she was going to hear me over their noise. I stood there wondering if I should just wait for her or if I should get her attention and tell her immediately.

In answer to my question, I heard Mama say to Daddy, "And you are a terrible father! You never do a damn thing with your kids!"

Now was the time! I tugged on Mama's skirt to get her attention. She looked down at me again with those same loving eyes. I quickly promised myself that everything would be okay.

"Do you need something, sweetheart?" she said.

She rarely called me sweetheart. This fight was indeed serious. I looked back at her, but I could not look her in the eyes because it was too intense. I took a deep breath and jumped in.

"Mama, Daddy puts his hands inside my panties, and I don't like it, and he hurts me," I stated forcefully, loudly and clearly. I thought that should be enough information at first. I could always tell her later about all the other horrible things Daddy did to me.

I was certain this fact would further her cause against Daddy, especially since she thought he was a bad Daddy. She stared at me; gone was the loving look.

The moment hung in the air with the heavy cigarette smoke. I was holding my breath and felt my legs getting shaky. I thought, "Why isn't she saying anything? Oh, my, God! Why isn't she saying anything! I know she heard me! Oh, my, God! Say something,

Mama...anything...just say something, please, Mama!"

I stole a sideways glance at Daddy. He was stone still. Not even his foot was moving, which he always twitched as he lay there. I thought, "He heard me, too. I know he heard me! They are both going to ignore me! Oh, my, God! What does this mean? What does this mean?"

Her stare turned into a glare. I had to look down. The shame I experienced in that moment crushed the very essence out of me. I had nothing left; I was gone; nothing; I was finally nothing. I wished I had stayed close to the door. I wanted to get out of there before she started to ask me questions.

Finally, without saying one word, she turned her head away from me and walked into the kitchen. Their fight was over.

I stood there looking at Mama's backside as she began to take out some cooking pots to make supper. She asked Daddy what he wanted to eat, and, as usual, he said he did not care what she cooked.

Nothing, she said absolutely nothing to me. I stood there for a couple of more minutes to make certain she was not going to acknowledge what I had said to her with more than just a stare.

I didn't understand! She had heard me. There was absolutely no doubt in my mind that she had heard me, and she said nothing – nothing! I felt dizzy and light headed. The shame was consuming. I was so glad Daddy was behind his book.

Nothing, she said nothing, ever. I made my legs move carefully toward the door. The room was spinning around and melting away. I felt like I was going to disappear into nothingness which I would welcome at any time. I quickly scrambled out the door and ran for the meadow. It was my turn to cry. It was my turn to howl. My mind was in a jumble. The world did not make any sense to me. I felt lost and totally abandoned. I couldn't get my mind to think anything that made any sense at all. The rules of the world no longer seemed to apply to me.

I lay in the cold, brown grass looking up at all the dead looking trees. They were spinning around so fast that they began to look like a bunch of twigs whirling around in a circle. I put my hands down to my sides and grabbed a handful of earth and held on for dear life. I closed my eyes and tried to slow my brain down. I concentrated about my pine tree sanctuary that was all mine. The pine trees always made me feel calmer and safer. Slowly, I started to get control back. My thoughts began to follow my lead.

As I calmed down a little and was able to think about what had happened, one fact became crystal clear to me: Mama had already known how Daddy was hurting me.

CHAPTER SEVEN

REVERBERATIONS

I WAS NEVER QUITE THE SAME AFTER TELLING MAMA ABOUT DADDY. The world seemed very different to me. Now, I knew that Mama knew what Daddy was doing to me because I had told her loud and clear. She knew, and she allowed it to happen. I was more terrified than ever before. Daddy had been right about Mama after all because she seemed very mad at me, and I felt like a tattletale. She was cold and distant to me. It seemed like Mama was no longer attached to me in any way. She treated me like an unwelcome stranger. I began to believe that she had known all along what Daddy was doing to me and that, somehow, she was helping him.

I expected some sort of punishment from Daddy for doing what he always warned me not to do, tell Mama, but as of yet, he had done nothing to punish me, nor had he said a word to me about it. I wanted him to just get it over with because the waiting and wondering about what he was going to do to me was torturous. Maybe that was his plan all along.

I felt as though neither one of them loved me or truly wanted me around them. I wondered if Daddy touched me to torment me, which led me to think that maybe what they really wanted to do was to kill me. I was afraid all the time. Everything in my world became suspect.

I watched Mama much more closely than I ever had before. Now that I knew she was in on it, I was convinced that she must be trying to harm me, too.

A couple of weeks passed from the time I told Mama about Daddy, and still everything felt strange to me. One morning when Mama woke me up for breakfast before school, she was smiling and humming a tune. She looked chipper and her voice sounded cheerful. There was no known reason for Mama's increased level of happiness, so I went on immediate alert. I did not trust her. She acted like her argument with Daddy had never happened. She never said a word about Daddy touching me; it was as though my confession had never occurred. Her unexplained good spirits convinced me that she was trying to trick me or hurt me somehow.

I got up from the couch, folded my blanket, and put it away in Mama's room. I watched every step I took looking for danger around every corner. I went to the kitchen and sat down at the table. Mama had my corn flakes poured in the bowl. She never poured my cereal for me.

Charlie was already sitting at the table when I sat down. He was half done with his cereal, and he teased me because I was so slow to rise. Mama was busy at the sink washing dishes. She had to heat the water on the stove top to do so; therefore, it was constantly covered with pots full of water. Soon our ability to have water would be even worse because it was the second week in November and already the weather had turned much colder, so the water pipes would freeze any day now. They froze up every winter.

Poor Charlie had the chore of bringing in water from the well. Mama and Daddy made Charlie take a bucket with a long, long rope on it and throw it down the well to scoop up water to bring inside. Most of the time, Charlie would have to find a big rock to throw down the well first in order to break through the ice that had formed so the bucket could get through it. Sometimes he let me help him throw the rocks down, but not often, because he said he was too afraid that I would fall in. The well was located a few steps beyond the front door. It was nothing more than a big, dark hole in the ground with a heavy cement cover that Charlie had to move and put back each time he was sent for water. He made a lot of trips to the well everyday even when it was so cold outside that his face would feel frozen within seconds, and his eyeballs would sting from the cold wind. It was northern Minnesota, after all.

I looked at my bowl of corn flakes that were already soggy because Mama had poured milk over them before she even woke me. I was certain she did that type of thing on purpose. I knew better than to complain about it. I picked up my spoon and asked for sugar.

"There is no sugar, Emily. We are out. Charlie got the last of it. That's what happens when you don't get out of bed first," Mama said.

Charlie looked shamefaced and whispered to me, "Mama had already put the sugar on my cereal before I got in here."

I knew that already, but I was glad Charlie told me. He felt bad about it, but it wasn't his fault. He looked like he was having trouble eating the rest of his cereal.

"I know that, Charlie. I know you would have shared it with me," I whispered back to him.

Charlie briefly smiled and then looked sad while he sat there finishing his cereal.

I accepted the fact that I had to eat soggy corn flakes with no sugar. It wasn't the first time this had happened. I would eat it quickly so that I would not get into trouble. I really was not hungry. I picked up a huge spoon of corn flakes and put them in my mouth. I didn't even have to chew them they were so soggy. They tasted like wet paper. I went for the next spoonful, wishing they were all gone, and when I almost had the spoon to my mouth, I stopped dead. I saw a blackened corn flake sitting right on top of the other ones on my spoon. "So that's it," I thought. "She is trying to poison me. Why else would I suddenly have a dark corn flake? Mama must have put poison on it and put it in my bowl thinking I would not see it." Maybe it was just a burnt corn flake, but I had never seen a burnt corn flake in my bowl before. It looked out of place sitting on the top of the other mushy corn flakes on my spoon. She must have done something to it. I was deeply afraid of the spoonful I had already eaten and even more afraid of all the cornflakes I had left to eat. I needed a plan and I needed it fast.

I looked for more dark flakes, but I didn't find any. I ate quickly, threw on my clothes and jacket, and quietly went out the door. I ran behind the house as far as I dared. I had forgotten to put on my shoes in my haste and it was cold outside. A light layer of misty snow covered the brown grass. My feet were burning cold, but I ignored them. My stomach was churning. I stuck my finger down my throat and made myself throw up the corn flakes. I won this time, but what about the meals to come? I would never be able to eat the same way again.

Everything Mama cooked from that day forward I examined very carefully. I watched closely to see if everyone else was taking their food from the same place mine was coming from or I would ask Mama if she wanted some of mine to see what she would say. If anything tasted even slightly funny, I would sneak off after eating and throw it up. Mama never caught me.

It was hard living with Mama and Daddy feeling like neither one of them loved me, wanted me, or would protect me, but it became normal to me. It was all I knew. There was no hope of anybody ever coming to save me from Daddy. He would go right on touching me, hurting me, and making me touch him. There was nothing I could do to save myself. I tried to convince myself that Mama was not trying to purposely hurt me, and I wanted to believe with all my heart that she was not helping Daddy hurt me. I tried so hard to forget about the day I told her about Daddy, but the memory wouldn't go away. It wouldn't fade. No matter what I told myself, I kept coming back to the same thought: they both enjoyed hurting me, and they didn't care how it made me feel.

I saw everything Mama and Daddy did as some sort of scheme to hurt me. Things that had happened many times before now took on a much more sinister flavor to them, especially when it came to the cockroaches.

Mama said that we had lived in a southern state called South Carolina before Daddy was transferred to New York. I could remember a little bit about South Carolina, but I was too young to remember much. Mama said that was where the cockroaches came from, and we had not been able to get rid of them since.

Cockroaches had been a part of life from as far back as I could remember. I hated them. They were creepy, disgustingly, ugly things that were everywhere and in everything; they made my skin crawl. I was always so afraid that one of them would dart out of my coat or lunch bag that I brought to school. Thankfully, that never happened. It was bad enough that the word had gotten out that we had the hideous things in our house. Charlie and I were teased cruelly about them, but as long as no one actually ever saw one on us or on our things, we could deny their existence.

No one else we knew in Minnesota lived with cockroaches. Mama said it was a southern thing. She despised the cockroaches, and they always seemed to make an appearance whenever she had guests over for a few hours. She was embarrassed by them and would offer her guests a lengthy story as to why it was not her fault there were thousands of cockroaches in the house. She would explain that they were nearly impossible to get rid of because you could not kill the "buggers." Mama said that even if you froze a cockroach solid in the freezer, it could still come back to life once it thawed. Her guests would always look wide-eyed with awe when she told them that cockroaches could live quite a while even after you chopped off their heads. She said they would probably be the last surviving creature on the earth once all the rest of us were gone.

One afternoon Mama was making a cake with choco-late frosting for her friends that were coming over to play cards with Daddy and her. They played a game called Pi-nochle. Eventually, they had to teach Charlie and me how to play because, for some reason, their friends and our rela-tives stopped coming over altogether. I was sitting at the kitchen table doing homework and watching her out of the side of my eyes. The cake was for her friends, so Charlie and I would not be getting any.

The cockroaches loved to live in the cracks of the walls, but they also crawled on everything else, including the kitchen counter where Mama was putting together her cake with chocolate frosting. I saw the cockroach getting close to Mama's bowl of frosting. I figured it was hungry and looking for some food. I waited for Mama to kill it, but she was con-centrating on frosting her cake perfectly. She had to impress her guests with her cooking talents. The cockroach made it to the edge of the bowl unseen by Mama. Its head was mov-ing and its feelers were wildly dancing in the air checking out its surroundings. Mama put her spoon back in the bowl to get some more frosting for her cake, and as she lifted the frosting out of the bowl, a big glob of it fell to the side, and landed on top of the cockroach, smothering it completely.

Mama still did not know the cockroach was there. I was not going to tell her because she would twist it around somehow and make it my fault that the cockroach had got-ten that close to her cake and frosting. Mama looked at the glob of frosting sitting on the kitchen counter next to her bowl. Then she looked inside her bowl to make sure she still had enough frosting left to finish her cake. She must have decided she had enough because all of a sudden she put her finger on the spilled frosting, scooped it up, cockroach and all, and put it in her mouth!

I was shocked. For a moment I felt guilty, as though I should have told her or intervened somehow to keep her from eating the cockroach, but that feeling passed quickly enough. As she sucked the frosting down her throat, she finally reached the cockroach. It was still wiggling around in her mouth, but it frightened and disgusted her so much that she caught it and snapped it in half with her front teeth without thinking first. She spit it out forcefully, and it landed in two pieces in the middle of her freshly frosted cake and stuck in the frosting. She was horrified but not so much about almost eating the cockroach as she was that it had landed on her cake. She dug it out of the frosting and was able to get most of it out, except she couldn't find one of its feelers and wasn't certain if she ate it or if it was lost in the frosting somewhere. She smoothed the area out where it had landed and said nobody would know the difference. She served it to her friends that evening. This was one time that I did not envy the cake they were eating.

As I started to fall asleep that night, I thought about Mama with the cockroach in her mouth. I smiled to myself. That was the most fun I had had in a long time. Unfortunately, my glee was short lived. Mama came into the living room with a can of Raid. Raid was what she used to try to kill the cockroaches, and it worked on some of them, but one can was never going to be enough to get all of them.

She started spraying the room with the Raid. She laid heavy amounts of it on the walls and up by the cracks. She was mumbling to herself about how much she hated cockroaches, and when the can of Raid was empty, she went back to her bedroom. I was wondering why she had waited so late at night to come out of her bedroom to spray for them because Mama usually sprayed for them during the day when Charlie and I were at school or at least when we could go outside. The room was thick with the smell of the killing spray. It was so thick that I could taste its awfulness in my mouth from breathing it in through my nose. My nose was burning from it and my throat felt sore. My curiosity about why Mama waited until bedtime to spray was satisfied when I felt the first thump. The cockroaches were crawling out onto the ceiling, succumbing to the Raid, and falling on me!

I had a sheet and a very thin, ratty blanket as covers. I quickly got up and wrapped my blanket around me tightly so the cockroaches could not get in. It was bad enough that Mama told us countless times that when we slept at night cockroaches crawled in our mouths and pooped, but at least I was sleeping then and knew nothing about it. Before I could get back on the couch and cocoon under the covers, one of the disgusting creatures fell from the ceiling and became lodged in my hair. I was feeling hysterical. It was like I was in some horror movie with cockroaches attacking. I grabbed the cockroach and pulled it out along with several strands of my hair, jumped on the couch, and wrapped myself in my ratty blanket. It was the only protection I had that night.

As I lay there, listening to cockroaches falling from the ceiling and landing on me, I figured it out. She had waited until night time to spray because she knew how the cockroaches would come out and die. She did this on purpose to horrify me. She was trying to get even with me because she knew I was watching earlier when she almost ate her chocolate covered cockroach. She must have seen the brief grin on my face when she snapped the cockroach in half with her teeth, and that was all she would need to convince herself that it was my fault. Mama often found a way to punish and hurt me without ever saying that was her intention.

I could not sleep, so I imagined the falling cockroaches jumping over a fence like sheep, and I tried counting them, but sleep would not come. Cockroaches simply are not sheep. I lay under my blanket for hours listening to the cockroaches fall, knowing that they were not all dead. In fact, most of them were just stunned and dizzy from the poison, and as soon as it cleared up a bit in there they would all start to crawl again, which meant they would be crawling all over me in no time. I tried so hard not to cry, but I could not hold it back. I started crying quietly to myself. I knew tears would never help, they never had, which is why I tried so hard never to let them fall.

Finally, between my tears and the tormenting sound of the cockroaches falling on me from the ceiling, plop, plop, plop, plop, I started to drift off to sleep.

CHAPTER EIGHT

JESUS LOVES ME

"JESUS LOVES ME! LOVES ME STILL 'THO I'M VERY WEAK AND ill. That I might from sin be free; bled and died upon the tree. Yes, Jesus loves me! Yes, Jesus loves me! Yes, Jesus loves me! The Bible tells me so," I sang as loudly as I could with the other children in Sunday School. I loved Sunday school, and I loved Jesus because I was absolutely positive Jesus loved me. I could feel his love for me every time I went to Sunday School. Sometimes, though, when I was at home I worried that God, who I learned was Jesus' father, wouldn't love me anymore because of what Daddy did to me. God can see everything, and Daddy said it was my fault that he hurt me. I prayed to God and told him I was sorry all the time. I asked him how to make Daddy stop, but he never answered me. The minister told everyone that God was a loving God, and he was forgiving. I prayed that was true. I wanted to go to Heaven. The other place scared me.

I loved singing about Jesus' love for me, but I did not really care for having to stand up in front of the grown-ups every Sunday and singing for them before their service began. It felt funny being stared at, but at least Daddy was never there. Daddy said he hated church. He thought it was stupid, and he told Mama the only reason she went to church was to try to impress people and be something she was not. I don't know what that was, but Daddy said that most people went to church to impress others. I thought Daddy used that as his excuse not to go, and, I figured, he was afraid that God would see all the bad things that he did. Maybe Daddy didn't know that God could see everything, everywhere.

Mama taught Sunday School with another lady, named Mrs. Polanski. She was very nice, and I liked her a lot. Mama acted really nice to her when she saw her, but when we would get in the car to go home, Mama would say mean things about her. She said she was "dumb" because her last name ended in "ski." I could not understand why that made her dumb, and she did not seem dumb to me at all. She was always very sweet to me and gave me big hugs. They felt so good. Mama and Daddy never hugged me.

Most of the time, Mama allowed me to stay in Mrs. Polanski's class. Mama did everything she could to avoid me. She never really did like me close to her, but since I told her about Daddy, she shunned me even more.

Mrs. Polanski taught the preschool children, and she let me help her take care of them. It was Christmas time, so we had been making decorations for the church's Christmas tree and getting ready to put on a play Christmas Eve night. I wanted to be Mary. Oh, how I hoped I would get to play Mary. I told Mrs. Polanski, who was making all the costumes, the part that I wanted, and she said she would talk to Mama about it. She smiled at me when she said it, so I thought that meant I was going to get to do it. I kept my fingers crossed and could hardly wait to find out.

As soon as church was over, Mama told me to grab my coat because we had to leave right away. Usually, Mama stayed around for a while and talked with all the other ladies. She acted nice when she was around them. Whenever we were there, Mama used a different voice and laugh than what I usually heard her use. I thought she must have saved it for Sundays because I only heard her use it when we were at church and, also, sometimes if a lady from the church stopped by our house.

Mama said the church we went to was called a Baptist church. She said it was okay to go to a Lutheran church, too, but never to go to any other church. I asked Mama why, and she told me, "Because I said so."

I was worried about all the people who went to other churches, so I asked Mama if they believed in God. She said I was being stupid, and that, of course, they did. I didn't say anything to Mama, but I thought, "That does not make any sense to me at all. If we all believe in the same God, what difference does it make what church we go to? If it is okay to go to either a Baptist church or a Lutheran church, then why are they called by two different names?" It all confused me. Lots of times, I couldn't understand grown-ups, and I didn't dare ask too many questions. I would get in trouble for doing that.

When we got in the car, it was so cold that the seats felt stiff. My legs were frozen immediately, and I wished I had had thicker tights to put on under my skirt. I rubbed my legs to help warm them, but my hands started to freeze right away. I had forgotten my mittens at home. Mama tried to start the car, but the car sounded sick and made a whirr, whirr, whirr, sound. Mama tried again, but it did the same thing.

"Stay here, Emily. I will be right back. I have to get some help for this f'n piece of shit your Daddy calls a car and loves so much," Mama said.

"Can I come with?" I asked.

"What did I just tell you?" Mama responded.

"It's cold out here!" I wailed.

"Knock it off, and quit being such a baby. Jesus H. Christ! I swear sometimes, Emily, you drive me up a wall. I will be right back. You won't freeze in a couple of minutes,"

Mama said in her regular voice, although we were still at the church. I guess it was okay, though, because no one except me could hear her. I missed her Sunday voice.

Mama was gone for more than a couple of minutes, and I began to worry that she had forgotten about me freezing in the car. I sat on my hands to try to warm them. I didn't dare tell Mama that I had left my mittens at home because she would just call me stupid anyway, and forgetting my mittens was a pretty dumb thing to do. It was so cold in the car that I could see my breath. The windows had all fogged up from my breathing, so I had a hard time watching to see if, and when, Mama was coming out. I was getting so cold that my legs started to hurt, and my nose and ears tingled painfully. I had to go inside. I couldn't wait any longer. The man on the radio had said it was going to be cold all week and 10 degrees on Sunday. I thought, "That's pretty cold."

I got out of the car and headed toward the church. I was going to be in a lot of trouble for leaving the car, but maybe Mama would understand. I stood just inside the front door of the church, so I could see when Mama went to the car. I waited and waited. I decided she must be downstairs with the other ladies. I started to head for the stairs when I heard Mama's voice. It sounded all sing-song and nice. I peered around the corner, and there was Mama talking and giggling with a man who went to our church, but I didn't know him. He had his arm around Mama's back, and they were heading out the side door to the car.

"Mama!" I yelled. "I am right here."

Mama stopped abruptly. She whirled away from the man, who took his hand off of her immediately, and she glared at me, asking, "What are you doing in here? I told you to wait in the car."

Mama was using her church voice, but I could tell by the look on her face that she was mad at me.

"I was getting too cold, Mama," I explained sheepishly.

"Go and get back in the car, Emily," Mama ordered.

I ran out ahead of Mama, got in the car, and waited for her. She got in the car a couple of minutes later. She said the man was a friend of hers, and he was going to jump the car for us. I wondered what it meant to "jump" the car, so I was kind of excited to see what would happen. I wanted to ask Mama how he would make our car jump, and how jumping it would help our car get started, but I was already in trouble with Mama, so I kept my mouth shut.

When the car would not start at home, Daddy said it was because the battery had gotten too cold, so he would bring it in the living room and attach it to this whatchamacallit that kind of looked like a battery itself. Daddy said the whatchamacallit "charged" the battery and would make it work again. Daddy never said anything about having to jump the car to get it to work.

"When he is done, you and me are going to have a little talk," Mama growled.

"Okay, Mama," I said quietly.

The man drove his truck over and parked it right in front of us. I thought, "He must be planning on making us jump backwards, because we can't jump forward with his truck in our way." I sat and watched quietly.

The man lifted the hood of our car, and then I could not see a thing he was doing. After a couple of minutes, he yelled out to Mama telling her to "Try it." Mama tried to turn on the car, and this time it worked. I never felt the car jump at all. I was very disappointed. Mama got out of the car, thanked the man, and gave him a long, long hug good-bye. He got back in his truck, smiled at me, waved, and drove off. He seemed nice enough. Mama got back in the car. We started driving home.

"When I tell you to do something that is exactly what I expect you to do. Do you understand me, Missy?" Mama asked.

"Yes, Mama," I answered.

"I am so sick and tired of you and your brother not doing as you are told! I have had it with you! You embarrassed me in front of Ted," she said.

"I'm sorry, Mama," I said.

"Well, sorry doesn't cut it, does it? You can go to bed two hours early for the rest of the week. How does that sound? Sounds pretty damn good to me," Mama said.

"But I was cold, Mama!" I said.

"Keep it up, and I will make it four hours," she said.

"I'm sorry, Mama," I said again, sadly.

Mama kept her word and sent me to bed early. I had to use Charlie's bed because Daddy was still lying on the couch. Charlie was so lucky to have a regular bed. I could not sleep, and the only toy I had with me was my Raggedy Ann doll, so I played with her. She loved me, and I loved her. I thought about the Christmas play and prayed, asking God to let me be Mary. When I finished my prayer, I heard Mama call for me.

"Emily, come out here, please," Mama said.

Mama was using her church voice, so, I thought, we must have company. I happily skipped out to the living room. To my joy, Mrs. Polanski was standing there holding a tape measure, a notebook, and a pen.

"Mrs. Polanski needs to measure you for your costume," Mama explained.

"Hello, Emily," Mrs. Polanski said smiling at me.

"Hello," I said. I turned towards Mama, and begged, "Mama, I want to be Mary, please!"

"No," Mama said.

"But, I really, really, really want to be Mary, Mama," I repeated.

"Emily, I said no," Mama repeated with her sing-song voice sounding a bit less sing-song.

I ignored the fact that Mama was getting upset with me. This was too important to worry about getting in more trouble with Mama, and besides, I knew that as long as Mrs. Polanski was there, I would be safe. It was after she left that I had to worry about.

"Whhhhhhyyyyyyy?" I whined.

"Emily, did we not have a talk earlier about you not doing as you are told?" Then she turned to Mrs. Polanski and complained, "Sometimes she simply refuses to do as she is told. I had to send her to bed early tonight because of it."

"Oh, Emily, sweetheart, you have to do what your Mama and Daddy tell you to do. You do remember the commandments that we have been learning, don't you?" Mrs. Polanski asked.

"Yes," I responded. I was so embarrassed by Mama telling on me that I started to cry.

"It's okay, sweetie. We all feel bad when we have done something wrong. What was the commandment about your Mama and Daddy? Can you tell me?" she asked.

I was not crying because I thought I had done something wrong. It was Mama who had done something wrong. She embarrassed me in front of Mrs. Polanski, and I feared she would never let me help out with the little children again.

I searched my memory for the Ten Commandments and thought, "One, Thou shall have no other Gods before me – that means I should only love one God...Two, Thou shall not make any graven image – I don't really know what that means. I will have to ask again...Three, Remember the Sabbath and keep it holy – that means to go to church on Sunday...Four, Thou shall not take the name of the Lord in vain – that means Daddy should not say, "God damn it and Jesus H. Christ" – I still wonder what that H stands for... Five, Honor thy Father and thy Mother. That's it. It is number five. I remember it. Oh...but, there is more...what is it about Mama and Daddy? It is something about living longer...honor them so I can live longer on the Earth that God gave me – I think that's it."

I had been chewing my lower lip while I thought about my answer without even knowing it. I stopped, smiled, looked up at Mrs. Polanski and proudly proclaimed, "Honor thy father and thy mother. It's number five."

"That's right!" she said, sounding very excited that I knew the answer. "Now, what does that mean?"

"I don't know," I automatically replied.

"Think for a minute, Emily. It will come to you. What does it mean to honor your mother and father?" she asked.

I thought for a moment, and, although I did not know exactly what it meant, I was pretty sure it meant I was supposed to do whatever my parents told me to do and that if I did, I would live longer on the Earth that God made for me, so I decided that was what I would tell her. I was so anxious to hear her sound excited again because I got the answer right.

"It means I am supposed to do everything Mama and Daddy tell me to do, and then I will live longer on the Earth that God made?" I answered as a question. I hesitated a moment and then added, "And, if I do not do what Mama and Daddy tell me to do, God will be mad at me."

Mrs. Polanski clapped her hands, and smiled, "That's exactly right, Emily! I am so proud of you! You are so smart!" She gave me a big, big hug.

Mama had been standing behind Mrs. Polanski the entire time with her arms crossed and a mad look on her face. The minute Mrs. Polanski turned around to talk to her, though, Mama smiled.

"What part do you want her to play? It would have been fine with me, by the way, if she had been Mary, but I did not get a chance to talk to you about it," Mrs. Polanski said to Mama.

"No, she's too little to play Mary, and besides, she doesn't deserve to get the part she wants when she can't seem to do as she is told," Mama stated.

"I understand," Mrs. Polanski said with a sound of concern in her voice. "What part would you like her to play?"

"What animal parts are there?" Mama asked.

"I don't want to play an animal, Mama. They don't talk," I cried.

"Emily, either, you will play an animal or nothing at all. Do you prefer to sit in the audience, while all the other kids are having fun wearing costumes and being in the play?" Mama asked, taking my face in her hand and holding it sternly.

"No, Mama," I replied. I thought, "Maybe being an animal wouldn't be so bad. I wouldn't have any talking parts, but the costume would be fun, and I could still make the sound that the animal made."

"We need a sheep, a donkey, a cow, and a camel," offered Mrs. Polanski.

"Can I be a sheep?" I asked hopefully.

"Certainly, yes, you can," Mrs. Polanski answered so fast that Mama did not have a chance to say no. Otherwise, I am certain, Mama would have made me be a donkey. Mama did mean things to me more often since I told her Daddy touched me; at least it sure appeared that way.

"Thank you!" I said, throwing my arms around her.

"Let's get you measured, little lady," Mrs. Polanski said smiling at me.

While she measured me, I daydreamed that she was my Mama. I wondered if she was this nice for real, or if she just put on a happy, nice face for when she was around other church people like Mama did.

As soon as she was done measuring me, Mama sent me back to Charlie's bed. Later, after Mrs. Polanski left, she told me I could go to bed three hours early the rest of the week for back-talking her about wanting to be Mary in the play.

Even though I had to go to bed three hours early, the week seemed to go by fast, and before I knew it, it was Sunday again. Mama had allowed me to wear my favorite dress, which made me feel a bit better about standing up in front of everyone singing, "Jesus loves the little children, all the children of the world. Red and yellow, black and white, they are precious in his sight. Jesus loves the little children of the world. Jesus died for all the children, all the children of the world. Red and yellow, black and white, all are precious in his sight. Jesus died for all the children of the world!"

I was so happy to be back in church where I was promised the love of God and his son, Jesus. I sang so loudly that I thought my lungs might burst. There were so many things going on at the church during Christmas time. Soon it would be time for the play, and I was excited because after Sunday School, everyone had planned to go over to another church for a visit and brunch. Mrs. Polanski told me that brunch was a combination of lunch and breakfast. I wondered what I would be eating at a brunch, but, mostly, I was excited to see other children and the church. The only thing I was sad about was that Charlie was not with us. Charlie hardly ever came to church with Mama and me. Mama never made Charlie go along, and I never understood why. Charlie told me he did not like going to church with Mama. I kind of understood. I think he was talking about how phony Mama seemed at church, but I missed him.

When the service was over, I went to find Mama. I saw her and ran up to her and tried to grab her hand, but she took it away quickly.

"I'm ready to go, Mama," I said smiling up at her, but really feeling hurt like my stomach was being squeezed and tied into a big knot because she would not let me hold her hand. Mama was becoming more and more distant from me. She made me feel like I was a germ, or I was contagious with some awful disease.

"I can see that, Emily. You are riding with Mrs. Polanski. She will need your help carrying some things in at the other church," Mama said. Then, Mama bent down and whispered in my ear, "And, you had best be good and do exactly as you are told...and, I mean it. Do I make myself clear?"

"Yes, Mama," I whispered back feeling like I had already done something wrong.

"Go find Mrs. Polanski. I will see you over there," Mama instructed.

So, I took off in search of Mrs. Polanski. I was glad I got to ride with her. I found her in the classroom putting things in a box to take with us to the other church.

"Emily, there you are. Can you help me get these things to my car, please?" she asked.

"Yes, what do you want me to take?" I asked. I loved helping grown-ups when they let me, especially if they were nice to me. It made me feel more grown-up.

"Here, you grab this smaller box and I will get the bigger one. We can't take too much because I drive a really small car," she explained. "Have you ever seen my car, Emily?"

"I don't think so," I said, realizing I had never even thought about Mrs. Polanski driving a car. To me, she had always been at the church when I got there, and she was there when I left.

"Well, wait until you see it. I bet it makes you laugh. It's called a beetle, and it is small," she said.

"I know what that is!" I said excitedly, while at the same time trying very hard to squash the memory of how I knew back into its own little box. "When I was about 5 years old, Daddy took me to a movie called The Love Bug, and the car's name was Herbie."

"That's it exactly, Emily. My car looks just like Herbie. Was the movie good? I never got to see it," Mrs. Polanski responded.

"I did not get to see the ending, but the first part of it was good," I responded honestly.

"Why didn't you watch the entire movie?" she asked.

I panicked. I thought, "I never imagined she would ask me such a thing. I can't tell her the truth...Daddy made us leave the movie early, so he would have time to hurt me before we had to go home...I can't tell her that! I will have to lie, and I am in church. Lying in church is like saying a triple lie. It is probably the worst kind of lie in the world. I am sure I am going to be in a lot of trouble with God, but if I tell her the truth, I still might be in a lot of trouble with God because Daddy told me not to tell anyone, and I am supposed to honor my mother and father. Besides, I already told once, and it made everything worse just like Daddy said it would do. Why is it always so hard to understand? No matter what, I am going to be wrong, and it is going to be my fault, but, I have to think of something, quick, quick, quick to tell her... Mama says I am a terrible liar; Mrs. Polanski will probably know I am lying. Oh, no! What if she tells Mama what I said! Oh, no! Mama does not know Daddy made me leave the movie early. I better think up another lie to tell Mama just in case Mrs. Polanski says something to her. I hate this...I hate it so much. Why does Daddy hurt me and make me keep secrets that make me be a liar? I do not like being a liar. It is much easier to remember what I have said when I tell the truth. I can't keep track of lies, and, then, when I goof up on a lie I have already told, I have to tell another lie that I won't remember either to fix the one I goofed up. Oh, I hate this! I really like Mrs. Polanski. I don't want to lie to her! Oh, how I wish I could tell her the truth..."

I was 5 years old the day that Mama told me I was going to be going to a movie with Daddy at the movie theatre. There were some things that no matter how hard I tried, I couldn't forget them, and this was one of those things. I had never been to a movie theatre before. Mama told me all about the popcorn, soda pop, and candy I would get because I had been a good girl, and Daddy wanted to take me out. She said Daddy wanted it to be just him and his little girl. As soon as Mama told me that, I didn't want to go, but if I told her that, I would have been in a lot of trouble. I had to go. I prayed and prayed and prayed to God asking that Daddy not hurt me when he took me to the movie.

Finally, the Saturday arrived when we were supposed to go. It was in the middle of the afternoon. Mama had dressed me up special because she said the movie theatre was on the air base, and she did not want Daddy to be embarrassed because of me. I was so frightened. I was afraid that we were not really going to a movie at all, and I made myself sick wondering where we were really going. After Mama got me all dressed up, I ran to the bathroom and threw-up as quietly as I could. I was glad she never found out.

Daddy took me by the hand, called me his big girl, and said we were going on a date. I didn't want to go on a date, although I didn't know what a date was. I wanted to stay home, but if I had to go then, I wanted to go to the movie.

The movie theatre was very close to our house. I was so happy when Daddy pulled the car into the theatre parking lot. We went inside, and Daddy bought me everything Mama had said he would: popcorn with loads of butter, candy, and soda pop. He let me pick where we sat, and I chose the first row, as close to that big screen as we could get. Daddy asked me if I was sure about that and I thought, "Why would anyone want to sit anywhere else, except for right up front?"

Before the regular movie started, the theatre played the National Anthem, and everyone stood up, put their hands on their hearts, and sang with the music. The men and women who had on uniforms, like what Daddy normally wore to work, had their hats off and were holding them over their hearts. The sound of all those voices singing so proudly made my skin get goose bumps all over it. After the singing was done, everyone sat down with a "humph." There was a lot of clicking noises and flickers of light, as many of the grown-ups lit their cigarettes, including Daddy. It became very smoky, very fast, but I was used to it from Daddy's smoking at home and in the car. Then, the movie started.

I had never seen anything like it before in my life. The screen was huge, and the sound filled my ears. I could feel the sound in my chest; it thumped through me. It was amazing! Daddy let me hold the popcorn, and I gobbled it down. My fingers became too greasy from all the butter to open my candy, so Daddy opened it for me. It was a big box of Milk Duds, the biggest box of Milk Duds I had ever seen in my life, and they were all for me. They stuck to my teeth as I tried to chew them, so I had to keep sticking my finger in my mouth to pry the caramel lose, and Daddy did not even yell at me to stop. I still was not sure what I had done to earn all of this, but I didn't care right at that moment. I was having too much fun. Maybe Daddy was not going to hurt me after all. Maybe this was Daddy's way of saying he was sorry and that he was not ever going to do it again. I smiled at him, and he smiled back. I was so happy.

"Emily, we have to leave in just a couple of minutes," Daddy whispered to me after we had been there a while.

I did not answer him. The movie was not over yet; I was not even done with my popcorn, soda pop, or candy, although I had planned on bringing at least half of everything home to Charlie. I stared at the screen but could not see a thing.

"Emmy, did you hear Daddy?" he asked.

"Yes, Daddy, but the movie isn't over yet," I whispered back with a slight whine in my voice. I was so frightened and disheartened. I told myself that I should not feel surprised. I knew all along that this was what was going to happen anyway, and, at least, I had gotten to see some of the movie, and I would still get to take my treats home with me to share with Charlie.

"I know, Emmy, but you did get to see most of it. It only has about 30 minutes left," Daddy said.

"Where are we going?" I asked, afraid of the answer.

"I thought we could go for a nice ride," Daddy said.

"Why can't we go for a ride after the movie?" I asked.

"Because Mama expects us home right after the movie, and if we are late, she will be really mad at you, Emmy. I don't want Mama to be mad at you," he said.

"Why do we have to go for the ride?" I asked.

"Emily, you ask too many questions. Stop it. We are going for a ride because I said we are going for a ride. Now, gather your things up. I will carry your popcorn," Daddy said as he stood up and hunched over so the people behind us could still see the movie.

I walked out behind Daddy with my head hung low, feeling as though life itself were going to come to an end. With each step I took, I asked God why he had forgotten me again. I had prayed over and over for God to stop Daddy from hurting me. I didn't understand how God could love me and let Daddy keep doing this to me. I decided I would have to pray harder and try harder to be a good girl.

I was so confused, though, as to what it meant to be a good girl. On my way to the car, I thought, "I don't like keeping Daddy's secrets; it's like lying, but I am so afraid that Daddy is right, and Mama will blame me, and maybe it is my fault. Oh, maybe that is why God does not answer my prayers. Maybe I am asking for the wrong thing because if it is my fault, then God has to stop me from making Daddy hurt me. Oh, how I wish I knew. I just can't figure this out. If only I could ask Mama, but I am so afraid of Mama. I feared that she would blame me and hate me, just like Daddy says. I don't think Mama likes me that much, anyway. I wish Mama could help me. I wish someone could help me, but if I tell anyone, they will hate me and blame me. I don't want other people to know about all the bad things Daddy does to me. What Daddy does to me feels bad – very bad. It's wrong. I just know it's wrong!"

When we got in the car, Daddy started to drive fast. I stayed next to the door and was very quiet. I watched out my window as the telephone poles zoomed by. I tried to count ten of them, but I could not concentrate on them. I was too worried about where Daddy was taking us and what he was going to do to me.

We did not drive very far before Daddy stopped the car and turned it off behind a very large, gray building.

"This is where I work, Emmy. It's Saturday, so there is no one back here," Daddy said. "Come over here, closer to Daddy. I want to give you a big hug for being such a good girl about leaving the movie early."

Daddy never gave me hugs – at least, not real hugs. If Daddy was going to hug me, it also meant that he was going to touch me in a bad way. I did not want to sit next to Daddy. I wanted out of the car. I wanted to go back where all the other people were in the movie theatre. I wanted to laugh again at Herbie, the car in the movie, and forget all about Daddy and Mama for a few minutes. I wanted to disappear and no longer be anywhere. I tried to wish myself to disappear many, many times, but it never worked. I ignored Daddy and stayed right by the door.

"Emmy, Daddy said to come over here. Come on now. Daddy took you to a nice movie, and I bought you all kinds of nice treats. Look, you still have leftovers you get to take home. You can give some to Charlie. He would like that. Now, come here. Don't make Daddy get mad at you. We have had a fun day, so far, haven't we? Let's not ruin it now, Emmy," Daddy said, as he patted the seat next to him to indicate where I was supposed to move to.

I tried to move next to Daddy because I thought it would be better if I moved, instead of Daddy moving me. If he did it, he was going to be mad at me and things were worse when he got angry. But I could not make myself move. I felt like I was paralyzed. I was trying to tell myself to move, but myself was not listening to me.

"I can't," I mumbled to Daddy.

"You can't what, Emily?" Daddy asked.

"Move," I mumbled.

"Jesus H. Christ. Sometimes, Emily, I really do not understand you. It's not as if you have a broken bone, now is it?" he asked.

"No, Daddy," I squeaked out in reply. Again, I tried to get myself to move over next to him, especially because I could hear he was getting mad at me, but I still could not get my body to move. It was stuck in place. It was trying to protect me. I was certain of it.

"Emmy, sometimes I think you enjoy pissing me off," Daddy said, as he grabbed me hard and pulled me over next to him. "There now, was that so damn hard?"

"No, Daddy," I said.

"That's a good girl. You were a good girl at the movie. Daddy was very proud of you. You are so pretty today, Emily. Did you know that?" Daddy said.

"Yes, Daddy," I replied automatically. I was not really hearing anything he was saying. I was scared, and at the same time, I was trying to go away in my head. It was the only way I could escape. I closed my eyes, and I tried to think about Charlie and how much we liked going sledding together. Charlie had tied two of our dogs to our sled and had them pull us. He laughed very hard as the dogs took off. It was a lot of fun. Charlie was so smart, and he made me laugh.

I heard Daddy pull the zipper on his pants down. I kept my eyes closed.

"Emmy, look at what you did to Daddy again," Daddy said.

I did not look. I did not open my eyes. Daddy grabbed my hand and rubbed it against his pee-pee.

"I don't know Emmy...it looks pretty bad this time. I think you are going to have to kiss it to make it better," Daddy said.

"Nooooooooo," I whined immediately. My body tensed in reaction to his touch and request. Kissing his pee-pee sounded like the worst thing in the whole, wide world to me.

"I kiss your boo-boos, don't I, Emmy? So does your Mama. You are supposed to kiss boo-boos, especially when you are the one that caused the boo-boo. It's hurting really, really bad, Emily. You have to kiss it. It is your fault it is like this. It hurts me. You have to help Daddy. Come on now; it's not that bad," Daddy insisted.

I never wanted Daddy to kiss my boo-boos. I never asked him to do it, either. Sometimes I wanted Mama to kiss them, but most of the time, she was grumpy about it and told me not to be a baby.

"You do not have to kiss my boo-boos," I offered.

"You don't like Daddy kissing your boo-boos? You are never too big to get your boo-boos kissed, Emmy. I want you to kiss mine, please. Please, do this for Daddy," he begged.

"No, Daddy. Please, no," I cried.

"Emily, you have to kiss it or it's not going to get any better, and then what are we supposed to do? Are we just going to stay here all night until you decide to do the right thing?" he asked.

I didn't know how to answer him, but I didn't care if

we stayed there forever.

"Emily, Daddy is trying to be nice to you about this, but one way or another, you are going to have to kiss my boo-boo. Now, come on. Let's get it done. You will see. It's not that bad. Just give it a quick kiss...see...here, right on the top of it," Daddy instructed as he pulled my body around and started to push my head down by his pee-pee.

"Nooooo," I cried, while also knowing I was going to have to do what Daddy told me to do. I closed my eyes tighter than they had ever been before. The closer Daddy pushed my head to his pee-pee, the more I could smell him, and it smelled terrible. I felt his pee-pee brush against my face.

"There it is Emmy. Now be a good girl and give it a little kiss for Daddy," Daddy said.

He continued to hold my head on it with force. My neck started to hurt. He rubbed his pee-pee across my mouth.

"Kiss it, Emily. Kiss it. Kiss it, now!" Daddy insisted.

I kissed it. I went numb.

"Oh, Emmy, that was wonderful! Such a good, little girl you are! Now, kiss it one more time for Daddy, exactly the same way you just did – so gentle and soft," Daddy said.

I kissed it again, but it was like I was not there. I did not even know how my body moved. I was gone. Something else was making it move, but I did not care any longer. Daddy's voice sounded like an echo that was far, far away. It reminded me of the Charlie Brown cartoons when the teacher would talk and all you would hear was "muwhaw, muwhaw, muwhaw."

"What a good girl!" Daddy said as he allowed me to sit back up. "I am feeling much better."

Daddy grabbed my hand again and wrapped it around his pee-pee. I did not try to fight it because I was not there anymore. He made my hand go up and down until something squirted out of the top of his pee-pee; he let my hand go after it came out. Then he told me to get back over on my side of the car; he took out his hanky and wiped himself off, and we went home.

How could I tell Mrs. Polanski why I did not see the whole movie? Even if I wanted to tell her, I could not imagine being able to get the words to come out of my mouth without feeling like someone had reached down my throat and ripped out my soul. As I stood there, trying to think of something to tell her, something other than the truth, I started to feel very sick to my stomach, which gave me an idea.

"I got a sick stomach from all the popcorn and candy I ate. I had to go to the bathroom, so I missed the end of the movie," I explained. I felt relieved that I had thought of something, but how much time had gone by while I stood there and remembered all the horrible memories? I did not know, but Mrs. Polanski did not act like it was a long time, so it must have happened in a flash.

"I am sorry to hear that, Emily. Next time, you will have to remember how it made you sick, and maybe don't eat as much," she advised, chuckling.

I laughed a little, and said, "I won't."

Mrs. Polanski's car was indeed very small. It only had two doors, and a tiny backseat. She asked me to sit in the back because she needed the room in the front seat to carry things. I didn't mind at all. It was kind of fun to be able to ride in the same type of car that I had seen in a movie. I crawled in the back seat and looked out the back window. Mama was right behind us. I waved at her, and she waved back, but she did not smile.

When we got to the church, the parking lot was over full, so we had to park down the street a ways. The church was large, and I could see it had beautiful stained glass windows in the main part of it, but we were all meeting in the basement, so I thought I probably wouldn't get to spend any time in there. Our church only had one little stained glass window. Mama said it was very expensive, and that is why we only had one.

Mrs. Polanski had given me a small box with lots of paperwork in it to carry in. She said it was some forms that she had worked on for the church. I told her it looked like she did a very nice job, although I really did not know.

"Look at all the people, Emily," Mrs. Polanski observed.

"I know! I have never seen this many people in the same place before. How many people do you think are here?" I asked.

"Well, it looks like there could be two hundred and fifty to three hundred people – maybe more. This church does have a lot of members, although seeing all of them together when we are so used to our little church is quite something, isn't it?" she said.

"Yes," I replied in awe.

When we got inside the church with our boxes, Mrs. Polanski pointed to a room down a narrow hallway.

"That is the room, right there, Emily, that I want you to bring your box to. Wait there for me, and I will be back in just a little bit, and then we can find the brunch area together, okay?" she instructed.

"Okay," I said as I headed toward the room. Inside the room were a desk, a chair, a small sofa, and a very large bookcase filled to the brim with books about Jesus.

I put the box down on top of the desk and then sat on the end of the sofa to wait. The clock on the wall read 10:45. I wished there was no clock in there because once you looked at a clock to watch the time, it seemed like time slowed down and things would take forever to happen. It was like what Mama said about a watched pot that never boiled.

After about ten minutes, I got up, went to the book-case, and found a book that looked interesting. I loved to read, and I would take every opportunity that came my way to look at a book. I sat back down on the sofa and started to thumb through the pages. I liked to look through the whole book quickly and then go back to the beginning and start going through the pages slowly.

I must've been right above the basement where the brunch was taking place because I could hear squeals of laughter from lots of children and the muffled sound of many voices all talking in hushed tones at once. I looked around the office to see where the sound was coming from, and I spotted a vent in the floor. I got closer to it, and bent down to listen. It was clear that the voices were coming from there. The children sounded like they were having a lot of fun. I could not tell exactly what they were doing, but I could hear the sounds of running back and forth, and, based on their laughter and squeals, I figured they had to be having a very good time. I could hardly wait to join everybody.

At some point, I must have fallen asleep because I found myself lying halfway on the sofa and halfway on the floor with the book dropped open on the floor next to me. I grabbed the book right away to make sure it was not injured, and it was not. I was certainly glad about that. I was surprised that I had fallen asleep because I did not realize I was even tired. I wondered where Mrs. Polanski was, and then I looked at the clock, and I couldn't believe what time it read: nearly 12:30 PM. Where was Mrs. Polanski?

Maybe she had stopped by and left me there because I was sleeping, but that didn't sound right because she knew how much I had been looking forward to seeing everything and meeting everybody – even though I was very shy. Mama told people I was "painfully shy." She was wrong about that because I never felt any pain when I met other people, but I was shy. I was always worried that no one would really like me, and I worried that somehow people would be able to tell that Daddy hurt me just by looking at me. That really scared me.

I wanted to leave the room to go and find Mrs. Polanski because I was worried something might have happened to her, but then I remembered Mama's warning about doing what I was told to do, and Mrs. Polanski had told me to wait in the room for her and that she would be back to get me. I didn't want to get in trouble with Mama again for not staying where I was told to stay.

After a few more minutes, I started to cry. I decided Mrs. Polanski had simply forgotten all about me. It made my heart hurt. I got a really sad feeling deep in my stomach. I felt so dejected and unwanted. I had thought I was important to her, but I guessed I was not. I could never trust grown-ups, or anyone for that matter. How could she have just forgotten about me?

I was sitting on the couch, sniffling, when Mrs. Polanski opened the door. She had a concerned, hurried look on her face.

"Oh, my goodness, Emily! I am so, so, so sorry, sweetheart!" she said as she ran toward me and tried to hug me, but I rolled myself up in a ball so she could not hug me the normal way. "Oh, sweetie. I do not blame you for being mad at me. Oh, please do not cry."

When she touched me, for some reason it made me cry even harder. I was mad at her, but I was also so happy to see her, and I did not know which to show her first – the mad me or the happy me, so I let my body decide, and it decided to be mad at her.

Mrs. Polanski sat down on the sofa next to me to explain what had happened to her. I tried my best to listen to her, but her words got mixed up with my feelings of desolation.

"Oh, honey, there is no excuse for me forgetting you in this room. I can't believe you just sat in here and waited for me. I got side-tracked by a big group of children on my way back to you – they – they said they needed my help for just a minute, and it turned out to take more than a minute, and then – then, the minister from this church came over, and we got to talking, and I – I totally forgot about you and me bringing things to this office. Oh, I hope you can forgive me. I am not used to having a child with me. I don't have any children, you know, Emily. You – you must be starving. Oh, gosh, I am so sorry. I feel so bad. The food is already put away. We ate right away when we got here. I am going to go and ask your Mama if I can take you out to lunch, okay? Just – just the two of us, wherever you want to go."

I had never heard Mrs. Polanski stutter before, and she truly did look like she felt bad. Maybe she really did. It made me feel a little bit better the way she said she was sorry and that she wanted to take me out for lunch. She reached for my hand, and, in my pathetically dejected state, I hungrily grabbed for it, but my feelings for her had changed: She had forgotten me. I could never trust a grown-up, but Jesus loved me. Yes, Jesus loved me. This I knew…

CHAPTER NINE

THE CHICKEN SHACK

APPEARANCES WERE EVERYTHING TO MAMA, AND SHE WORKED hard to maintain them. For the entire world to see, I was a very happy, smart, contented child who loved her Mama dearly. I learned to act my roles early on and knew the consequences if I did not fulfill Mama and Daddy's expectations.

Valentine's Day had passed with no special meaning in my house. Mama was busy in the kitchen because she had three lady friends coming over to visit for the morning. When they arrived, they all went into the kitchen and sat around the kitchen table. Mama yelled for Charlie to get a bucket of water so she could make her friends some coffee or hot chocolate.

Charlie grumbled, but he slowly got up and put on all his winter clothes in order to go out and put the bucket down the hole in the ground. Charlie hated it when Mama made him do things like this for the friends she was having over, and he let her know it. He was so much braver than I was. Charlie did not care if Mama hurt him; he was going to complain no matter what.

I was sitting in the living room, curled up on the couch under my blanket when Charlie came back in. It was cold in the house because it was very cold outside. We were both watching Saturday morning cartoons. My favorites were Bugs Bunny and Road Runner. When Bugs Bunny was over, I decided I was thirsty, so I went into the kitchen to see if there was any more water in the bucket. It felt warm and slightly steamy in the room from the water Mama had been boiling. In a way, it was a rather comforting feeling. The smell of the hot chocolate was delicious, and my stomach growled because I had not eaten yet. Charlie and I loved hot chocolate, but Mama rarely shared any when she had friends coming over. She said she had to save the hot chocolate mix for them.

I found myself standing close to Mama and without thinking I said, "Mmmmmmmm...that hot chocolate smells so good. I wish I could have some of it just this once."

I think I must've embarrassed Mama by adding the "just this once" part. I did not realize how it sounded until it was out of my mouth and hanging in the room with strings of innuendos attached to it. Without blinking an eye or missing a beat, Mama slapped me hard across the mouth and nose. She called it "back-handing" me, and she was quite good at it. I cut the inside of my mouth and bottom lip with my teeth, and my nose started to bleed.

"Children are to be seen and not heard. You never speak unless you have been spoken to first," Mama coldly instructed me.

The friends she had over looked stunned. I was so ashamed that all I could do was steal a quick look at them. Mama told me to grab an old rag for my face and get outside. I held the rag to my face, and as quickly as I could, I scrambled out the door bundled up in my winter clothes. I tromped over to the chicken shack that was left there from the days when Grandma had raised chickens.

The chicken shack was out behind the house, past the

sewage hole, which was created by the water that drained from the kitchen sink. Daddy had hooked up a pipe to the sink and cut a hole in the wall so it could drain outside in the yard directly behind the house. In the summer, it formed a cesspool of stink and bugs.

The chicken shack was past the outhouse. I debated using the outhouse as I shuffled by it, but decided it was much too cold out to pull my pants down. I can hold it, I thought. I had gotten very good at "holding it" to avoid any extended times in the bucket room where Daddy could find me by myself with my pants down.

Being in the chicken shack always reminded me of when Grandma allowed me to help her feed the chickens and to feel underneath them for eggs. Finding the eggs was my favorite part because every time I found one under a chicken, Grandma would act as thrilled as if I had just completed some miraculous feat.

The chicken shack sat there looking like a frozen leftover from days gone by. After Grandma moved away, Mama said chickens were dirty animals, so she told Daddy to chop off their heads so that she could clean them and use them for soup. She said that is all they would be good for because they were "tough old birds." I had begged Mama to stop Daddy from killing the chickens. I promised her I would take care of them, and I said I did not care that they were dirty birds, although I did not think they were dirty at all. Mama told me to shut-up.

I didn't want to watch Daddy chop their heads off, but I couldn't help myself. Daddy took the chickens out one at a time, and he laid their necks on a log he had placed on the ground close to the chicken shack. He held the bird down with his foot, and he had the ax in his hand. He brought the ax down fast and hard. It made a horrible sound against the wood, and the head of the chicken popped off. I thought there would be more blood. That was all I could think right at that moment. I felt so sad to lose the chickens and my connection to Grandma through them.

The chickens would run around for a couple of minutes after their heads were chopped off before they finally fell down. I quickly learned where the saying Mama used, "You are running around like a chicken with its head cut off," came from. It was grotesque to watch: the chickens looked like they were desperately searching for their severed heads. Daddy must have gotten tired by the time he got to the last chicken because the head of it did not pop off all the way when Daddy slammed the ax down on it. The chicken started running wild through the grass with its head bobbing up and down alongside its neck. It was horrific. Daddy thought it was very amusing, and he laughed and laughed. I felt sick to my stomach and so sad for all the chickens.

The chicken managed to get itself under a shed that was so low to the ground Daddy could not reach under it because he was too big and would not fit. He told me to go and get the chicken. I sat and stared at Daddy for a minute. I couldn't believe that he had just told me to go and get a dead chicken that was stuck under the shed, but didn't know it was dead because its head was still hanging on it. There was nothing I could do. I had to go and get it. I crouched down on my hands and knees and felt around for the chicken. It was still trying to run around under the shed, but since it did not have enough room, all it ended up doing was bouncing up and down hitting the bloody stub of its neck on the bottom of the floorboards to the shed. It was a bit difficult to grab at first, but then I finally got hold of it and felt its head bounce off my hand as I tossed it back out on the grass as fast as I could. Daddy doubled over laughing at me. I felt wretched.

Mama had a huge pot of water boiling in the kitchen when Daddy brought all the dead chickens in. One by one, Mama put them in the boiling water for a couple of minutes. She said that helped to loosen up the feathers for her so she could pull them off. That might be so, but the smell was tremendously bad. Actually, it was so bad that it was more of a stench than it was a smell. Then she laid the chickens on the table and started pulling their feathers off. They looked so naked when she was done. After she got all the feathers off, she said she had to clean out their guts. Oh, my goodness, I had not thought of that at all! Mama grabbed a bird and opened up a hole somehow down between its yellow, rubber looking legs. She shoved her hand up the hole and grabbed the chicken's guts. As she pulled them back out of the chicken, the chicken made a clucking sound! I had been standing by the kitchen sink, and I nearly fell over when I heard the bird make noise with no head on it or life in it for that matter. Mama laughed and said the sound was caused by air left in the chicken that was pushed through its voice box when Mama grabbed out its guts. I guess both Mama and Daddy thought the killing of the chickens was some sort of funny thing to do. I did not. I thought the whole process had been utterly disgusting. I never ate any of the chicken that came from Grandma's chicken shack. I simply could not do it.

At least Mama and Daddy did not tear down the chicken shack. It was a small building, but Grandma and I could fit in it together if we squeezed when we went inside to look for eggs. The chicken shack was lopsided and crooked. Grandma said that Grandpa had built it for her "grudgingly." I had no idea what grudgingly meant, but by the way Grandma said it, I could tell it was not a nice thing.

The door was made out of three wide and thick slabs of wood planks nailed together. It did not have a handle on it, but it did have a piece of rope that was looped through a hole in the wood that was used as a handle if needed. I stood at the door freezing from the cold wind and could feel my body start to shiver. I tried pushing the door open, but it was blocked inside by snow that had built up from blowing in the windows. I was determined though; I had to get inside and get out of the wind because there was no way I was going to turn back and go inside the house. Besides, Mama had ordered me out. If I went back in so quickly, I would be in more trouble. The order to go outside was a punishment Mama often used in the winter time. In the heat of the summer, it would be just the opposite. The unspoken rule was that I had to stay outside long enough for the cold to start seriously freezing me. She wanted to see blood red cheeks, red fingers and toes, and frosty white ears. Mama used everything she could find to her advantage.

I was finally able to get the door pushed in just enough for me to slip through it. I closed the door and sat on the back side of it with my legs bent up by chest and my arms wrapped tightly around my legs. The chicken shack provided some shelter but not much. As I sat there, I looked around remembering the good times I had had with Grandma. It made me feel just a little bit warmer inside thinking about her.

The cages for the chickens were still there. They were stacked three high and covered the length of three walls. Grandma had a lot of chickens in there sometimes. Most of the cage doors were flung open and bent, and some were hanging on by one hinge. On the very top of every wall above the chicken cages was a long thin window with no glass in it. The windows were there to provide fresh air for the chickens, and chickens did not need glass in their windows, Grandma told me.

Everything was so frozen now and deserted, although there were still remnants of the chickens to be found. There was a layer of ice and snow that had built up on the floor, and there were chicken feathers sticking straight up out of ice, frozen in place. They would probably never get all the chicken feathers out of the chicken shack even if they tried. The bottoms of the cages were littered with chicken poop and more feathers. Grandpa had tried to convince Grandma and me that chicken poop was very valuable to some people in other countries. I laughed on the inside when Grandpa said poop was valuable; I didn't dare laugh out loud at him because he was quite serious about it. Maybe that is why he left the chicken poop there, although I could not imagine Grandpa coming back and scooping it out anytime soon or ever.

The air inside the chicken shack was cold, crisp, and clear. The open windows provided ventilation and also allowed the snow and ice to get in. I could feel crystals forming inside my nose, and my breath looked like smoke. It reminded me of the smoke from Daddy's cigarettes, except it disappeared a lot faster, and it didn't stink and make me cough. During the summer, I avoided going to the chicken shack because in the heat of July it smelled terrible! No one would ever clean it out, and I was too small to even try. The chicken shack would sit there just like it was until one day it would simply fall down.

The cold was starting to freeze my hands, and my bottom was beginning to feel numb from sitting on the ice packed floor; however, I did not want to go back into the house until Mama's friends left. I felt too ashamed to face them again, and I certainly did not want to have to give them a hug and a kiss goodbye, which was a standard expectation from Mama when she had guests over.

Charlie and I were expected to pretend everything was wonderful in our family. We did a lot of pretending in our house. I wondered how Mama could think she had a chance of making her friends believe we had it good. It was embarrassing having cockroaches and no toilet or bathtub. I always tried to hold it while people were over because I did not want anyone actually seeing me going into the room where the bucket was kept. Likewise, I noticed that no one who came to visit us ever used our bucket to go the bathroom while they were there.

I held the rag to my nose and pinched it while I put my head back in an attempt to stop the bleeding. Mama had taught me how to do this following her numerous other back-handings. Her slaps were very unpredictable, and there were many times that I had no idea what I had been back-handed for, and she rarely gave explanation. The blood seemed to slow down. My nose was throbbing and felt ten times bigger than its normal size. My bottom lip was swollen, and I could taste my blood inside my mouth as I sucked on it.

When my nose stopped bleeding completely, I used the blood soaked rag to scoop up some of the snow that had been behind the door and held it to my lip. I thought it might help somehow because when I would get a lump on my head from a fall, Mama would put a butter knife in the freezer and then run the cold sides of the blade over the lump. I assumed the snow would work on my lip in the same manner as the cold butter knife did on my head. The times when Mama was kind and gentle were rare and cherished by me.

In the winter my toes would be the first thing on my body to start to freeze, and sitting in the chicken shack was no exception, plus I had forgotten to put on some socks before I put my boots on, so my toes were already starting to tingle from the cold. I couldn't hold out much longer there. I wished I could lie down, fall asleep, and die from the cold like the girl in the story my teacher had read to all of us before Christmas.

The story was called "The Matchstick Girl." She was a little girl who had to sell matchsticks in the street for a penny, and if she went home without selling any, her daddy would beat her. One night she didn't sell any matchsticks, so she decided not to go home, and she used her matches to try to keep warm. She started to see her grandma who was up in Heaven each time she lit a match. Her grandma was the only person who had ever truly loved her and had been kind to her. That night her grandma took her to Heaven with her. In the morning, people found The Matchstick Girl and said she must have frozen to death.

The story reminded me of my grandma. She was the only person who had always been kind to me. I wondered what it would be like in Heaven. At least I would be away from Daddy. I wondered about that all the time.

However, on this day, I was not going to be going to Heaven. Finally, I had to get up and go back in the house; my toes hurt so badly that it hurt to walk. My plan was to hide in the room where we kept the bathroom bucket. Hopefully, I could just be alone in there, and Mama wouldn't notice I was back inside the house. I slipped in as quietly as I could, but my boots were loud with the squeaking from the snow and cold. Mama saw me immediately; she told Charlie and me that she had eyes in the back of her head. I guessed her eyes must not work that well because there was a lot my Mama never seemed to see. I should not have come back in, but I guessed it was better than having my toes fall off, which Mama warned us about constantly. She called me over to her and her friends who were all still sitting at the kitchen table.

"Emily, I want you to apologize to these nice ladies for disrupting our visit together," she said in her command voice.

I stood next to Mama knowing that I would have to look at the three ladies when I apologized – that much would be expected. My head was so far down that my chin was resting on my bony chest. My head was heavy with shame, and I wondered if I could even pick it up. I must have looked so ugly with my swollen nose and puffed up lip, and I could feel dried blood on my face in the area between my nose and my upper lip.

My heart was beating rapidly, and I was a bit dizzy. I had to find the strength just to get it over with, so I slowly lifted my tremendously heavy head, looked at the ladies with my eyes brimming with shameful tears, and meekly said, "I am sorry." I quickly put my head back down to study the rotten boards that made up our kitchen floor.

"What are you sorry for, Emily?" Mama asked.

I was not going to get out of this easily. Mama had not shamed me enough in front of her friends. She needed to feel the power of her position as my Mama. Charlie and I knew she had the power over us as she often reminded us, "I brought you into this world and I could take you out," or she would threaten to take us to an orphanage. Of course, along with her threat of the orphanage, she would tell us horror stories of what it was like to live in one. Still, it sounded better to me than living with Mama and Daddy.

I looked up again and said, "I am sorry for disrupting your visit with my Mama." I thought using the same words Mama had used would be a sufficient enough of a response.

"And how did you disrupt our visit?" Mama queried.

By this time, I was getting used to the intense feeling of shame in front of the ladies. Throughout this entire dialogue between Mama and me, they did not say a word. Instead, when I looked in their eyes, I saw compassion and sadness for me, which gave me some comfort, but at the same time, it also made my position that much more real to me.

"I disrupted all of you by sassing you, Mama. I am very sorry," I responded with the correct amount of contriteness.

"Go sit on the couch," Mama commanded.

Charlie was in the living room sitting on the broken recliner still watching the Saturday morning cartoons. I had forgotten about them. I had missed most of them and felt the sting of the loss. Now, I would have to wait until next Saturday to see cartoons again.

As I sat there on the couch, I took off all my winter clothes and my boots. I held my toes tightly in my hands. They were still burning cold and red. It seemed I could not get them to warm up. I wished I could get up and go and get a couple of pair of socks for my feet, but I had been commanded to sit on the couch. If I asked Mama for permission to leave the couch to get socks and explained quickly how cold my toes were, she would tell me it was my own stupid fault and to sit there and be quiet. I decided to sit on my feet, hoping that covering them with my bottom would provide them with enough warmth.

At least my cold feet were taking my mind off my

throbbing, swollen lip and tender nose. Charlie was having a hard time looking at me, though, which reminded me it must look bad. Charlie felt bad for me when Mama or Daddy would harass me. He knew what it felt like, too.

"There are only 15 minutes left of cartoons, Emmy. You can pick what you want for us to watch. Popeye is on right now," Charlie offered.

Charlie was trying to reach out to me and offer me some kindness. I do not know what I would have done sometimes without him.

"Popeye is okay," I mumbled and gave him a weak smile intending to convey a thank you.

"Okay, Emmy. We can go sledding later if you want... if Mama will let you," he added quickly.

"My toes hurt too badly anyway, Charlie," I said.

Mama and her friends entered the room. Mama went and fetched the coats for her friends that she had laid across her bed when they had arrived. As they put on their coats, Mama told us to come and give each of them a hug and a kiss good-bye. I stole a quick glance at Charlie. He hated having to do this, and I mean hated. His face was all contorted with a disgusted look, and I feared for him if he did not get that look off his face, but he was able to quickly hide it. Years of experience of hiding what we really felt made it rather easy for both of us to do. I did not like the kissing and hugging of people when they came and left either, especially since I didn't know most of them. I recognized them, but I did not know them.

We got up, went to the door, and gave our fake hugs and kisses good-bye to the ladies that we did not really know. It felt awkward because I didn't think they wanted to touch us anymore than we wanted to touch them.

Mama said her good-byes and closed the door. She slowly turned around and smiled at Charlie.

"Charlie, I have some hot chocolate left over that you

can have. Come in the kitchen right now and drink it," she cooed.

Charlie had no choice. He had to go because if he didn't, he would be in trouble. I watched him sitting at the kitchen table with the cup of hot chocolate. He picked the cup up slowly and took a drink, while Mama turned around to start washing the dishes from her friends' visit. Charlie turned toward me, smiled, and spit the hot chocolate into the garbage can sitting next to him. He did this a couple of times until Mama left to go to the bucket room. Charlie then held up the cup triumphantly and poured the rest of it down the drain. He turned to me and grinned from ear to ear as though to say, "We win."

CHAPTER TEN

THE PLAYGROUND

SCHOOL WAS ALWAYS AN ESCAPE. I LOVED MY TEACHERS. THEY looked so clean and beautiful. They were nice to me even though I smelled bad. The other kids at school would make fun of me saying that my hair was so greasy they could fry an egg on it and that I smelled like poop. How could I tell them it was not my fault? And I doubt it would have made any difference. The teachers noticed how dirty I was, too, but they never said a word. They accepted me regardless of how dirty I was or what hideous clothing Mama had put me in for the day.

Mama took us to get a bath once a month or so. She would take us to our Great-Aunt May's house where there was a bathroom with a toilet and a bathtub with water that worked all year long. She even had a basement with a bar in it. The living room had the most beautiful orange and red shag carpet that we had ever seen and a big console television set. We thought she must be rich. Charlie and I loved going there because Great-Aunt May had a slot machine in the basement; she always had a nickel ready for us to play it. We never won, but it was fun trying.

Even though the other kids would often tease me, I still loved going to school; Daddy was never there. Most of the time, Mama was not there either. School became a place of fantasy and daydream for me. I could be whoever or whatever I wanted to be in my mind. I was free at school; free from Mama and Daddy.

I was in the second grade, and Ms. Erickson was my teacher. She was very tall and very thin. She had short brown hair and black rimmed glasses. She looked much younger than Mama, and she had the nicest voice I had ever heard. I loved her immediately, although she never knew it. She called me "honey" and spoke kindly to me; it was as if she was afraid I would break if she spoke to me in any other way. I sometimes would sit in class and daydream that Ms. Erickson was actually my mama and that when class was over she would take me home with her and we would live happily ever after. I could never tell Ms. Erickson about Daddy. I was too afraid she wouldn't like me anymore if she knew what Daddy did to me. She might think it was my fault, too, like I was certain Mama did.

The other kids always seemed so different from me; I cannot explain how really – just different. I was shy, but mostly I was afraid if I made friends they would find out about Daddy. I could never have a friend spend a night at my house like the other girls talked about. I was too afraid Daddy would hurt them or they would see what Daddy did to me nearly every day and every night, and besides, the bucket we used for a toilet and the cockroaches were too embarrassing.

On the playground, I kept my distance from most kids although I wished fervently that I had some friends. Once in awhile, someone would tease me and play jokes on me. One day, we were all outside for recess, and it was especially cold; I was swinging on the swing set. It had eight swings on it, and it was made from metal. The seat of the swing was made from some sort of cloth, so that when you sat on it the seat would wrap up around the side of your thighs and your butt would hang over the other side. The teachers said it made the swing safer, but it hurt to sit on, and it made your legs stick out at funny angles. I missed the straight wooden seats.

I was swinging high in the air when I noticed a couple of boys and girls coming toward me. I figured they were probably going to try to get the swing from me. I debated getting up and leaving before they got there, but they were too close for me to make a clean departure. They walked right up next to me and dared me to put my tongue on the metal leg of the swing set. They promised to be my friends if I did it. I did not understand what the big deal was about putting my tongue on the swing set, although I did think it was kind of a strange thing for them to ask me to do. The kids were so nice to me in that moment, and the possibility of having them for friends excited me. I would have someone to play with on the playground, and maybe they would pick me during gym class to be on their team when we played dodge ball. Dodge ball would be a lot more fun if I were not the last one picked for a team and the first one hit with the ball. Licking the swing set seemed a small price to pay for the chance of having them as my friends.

I got off my swing and stood by one of the legs of the swing set. The kids all gathered around me. They seemed so thrilled about what I was going to do. More kids started to gather around to see what was happening. They began to cheer me on, and in that moment, for the first time in my life, I felt like a hero; I was caught up in their enthusiasm. I looked over all the smiling faces and listened while they cheered my name. I didn't even realize, prior to this, that they knew my name. The smile on my face was so big that I could feel it. Under my fans' watchful, admiring eyes, I turned toward the leg of the swing set. I got close enough to it so my tongue could reach it. I planned on licking it quickly and then turning back around toward my new friends to see what I could do next to amaze and delight them. My tongue hit the leg of the swing set and stuck in place. I could not move it. I tried ripping it back off, but all that did was make my tongue hurt. I was stuck there with my tongue hanging out of my mouth freezing and feeling like a nincompoop.

The kids were wildly laughing and pointing at me. Suddenly, they went from cheering me on to calling me names. They called me stupid, and yelled that I was a moron. They were right. How could I have been so gullible and fallen for their game? I should have known they were up to no good. More kids gathered around and joined in the laughter. I tried so hard not to, but I started to cry. This made the kids laugh at me even more; they called me a baby. I felt so low and so embarrassed that I was nearly ready to faint. I wondered, "What will happen if I faint with my tongue stuck to this swing set? I bet the dead weight of my body will rip my tongue right off. Will the kids feel bad if I faint and fall? At least if I faint, I will not be able to feel my tongue ripping off." Even better, if I fainted, I could get away from the sheer feeling of mortification that I was suffering. It seemed as though there was no one in the world that I could ever trust.

I wondered where the playground lady was and why she did not come over to save me. I hoped she would not forget about me and just leave me stuck to the swing set when recess was over. Would anyone even notice that I had not returned to class? A girl emerged from the crowd. I knew her; she was in my class. She seemed just as quiet as I was, and I didn't think she had any friends either. Her name was Josephine, and kids teased her because she was chubby and wore glasses. It was not a good thing to be different in school.

Josephine came up to me and put her arm around my shoulder. She whispered in my ear, "Don't pay any attention to them. They are just being stupid. It's going to be okay. I am going to go and get the teacher."

She was like an angel sent to me from God, and I had not even prayed yet. I immediately settled down, stopped crying, and felt some strength returning to me. The kids noticed that they no longer had the same effect on me. Some of the kids seemed to lose interest after that and wandered away. I was sure the rest of the kids would scatter the minute they saw the teacher coming, and they did.

"What happened?" said Ms. Erickson.

I could only grunt in reply.

"You poor thing. Stay right there – oh, it's not like you can go anywhere anyway – I will be right back with a bucket of warm water," she stated.

"What will that do?" Josephine asked. I was wondering the same thing.

"I will pour the warm water over Emily's tongue until it lets go of the swing set. Don't worry, Emily. I will hurry," she explained.

Josephine stayed with me while Ms. Erickson ran back into the school. She didn't talk to me at all, but she did stand close, and I felt protected. I hoped this meant we would be friends; if so, my humiliation would have been worth it.

Ms. Erickson came back and poured the warm water over my tongue, and my tongue magically released from the swing set. Ms. Erickson was so smart. I hugged her, and she hugged me right back. That felt so good. Recess was over, and the other kids had already gone back in to class. Josephine and I walked back inside the school with Ms. Erickson.

When we got inside, Ms. Erickson stopped me out in the hallway.

"How did you end up with your tongue on the swing set, Emily? Did someone make you do it?" Ms. Erickson asked.

"I don't know Ms. Erickson. No one made me do it," I quietly replied. My tongue hurt so bad that I was surprised I could talk at all. Technically, I was not lying to Ms. Erickson. No one had made me do it. I felt so humiliated that I started to cry again. Ms. Erickson put her arm around me and said she was going to call my Mama to come and get me. She thought it would be best if I went home.

"I don't want to go home, Ms. Erickson," I managed to mumble.

"I think it is best, Emily. You are too upset to stay in school today, and besides, I can tell your tongue is very sore and hurting you," she explained.

At least it was early afternoon, so Daddy was at work and could not come and get me. I didn't know who would pick me up though because Mama did not have a car when Daddy was at work. We only had one car.

"Do you know what happened, Josephine?" asked Ms. Erickson.

I shot a quick look at Josephine that I was hoping said to her, "Please do not tell." I was desperate that Ms. Erickson not find about my shame, and besides, if she did know, she would punish the kids involved, and then my life at school would become insufferable.

"No, Ms. Erickson. Emily was already stuck to the swing set when I saw her," replied Josephine. Maybe that was true. I did not know. I would have to find out later.

"I want you to go to the nurse's station, Emily, and wait there for one of your parents to come and pick you up. Josephine, you can walk with her to the nurse's office, but then you have to come right back to class," said Ms. Erickson.

We started down the hall toward the nurse's office walking very slowly. Our school was new. It had been built during the last year. It was beautiful and still smelled new. It was so nice to leave my house and come to the new school. The floor was made up of tile that looked like bricks. It was shiny and slippery if you came in on it with wet feet. We tried keeping our feet inside the blocks, avoiding the cracks around them while we walked. Josephine started to chant,

"Step on a crack..."

I joined in and in unison we sang, "And break your mother's back!" We looked at each other and giggled. We were friends.

Sometimes I slipped and stepped on the cracks, and I would feel guilty because I was not sure if I had done it on purpose or not.

We chanted and walked a little further, when I turned to Josephine and said, "Thank you."

"You are welcome. Those kids are so mean," she said.

We were quiet for a few steps, and I struggled to think of something to say. I did not want to lose her as a potential friend. She had stuck her neck out for me and saved me. No one, besides Grandma, had ever done that for me before. Then I remembered that Josephine liked to draw, and she was very good at it. I saw her drawings when she left them on her desk, and sometimes Ms. Erickson hung them up in the classroom. Josephine was truly very talented.

"I love your drawings," I commented.

"Thank you," Josephine said.

"I would love to learn how to draw like that. Maybe sometime you could teach me," I ventured.

"I would like that too. You could come over to my house after school someday. Maybe you could ride the bus home with me," she offered.

That sounded wonderful – nearly too good to be true.

"Where do you live?" I asked.

"I live on the air base. My dad is in the Air Force. Do you know about the base?" she responded.

I was suddenly downhearted.

"Yes, my Daddy is in the Air Force too, but we do not live on base. We live in a house that my Grandma and Grandpa used to live in. It's not too far from here. I will ask my Mama if I can ever come over, but I don't know if she will let me. I have never gone to another kid's house before," I replied.

"Okay," she said.

We stopped in front of the nurse's office, and Josephine turned around to go back to class. I watched her as far as I could and felt thankful that she was there for me today. I also felt angry and cheated. If I told Mama about Josephine and her dad, she would want them to come to our house to meet her. I would be so embarrassed in front of Josephine if she saw my house, and I was certain she would no longer want to be my friend.

I waited for over an hour in the nurse's office when the nurse told me Daddy was waiting outside in the car for me. I looked at the clock which read two-thirty. I studied my feet as I walked to the car. Daddy had to have left work in order to pick me up. It was too early in the day for him to be done working. I would be in trouble now.

Daddy was staring straight ahead as I approached the car. I quickly grabbed the back door, opened it, and got it. We just sat there. Daddy didn't move the car. I didn't dare to speak. I rested my head against the door window and watched as the warmth of my breath cleared a spot that had been covered with frost. I waited. I felt tired, defeated, lonely, and scared, but I always felt scared when around Daddy.

"Get in the front seat, Emily. Now!" yelled Daddy.

"Dear God, why me? I don't want to be in the front seat next to Daddy. Please, God, help me! Please, God," I prayed. God wouldn't be there to save me. I didn't expect I would get two miracles from God in one day, and I was thankful for the one miracle of Josephine.

I got out of the back seat and moved to the front. I sat as close to the door as I possibly could. I knew what it meant to be in the front seat with Daddy. This was not a good day.

Daddy started to slowly drive off.

"How stupid can you possibly be, Emily? You stuck your damn tongue on the swing set? What kind of moron are you? You are just like your mother – dumb as a box of rocks. I had to leave work early because of how stupid you are – do you realize that?" Daddy asked.

Daddy was not really looking for an answer, so I stayed quiet. I leaned my head on the window and felt the coolness of the glass against my face. There was no frost left on this window. The car heater must have cleared all that off. I tried thinking about Josephine, while also paying very close attention to what Daddy was doing and saying. It was only a matter of time before he was going to make me move closer to him. Suddenly, Daddy pulled the car over to the side of the road and stopped. I became hyper alert; my heart reacted immediately, thumping hard within my ribcage. I knew this was coming, yet still my body always reacted to it when it arrived. I would never get used to it; it would never stop.

"Move over closer to Daddy," Daddy said in a bit kinder voice.

I sat still. He would have to drag me next to him. I grabbed hold of the car door with both hands. I pressed my feet hard into the floor of the car, looked out the window away from him, and braced for the assault.

"I said move closer to me, Emily," Daddy repeated.

I sat still waiting...waiting...waiting... .

"You really want to play this game with me today? After you have already made me miss work and made me pissed off? You really want to go there, Emily? You are a stupid, stupid girl. Get over here!" Daddy yelled.

I was stupid. I was stupid for doing what the kids had asked me to do. If I had not done that, Daddy would not be here right now, and I would not have had to cling to the door with all my might knowing that it was a losing battle any-way. I continued to ignore Daddy, while listening to every sound he made.

"That's it!" he yelled as he grabbed my arm. He pulled hard and pinched my arm.

"Stop," I yelled through my tears and sobs. "Please, stop!"

Daddy slapped my head. Then he grabbed my leg and arm and roughly pulled me. I couldn't hold on any longer, and my hands gave way as he dragged me next to him.

"Quit your damn crying before I give you something to cry about. When I tell you to do something, you damn well best do it the second I tell you to do it or I will beat you until you can't sit down! Do you understand me?" he questioned.

"Yes," I answered, while stifling my tears and getting control of myself before I got slapped for crying again.

Daddy slowly pulled back onto the road, and I noticed for the first time that we were not going in the direction of our house. Daddy would be taking what he called "the scenic route" home, which really meant he did not want to go home right away, so he drove the long way around. I settled into my fate.

Daddy reached across me and turned on the radio. As he was moving his hand back from the radio dial, he rested it on my leg. I was wearing a skirt, of course.

Mama had dressed me in an outfit that she had made herself. She had decided that she could save money by sewing my clothes. The skirt was a rusted orange color, and Mama had sewed what she called "brick-a-brack" around the bottom of it. The brick-a-brack was the only pretty thing on the skirt, but it looked out of place against the ugly material. My top was made from a pair of old, black stretch pants that Mama did not like anymore. It was itchy and ugly. The seams on both the top and the skirt were uneven and there were threads sticking out that I tried to break off as close as I could to the garment itself. I didn't know where she got the patterns from, but most of the cloth she got from cutting up her old clothes. She said with the money she saved by making my clothes, she could go out and buy herself some new ones. I was teased cruelly at school because of what Mama made me wear. I told her about the teasing, and she said people who learned how to save money should be proud. I could not understand how we saved much money. She seemed to be buying herself more clothes than I had ever seen her do before.

Daddy let his hand rest on my knee while he continued to drive and listen to the country-western music on the radio. He was humming along to a song. I was petrified. I tried thinking about Josephine again. I decided we could be friends at school even if we could not go to each other's house after school or on the weekends. I would have to talk to her about it and see what she thought.

"So, are you at least sorry for what you have caused, Emily? I have missed two and a half hours of work because of you and your stupid, idiotic behaviors," said Daddy.

"Yes, I am sorry," I replied. He had no idea how truly sorry I was at that moment.

"Good. You should be," he stated, as he slowly started to move his hand up my leg.

I squirmed trying to get away. Daddy grabbed my leg and pinched it hard. There would be a bruise left there.

"What did I just tell you, Emily? You do as you are told! I told you to sit here and sit here you will! Do you need a spanking?" he asked.

"No," I replied.

My leg was throbbing from the pinching, and I wanted to rub the spot that hurt, but I could not reach it because Daddy's hand was in the way.

He continued to hum to music on the radio. The radio was quiet for just a moment, and Daddy stopped moving his hand. The music started again and so did Daddy. He was singing now and appeared to be totally engrossed in the song.

He moved his hand all the way up my leg until he got to my panties. He had to twist his hand around and lean forward over the steering wheel to be able to do what he wanted to do. He was looking straight ahead as he pulled my panties aside and found that spot where he could jam in his finger. I tried sitting higher so he couldn't reach it, but he pinched the top of where I go potty very hard, and it stung so bad that it brought tears to my eyes. I had to sit normally.

I shut my eyes, but I could not shut my ears. Daddy was singing with the man on the radio, "I tried so hard my dear to show that you're my every dream, yet you're afraid each thing I do is just some evil scheme."

I knew the things Daddy did were part of an evil scheme. I wondered if this song was about men like Daddy.

When Daddy got to the chorus of the song, his voice boomed as he sang. He also jammed his finger in and out of me to the rhythm of the music. He was particularly rough and mean about it. I wondered if he was being so mean as a way to punish me for causing him to leave work early and not minding him right away when he ordered me to sit next to him. Thank goodness the angle of his hand would not allow him to get his finger in very far; still, it hurt – it hurt so much.

I sat there pretending that it was not happening. Daddy didn't really have his finger in a place that felt wrong for a Daddy to have his finger in. I didn't really have a shameful day at school; in fact, all the kids really liked me. It was not working. I could not even pretend in my head while Daddy was keeping time to his music by ripping his finger in and out of me. I gave up trying and just sat there with my eyes closed, holding back the tears and willing myself not to yell at him to please stop. It will be over soon, I told myself; this ride cannot last forever.

Finally, I felt the car turn, and I heard the familiar

sound of the dirt road we lived on. I could smell it, too. It smelled much different from the paved roads. I liked it. It smelled like the earth. I opened my eyes slightly to make certain I was right. I was right; we were nearly home.

Daddy turned his blinker on to turn into our drive-way, but he still had his finger inside me. The pine trees that I loved so well in the yard hid the car from the house as we sat there waiting to turn; otherwise, Daddy would have told me to get over by the door already.

"Do you remember what I said now, Emily?" asked Daddy. I had no idea what he was talking about, but I said yes anyway.

"What do you remember, Emily?" he queried.

"I don't know," I honestly replied.

Daddy took his finger out of me. I let out a breath of relief, knowing that soon it would be over. Instead of moving his hand away, and placing it back on the steering wheel, Daddy pinched me again by where I go pee, harder than he had the first time. He pinched me three times while telling me what to remember.

"You had best do as you are told! When I tell you to do something, you do it!" said Daddy.

The pinch was so hard that I winced. I tried not to, but I could not hold back from asking him to stop.

"Daddy, please stop! That hurts!" I begged.

"And that's another thing. You never, ever, tell me what to do! Do you understand that!" he reiterated with his second pinch.

"I'm sorry...I'm sorry," I cried.

"You just remember this is your entire fault. You brought this on by being stupid today. And you had best not tell your Mama about our car ride home, or she is just going to be even madder at you than I am certain she already is. Do you understand me, Emily?" Daddy asked and then pinched me hard with a twist at the end for good measure.

"I understand," I replied.

"Move back over by the door, and when we get to the house I suggest you go inside and tell your Mama you are sorry for being so stupid because she is not happy about having to call me at work to come and get your idiotic ass," ordered Daddy.

"I will," I promised.

Daddy pulled up into the driveway; I got out of the car, looked toward the house, and saw Mama standing in the window with a mean look on her face and her hands on her hips. I felt a deep sigh of despair escape my lips as I walked as slowly as possible to the house, examining in great detail everything on the ground.

With each step I took, I thought, "Does Daddy touch me to punish me? It feels like he is trying to hurt me, but sometimes when he does, he looks more like I am hurting him. His face gets all scrunched up when the white stuff comes out of his pee-pee. Is touching me hurting him? Is this really my fault?

I entered the house and looked at Mama. There would be no answers for me here.

CHAPTER ELEVEN

KUM-BA-YA

THE KIDS AT SCHOOL NEVER SAID ANOTHER WORD TO ME ABOUT what had happened on the playground. I was grateful for their short attention spans. Josephine and I continued our friendship throughout the rest of the school year, while winter quietly gave way to spring. Near the end of the school year, Josephine told me her father had been transferred. They would be moving over the summer, and I would never see her again. Strangely, I felt nothing when she gave me the news. It was as though I always expected bad news, and I had grown accustomed to it. I would miss her, but I could not allow myself to feel the pain from her loss.

Spring was my favorite time of year, even with the bad news from Josephine. It was April Fool's Day when Ms. Erickson called me up to her desk. I had been expecting someone to do something to me all day but certainly not Ms. Erickson.

She told me that I was to stay after school and go to Girl Scouts. I was so excited! I got to go to Girl Scouts! The rest of the day seemed to slow down, and every 'tick-tock' of the clock echoed in my ears. It became maddening until I finally had to hang my head down and plug my ears with my fingers. The ticking reminded me of the story "The Tell-Tale Heart" by Edgar Allan Poe, and it filled me with a sense of dread. I had read the story over the Christmas break. Daddy had a stack of books next to the couch which we were not supposed to touch, but Charlie and I looked through them one afternoon anyway. On the bottom of the pile was a book with a hardcover, which was strange for Daddy because he nearly always read paperback books with no covers and often times no backs either. The hardcover book was made from leather with fancy scrolling across it. It looked very old. On the binding it said it was a collection of works by Edgar Allan Poe. I had heard of Mr. Poe before somewhere, but I could not remember where. I loved to read, so I had probably read something about him. What I remembered the most was that his writing was supposed to be spooky.

The book was heavy and felt used. It made a creaking sound when I opened it, as though it was trying to warn me that the stories inside were scary. Usually I do not like reading scary stories, but it seemed like the book was already sharing its secrets with me before I turned the first page. Daddy was at work, and Mama was in the kitchen, although she never paid any attention to what I read anyway, so I grabbed the book and curled up on the end of the couch with it.

I decided to let the book tell me what story to read. I closed my eyes and opened it up in the middle. I opened my eyes and had to turn a couple of pages to get to the beginning of a story, and "The Tell-Tale Heart" was the first one I came to. It was the only story I read, and I read it over and over again trying to understand it. The story did scare me but not because of the story itself; it scared me because it reminded me of me, and I could not quite understand how.

"The Tell-Tale Heart" was a very short story about a man who killed an old man that he lived with just because he did not like the way his eye looked. He chopped him up and buried him under the floor in the old man's bedroom.

He thought he was really smart and that he had gotten away with it, but then the police came, and he started to feel very guilty about what he had done. He was sure he could hear the old man's dead heart beating from under the floor boards, and he thought the police could hear it too, but they didn't. In the end, he gave himself away because the guilt he was feeling made him crazy, and so he confessed what he had done.

At the very end of the story, when the man was feeling extremely guilty, he said, "Almighty God! – no, no! They heard! – they suspected! – they knew! – they were making a mockery of my horror! – this I thought, and this I think. But anything was better than this agony."

I read that part over and over again. I thought, "I feel the same way! I know Mama must hear what Daddy does to me. I know she knows! They are mocking me!" The story did not make me feel any better though, because the man in the story was a bad man. I wondered, "Does this mean I am the bad one?"

After I read it several times that afternoon trying to figure it out, I threw the book down in frustration – then I quickly picked it up and put it back where I had found it. I did not want to get in trouble for touching it. I felt more lost than ever, and I never touched the book again. I promised myself to never read anything from Edgar Allan Poe again. He was too spooky for me.

My fingers were still stuck in my ears when Ms. Erickson told me it was time to go. I looked up at the clock, grateful to see that it read 3:30. I buried my thoughts about the dead, ticking heart under the floor boards deep in my head and quickly left my seat. I was anxious to get going.

Ms. Erickson told me the Girl Scouts were meeting in another classroom, and she took me there. I walked in quietly with my head down. I was excited, but, as usual, I was also very afraid of anything new. I saw several girls who were in my grade, but they had different teachers. They were all sitting around in a half circle, and there was a big lady in front of them talking. I couldn't quite see her face yet, but I could hear her. My sense of dread had been right. I wanted to turn around and run out the door. I wanted to find Ms. Erickson and tell her there had been some sort of mistake and that I did not belong there. It was useless. I joined the other girls, sat down, looked up at Mama, and smiled my best smile for her.

Mama had decided that she was going to be a Girl Scout leader. This was a disaster. Mama told all of us that we would meet in the same room once a week, and that each one of us had to pay dues of 50 cents a week. She explained that would help pay for all the fun things we were going to do. I couldn't imagine my Mama and fun together. I was certain there must be a trick in this somewhere.

Each week we met, and each week Mama treated all the other girls the way I had always wanted her to treat me. I never knew Mama could be so sweet. All the other girls said they were jealous of me, and they wished their mamas were like my Mama. It was amazing to me! Mama tolerated me in the group, but she never went out of her way to be nice to me. I was certain it was because of what Daddy did to me.

"I can't spend any time with you while we are at Girl Scouts, and I certainly can't let you carry the flag in the ceremonies because I don't want people to think I am favoring you," she said.

Girl Scouts quickly became a misery. The minute all the girls were gone, Mama would become her old self again, and there was always something I had done wrong. She said I was an embarrassment to her. Daddy would show up at the very end of our group to take Mama and me home. He always had his uniform on because he came straight from work to get us. All the girls thought I had a very nice Daddy.

It was getting warmer outside, and I loved to be outdoors during the spring. The air always smelled so new and fresh; it was like anything was possible. At the Girl Scout meeting, Mama announced that she had decided we were all going to the Girl Scout cabin for the weekend. It sounded like fun, but I was afraid Mama would find a way to ruin it for me. I thought if I could just get away with the other girls and somehow hide in the group of them, then maybe she would let me have some fun. Well, at least I would be away from Daddy for a weekend.

When Girl Scouts ended, Daddy was there to pick us up. I sat in the backseat, and I could hear my parents talking. Daddy was mad at Mama, but I was not quite sure why, so I started listening even closer.

"You are such a stupid bitch. I don't know why you thought you had to start this Girl Scout thing in the first place, and now you want to drag me into this shit!" said Daddy.

"I am doing it for your daughter," Mama promptly answered back.

"Bullshit you are! You are doing it to try and look good in front of your friends and your damn sister, so you can say, 'Look at me – I am a big community involved person' – that's why you do it!" said Daddy.

"What do you want me to do? It's not like I can get out of this now. It's this weekend, and I am going to need your help. Christ! Why can't you just help! I can't take 25 girls to a cabin in the woods without someone with me. It's one f'n weekend, and I won't ask again," said Mama.

I could not believe what I was hearing. She was asking Daddy to go with our Girl Scout group to the cabin for the weekend for two whole nights. I had thought I would be safe there. I had thought since it was the Girl Scouts that Daddy would not be allowed. I wondered if I could stay home if I said I was sick. Mama would just drag me along anyway, and I knew it.

"Damn it. I will go with, but know this – I am pissed! Don't you ever volunteer me for any of your shit ever again!

If you want to get involved and pretend you are something you are not, be my guest, but do not include me in your shit!" yelled Daddy.

"Well, thank you, and I will never ask you again," promised Mama.

I thought it was awfully strange that Daddy accused Mama of being something she was not especially since Daddy pretended every day that he was not a monster. Mama knew it too – I knew she knew it, but she never said anything to him about it. I couldn't say anything. It would not do any good anyway. I had already learned that lesson. I started screaming so loud in my head that I was afraid for a moment the noise might escape through my ears, and Mama and Daddy would hear me.

I dreaded the weekend coming up – simply dreaded it. At school, the other girls in the troop were very excited about going to the cabin, and they talked about it all the time. The girls said they got new sleeping bags and pajamas for the trip. I had never had a sleeping bag before, and I doubted I was going to have one now. I thought about asking Mama if I could get one but decided against it. I would be bringing the pajamas I had been given for Christmas, which were not too bad, and my blankets that I used on the couch. I wished I could wash them before we left, but at least I could take them outside and shake them really hard to try to make sure there were no cockroaches in them.

The weekend arrived and, as I guessed, no sleeping bag. I was busy shaking my blankets outside behind the house when Daddy approached me from behind. I never saw him coming; usually I paid more attention and should have heard him sneaking up behind me, but I was just too focused on what I was doing and worrying about what was going to happen over the weekend.

Daddy came up behind me and draped his arms around my neck with his hands falling by my chest. I kept right on shaking my blanket out and pretended he was not there.

"You are going to be a good girl this weekend, aren't you, Emmy?" said Daddy.

"Yes, Daddy," I answered as I tried to squirm out of his grasp.

"Well, that's certainly not being a good girl. Quit squirming," he responded, as he used one of his hands to lift my skirt. He squeezed my butt cheek very hard. "You had best be a good girl this weekend. I will let you help me chop and bring the wood for the campfire your Mama has planned tonight, as long as you are good."

That was the last thing I wanted. I wanted to avoid being anywhere alone with Daddy this weekend. I was so afraid that if he tried to touch me while we were at the cabin, all the girls would see him and laugh at me and blame me. It would be so much worse than the shame I endured when the kids asked me to lick the swing set. The horror of it chilled me to my very bones.

"I don't want to help you with the wood, Daddy. I want to just be with the other girls," I offered in explanation.

"Well, isn't that just too bad? You will do as you are told, and you will help me when I tell you to help me," Daddy said, as he reached his hand around to the front of me, lifted up my shirt, and squeezed my nipple so hard that I cried out and instinctively put my elbow back toward his body as hard as I could, but I missed jabbing him.

"I knew you liked that," he said, as he turned to leave.

I continued to shake out my blankets, not wanting to move from the spot I was in. I was trembling. I had been afraid before but this was a new kind of fear. I thought, "What does he mean by saying he knew I liked that? I can't stand him touching me! It hurts! Can't he hear me? Does he really think I like it? I don't know what to do. He warns me to keep what he does to me a secret, but it seems like he likes touching me when other people are around, and they might see. Maybe he isn't worried about getting caught because it really is my fault! Dear God, please don't let the other girls see him touching me! Please, God, please!"

Mama yelled for me to get in the house and help her pack the food up for the weekend, so I moved quickly, sealing away my worries about Daddy to avoid trouble.

"Now, Emily, you know that all the girls will be working on badges this weekend," she said.

"Yes, Mama, I want to earn my outdoors badge. I love the picture on it. It is my favorite one of them all," I responded.

"You know that your Mama is the leader, so other girls and their parents will be watching closely to make sure that I don't give you the badges without you earning them, so when I sign off on the badges for the other girls this weekend, I am not going to be signing off on yours. I am going to tell everyone that I am giving you extra assignments to earn the badges; that way everyone will know I am not favoring you," explained Mama.

"That's not fair! I have almost already earned that badge, Mama! I only have one more thing to do this weekend, and I will have done everything!" I yelled.

"Don't you yell at me, and I don't care what you have done. This is the way it is going to be and that's it," she commanded.

"Why?" I questioned.

"Because I said so, that's why. The only reason I am telling you now is so that you don't create a big scene when I am signing off for the other girls. Do you understand me?" Mama said.

"Yes, Mama, I understand. Do you have to say it in front of all the other girls? They will tease me," I questioned.

"That's the whole point, you idiot. Yes, I have to say it in front of everyone. How else are they going to know," she responded.

The conversation was over, and I continued to help Mama pack up the food and other items in the car. At least Charlie was coming, too, so I would have someone there who understood how we lived. Charlie was not happy at all about going away for the weekend with a bunch of girls, especially a bunch of girls that were in the second grade. Mama did not care what he thought about things either.

The cabin was over an hour away. Everyone was quiet the entire trip, which was nice for a change: no yelling. Mama said the cabin was on the end of a dirt road by a creek. I felt excited as we turned down the road, straining my eyes to see it. Then there it was, and it was huge! I did not expect it to be so big, but I did not say a word because they would have told me I was dumb for not realizing the cabin would have to be big to keep all the girls in it.

The cabin was made of logs, and it was two stories high with a basement. It sat right in the middle of the woods surrounded by the largest pine trees I had ever seen. I imagined that someday my pine trees at home would grow as big. Off to the side of the cabin, I saw a big fire pit and large logs laid out in a huge square all around it. I thought that must be where we would have our fire, and we would sit on those logs when we did. Behind the cabin was a small creek. Mama was worried about the girls falling in it and drowning.

When we got out of the car, I took a deep breath. It smelled like pine and earth, and it was wonderful. It was that familiar, safe smell that I enjoyed when I was wrapped in the boughs of my pine trees at home. I loved it. I was so happy to be there, and in that moment I did not care that Daddy touched me or that Mama was the Girl Scout leader. In that moment, I felt good, and I was excited. I had learned that happiness usually came in moments, not in days, at least that is the way it was for me, so I tried to recognize, enjoy, and hold on to those moments when I was lucky enough to have them.

"Grab some bags and get them in the cabin," Mama ordered.

Everyone was helping unload the car, and I joined in. As I walked through the door of the cabin I was amazed. The kitchen was the first room I saw, and it was bigger than our living room and kitchen combined. Past the kitchen was what Mama called the mess hall. It was where everyone ate. It was big, too, and had beautiful tables that looked kind of like picnic tables for all us to sit on, and there were a lot of them all lined up in a row. On the other side of the mess hall was a great big open room with a massive fireplace made out of stone. It reached all the way up to the ceiling, and I could almost stand straight up inside it. It smelled like wood and campfire in that room and felt warm and inviting. All of the floors were made out of wood that looked like it had been polished to a high shine. The flooring was beautiful and made a clicking sound under Mama's shoes when she walked on it. Mama told me she was going to use the great room to teach the girls how to dance and skip to my lou, whatever that meant. I did not know Mama knew how to dance.

The other girls were starting to arrive. The stairs that led to the second floor were in the great room by the fireplace, so I quickly headed to them to have a look before anyone else got in the cabin. My sneakered feet landed softly on the worn, wooden stairs, and made no noise as I climbed to the top. Mama had allowed me to wear my sneakers because we were going to a cabin, but I still had to wear my Girl Scout dress uniform all weekend. A lot of the girls did not even have a uniform, and it made me feel silly wearing it around them. Mama said as the leader's daughter, I had to set an example. I hated being the leader's daughter.

At the top of the stairs, I found one large room with another smaller room at the end of it. In the large room there were two rows of beds. I counted 15 beds on each side. I had never seen so many beds before in my life! They were small beds, Mama called them cots, but still, it was something looking at all of them lined up in two rows facing each other. I was so delighted about the idea of all of us girls sleeping together in the same room. It would be like the sleep over I had never been able to have, nor had I ever been invited to one.

The other room was small and had one large bed in it. I assumed this must be where the leader was supposed to sleep. There was no door to the room; in fact, there was no privacy whatsoever in there. Mama did not like it when she had no privacy in her bedroom.

I chose a cot right in the middle of one of the rows. I did not know if this was a good idea or not. I thought for sure if I chose to sleep at the end by the stairs, Daddy would get me, but here in the middle it might be harder for him. I was worried, though, that he would still try; rarely did Daddy let a night go by without coming and hurting me after Mama had gone to bed. All I could do was hope for the best. If he did come, maybe in the dark the other girls would not be able to see what he was doing, and I could say he was just there to check on me. I had to think of something, just in case.

Mama yelled for me to get downstairs and help her. I quickly ran down the stairs. I wanted to avoid trouble as much as I possibly could during the weekend. Mama was in the kitchen and said that I had to help her cook supper. She was making sloppy joes. All of the other girls had arrived, so Mama told them they could go outside and play until supper time. She asked my Daddy to "keep an eye on them." I prayed that he would not touch any of them the way he touched me.

The girls ran outside as fast as they could go. I felt like they had not even given me a second thought being stuck in the kitchen helping to cook their food, but I forgave them for that because it was not their fault. As I helped Mama cook, I watched the girls having fun outside and wished I was with them. I saw Daddy, too, and he wasn't getting anywhere near the girls. He was over behind a big shed on the opposite side of the cabin from the fire pit. He was looking around all the firewood logs stacked there. I felt like I had a heavy rock in the pit of my stomach as I stood there watching him through the window.

Once supper was prepared and cooking, Mama let me go outside. She said it would be done in a few minutes, so I had best enjoy the time I had outside with the girls.

After supper, Mama said it was time for our campfire. She assigned two girls to bring graham crackers, marshmallows, and chocolate bars. She said we were making smores with them. I had no idea what smores were, but the ingredients sure sounded good to me. I was scared because having a campfire meant that Daddy was going to tell me any minute that I had to help him with the wood. I dreaded that moment and hoped he had forgotten he was going to make me help him. Maybe, just maybe, he had changed his mind.

I rushed out the door with the other girls. I thought it was best that Daddy not even see me because I was afraid that the sight of me might just remind him. I made it to the campfire area with the other girls and sat down on one of the logs surrounding the fire pit when I heard Daddy call me.

"Emily, get over here and help me with this wood! I told you before you were going to help me, and I know you remember," reprimanded Daddy.

Charlie was at the fire pit with Mama, and they were starting the fire with the wood that was already there, so it was no use asking if Charlie could do it instead. That never worked anyway. I had no choice but to go to Daddy.

Daddy was behind the big shed where tools were stored and the wood was piled. No one could see us back there, and we could not see them either. I was glad no one could see me because I was sure Daddy was going to touch me and hurt me. I kept my head down as I turned the corner to the back of the shed, and there Daddy stood waiting for me.

"Grab some of those logs there, Emily, and bring them over here so I can split them," he ordered.

My spirits soared. Maybe we really were going to work on the wood together! This was okay – I could do this. Daddy continued to chop wood for a few minutes, and then he sent me back to the big pile of wood to get more logs for him. I could carry only one at a time.

As I was bending over to pick up one of the logs, Daddy pushed me down onto the pile of wood. I scrambled up to my feet. Daddy pinned me to his body with my back next to him. I heard the zipper on his pants go down, and I tried to go away in my head. I pictured myself back at the fire with the other girls eating smores and having fun. Daddy turned me to the side, grabbed my hand and forced it around his pee-pee. I tried to pull it back; but Daddy wrapped his hand around mine and made it go up and down. It made me feel sick to my stomach. At least I was able to turn my head away from him, so I didn't have to look at it.

With his other hand, Daddy reached under the neck of my Girl Scout dress and started to pinch my nipples. He pinched them so hard and it hurt so bad! Whatever I did, though, I couldn't scream out. I couldn't risk the chance of someone coming back there to see why I was screaming. I closed my eyes tightly and continued to think about the fire and the smores. In the distance I started to hear all the girls singing around the campfire. Daddy kept moving my hand – faster and faster.

The girls were singing, "Kum-ba-ya, my Lord, come by here, oh Lord, Kum-ba-ya." They sounded so pretty.

I felt something wet all over my hand. Daddy stopped pinching my nipple and let my hand go. It was over. I ran to the creek to wash my hand. I felt so disgusted and sick; my nipples were hurting. After I washed my hands, I rubbed my chest to help it feel better.

"Carry this chopped wood over to your Mama, Emily," said Daddy, as though nothing had just happened.

I grabbed some wood and so did Daddy, and we both walked over to the campfire. I put the wood down and sat a little away from the other girls because I was afraid that somehow they could tell what had just happened to me.

We all began to toast marshmallows to make smores and started singing again. This part of the night would be good.

Later that night, I lay in my cot worried that Daddy was going to come and get me, but he never did. I figured he must have had enough earlier by the wood pile. I was thankful and finally went to sleep.

In the morning we all went outside to the outhouses. There were two of them, and in front of them was a big sink with a well water pump that had a handle on it that had to be pumped up and down to get the water to come out and empty into the sink. We all went to the bathroom and then started to brush our teeth. Mama had given me a toothbrush and a very small tube of toothpaste. I watched the other girls carefully to see how they brushed their teeth so that I did not make a mistake. I had never had a toothbrush before this weekend. Mama and Daddy always said they had false teeth by the time they were 22 years old, so they expected the same thing for Charlie and me.

Sometimes I would get really bad toothaches, and Mama would give me whiskey and tell me to hold it in my mouth over the tooth that was hurting and to swallow it when I was done. It tasted so bad and made me gag. It felt like it was burning all the way down. Mama would usually have me do that twice to my tooth. I really don't know if it helped the pain in my tooth because it made me feel so tired that I would just fall asleep, which was good too.

After I brushed my teeth, I ran my tongue over the front of them. I never knew my teeth could feel so smooth and good. I mentioned this to the girl standing next to me, and she looked at me funny. I guess she was probably used to the feeling because she brushed her teeth all the time.

The day was warm and bright. I felt full of energy and hope. I wanted to run free and scream joyfully as loud as I could, but, of course, I just stood there with the other girls. All of us girls and Charlie spent the morning outside investigating the creek but being very careful not to go in it. No one wanted to get into trouble. We walked through the woods and went by our campfire area. Charlie, being the oldest in the group, was kind of like our leader and protector as we ventured through the woods. It was a wonderful morning, and other girls were actually talking to me like I was their friend. I was happy.

After lunch, Mama said it was time to learn how to dance. Skip to my lou, she explained, was a dance. She showed all of us how to do it, and then she plugged in the record player and started the music. We all moved to the center of the room and started to dance like Mama had shown us. It did not take us long to learn the dance, and we were having fun!

My hair felt like it was flying through the air, and the room was spinning very fast as we changed partners going around and around in the circle. I was so happy I thought I might burst. I saw Daddy in a blur off to the side of the room, and even he looked like he had a smile on his face as he stared at me twirling around the room. This was the best time I had ever had at Girl Scouts, and I was thankful for it. I might have to put up with Daddy all weekend, but I would've had to put up with Daddy no matter where I was for the weekend. I would try as hard as I could to avoid him, and in the meantime, I wanted to suck out every ounce of joy possible.

By the time we went to bed that night I was so exhausted that I fell right to sleep. My normal worries about Daddy faded into the background; surely with all the fun we had had and Daddy not touching me here in the cot the night before, I would be safe going to sleep amongst all my new friends.

Hours later, Daddy woke me up and told me to be

very quiet because everyone else was still sleeping. The sun hadn't come up yet, and I wondered why we were getting up. I was instantly afraid. As we passed the room Mama was sleeping in, I heard her mumble thank you to Daddy. I looked at Daddy questioningly, but he gave me no response. Mama's knowledge of Daddy waking me and taking me downstairs with him did nothing to alleviate my fears.

When we got downstairs, he told me to wait in the kitchen while he went outside to use the outhouse. So I waited, wondered, and worried. Charlie was asleep in the great room on the floor. I could hear him snoring. Daddy said Charlie could sleep through a bomb going off.

When Daddy got back in he said, "I told your Mama that we would make breakfast for all the girls."

So that is why Mama said thank you. I did not know Daddy knew how to cook.

"What are we making?" I asked.

"I don't know, Emmy. What do you think?"

"I don't know how to cook, Daddy," I explained.

"Neither do I," he responded. "You sure looked pretty last night dancing."

I did not know how to respond to him. I wanted to go back to bed, back to the safety of my friends. I looked down to the floor and said, "It was fun."

I was still dressed in my pajamas, and my hair was rumpled from the deep sleep I had enjoyed. My eyes felt like I had crusty sleep in them, so I rubbed them until they felt clear. We were standing in the kitchen by the stove where large pans were hung from the ceiling. I kept staring at the floor.

"You looked so nice, Emmy, that I had trouble sleeping all night thinking about you," Daddy whispered.

I stood there quietly, with my head down. This was a different side of Daddy that I rarely saw. He was being nice to me. Why was he being like this? He was most dangerous when he was nice.

"You looked so grown-up dancing with the other girls," he continued.

Daddy moved closer to me, and I instinctively moved back a step. He moved closer again, and again I moved away. Suddenly, his facial expression changed, and he was no longer looking at me as though he thought I was pretty, and I felt pretty ugly.

"Okay, Emmy, have it your way. I was trying to be nice, but I guess that just doesn't work with you," Daddy growled through his teeth.

I had backed up enough to be right next to the kitchen door. My desire to run away overpowered my fear of Daddy. I opened the door and ran as fast as I could. I heard the screech of the screen door when it slammed shut as my legs carried me away. I wasn't even looking at what direction I was going. I could hardly see with the sun not up yet and the tears running down my face, but I didn't scream. How horrifying it would have been to me to have the other girls wake and see me running through the grounds away from Daddy.

Just as I saw the creek in front of me, I felt Daddy's hands grab the back of my pajamas. All was lost. I had no clue what I would have done anyway had I gotten away from him. I would have had to eventually go back, and he would always be there. It was stupid of me to run. Now, he was just angrier than he was before I ran out the door.

Daddy pushed me down to the ground. I tried to get up, but he pushed me down again, and this time he sat over the top of me with one leg on each side of me, pinning my arms under his legs and resting his weight on my belly. I felt like I could not breathe.

Daddy's face was red and he was breathing hard. He looked angry, yet he was smiling like we were playing some sort of game. Without saying a word, he reached behind him and ripped off my panties as fast as he could and threw them in the creek. They drifted a little way down until they got caught on a twig. I watched them while they clung to it, swirling around in the water fighting against the current to hang on, but it wasn't long before the twig gave way and the panties moved out of my sight.

I tried squirming, but I could not move. The look on Daddy's face really scared me. He looked like a whole new monster that I had never seen before. He held me tighter as I squirmed, so I stopped because it hurt, and I wasn't going to be going anywhere anyway. I gave up.

Daddy unzipped his pants and put his pee-pee in my face. I tried to look away. I closed my eyes as tightly as I could, but Daddy pinched my private area hard and told me if I did not look he was going to pinch me even harder. I opened my eyes to see his pee-pee so close to my face that it was blurry. The smell of it made my stomach sick, and I was afraid I might throw up, which would surely get me into more trouble.

"See, Emmy! See what you did! You are such a bad girl! You are lucky I don't tell your Mama myself what you make me do," Daddy sneered.

I lay there without saying a word. I thought about the night before and how much fun the dancing had been with all the girls. I recalled the smile on Daddy's face while he watched me dancing, except now it looked more sinister in my memory. I didn't care; I wasn't going to let him or anyone take away the fun I had had learning to dance.

Daddy held his pee-pee in his hand, and then he rubbed the top of it on my lips. He tried to push it into my mouth, but I held my teeth together as hard as I could, and I thought, "If he puts that in my mouth, first I will bite him as hard as I can and then I will throw up."

Daddy must have sensed my desire to bite him because he moved his pee-pee away from my mouth. He rested his weight back down on me, while still pinning my arms with his legs. He reached behind him again and started rubbing me where he had pinched me so hard just a moment ago.

"You like that, don't you, Emmy?" he asked.

I didn't answer. I closed my eyes, ignored him, and pretended I was far away floating down the creek and slowly going under the water never to rise again.

I could feel his hand touching his pee-pee again, and he was rubbing fast up and down, up and down. He started rubbing me the same way. It hurt. He rubbed me so hard that I thought for sure my skin must be bleeding. Suddenly, he lifted up on his knees, made grunting sounds, and squirted stuff out of his pee-pee all over my face. It was warm and sticky and smelled bad. Once it was out of Daddy he got off of me.

I didn't move a muscle. I felt like I would never be able to move again. The sticky stuff was dribbling down the side of my cheek and into my ear making my ear itch, but still I did not move. Nothing seemed to matter in that moment. I could hear Daddy zipping his pants up.

"Get up, Emmy, and go over to the creek and wipe that shit off your face," he commanded.

Still, I just lay there. His voice sounded like it was coming from some place far away through a long, dark tunnel.

"I said, get up!"

I blinked. I had movement again. I moved my head toward the creek and noticed the sun was just coming up making the sky look pretty and pink. The creek, I need to get to the creek to wash my face.

Daddy grabbed me by the arm and yanked me up off the ground. He straightened my night dress and brushed off the back of it. He took me to the creek and told me to get cleaned up quickly.

I scooped the water up into my hands and threw it on my face. I felt so sick; finally, I threw up. Daddy stood there watching me. When he thought I was cleaned up enough, he said we needed to get back to the kitchen to cook breakfast because it was getting late.

As we walked back, I trailed a step or two behind him. He looked like a giant of man.

"What are we going to cook together for breakfast, Emmy?" Daddy asked me cheerfully.

I didn't respond. Daddy stopped, turned, and looked directly at me. I said, "I don't know, Daddy."

"Well, it doesn't matter. When your Mama gets up, I will just tell her that we could not think of anything to make, so we went for a walk instead down by the creek. She can cook the breakfast herself. It's not like I want to be here anyway," Daddy said.

All I could think about was that Mama would eventually notice that one of my panties was missing, and then she would ask me to explain why. I had one pair for each day, and the day of the week was embroidered on each pair. Saturday's panties had floated off to freedom down the river without me.

As we approached the cabin, I could see the lights on in the kitchen, and I recognized Mama standing in there by the stove. She did not look happy. When we walked through the door, Daddy told her he couldn't find anything to make for breakfast, so we had gone for a walk down by the creek.

"Why is she all dirty with grass and shit in her hair," Mama whispered so no one else could hear her.

"You know what a klutz she is. She almost fell head first into the creek because she was running too fast and tripped. It's a good thing I was out there with her because I caught her just in time, didn't I, Emily," he asked as he turned to look at me.

"Yes, Daddy," I responded quietly.

"Go get dressed, Emily, and then get back down here and help me make some pancakes," Mama ordered.

I could hear her arguing with Daddy as I headed toward the great room.

"You never do what you promise! What is wrong with you? You are such a liar. You say one thing and then you do another!" accused Mama in a loud whisper.

"Shut your big fat mouth, you stupid bitch, or I will get in the car and leave right this second and leave your fat ass stranded here," Daddy ordered.

Charlie was awake in the great room. He smiled a little bit when he heard Daddy calling Mama a fat butt. It was kind of funny, I guess, but Daddy called us names too and it was not funny then. It was just plain mean.

I didn't hear another word about Daddy not cooking breakfast, and, for some reason, Mama never noticed that I was missing one pair of panties. I got lucky there, I guess.

That was the last day we were going to be at the cabin. We were scheduled to leave right after breakfast. Charlie and I helped load the car up when everyone was done eating. Charlie said he was glad to be going home because he couldn't stand being around that many giggling girls, and besides, he did not like sleeping on a wood floor.

I guess I was glad to be going, too, especially after what Daddy had done to me before the sun even came up, but at least here I had been able to have some really good times in between the bad times.

I had learned how to put the bad memories away in their own tightly sealed boxes far back in my mind so that I didn't have to think about them all the time. It was the only way I could have fun; it was the only way I could smile or laugh, although sometimes my laugh sounded hollow to me. It sounded like it was an echo of someone I could have been.

CHAPTER TWELVE

THE RED CHAIR

S CHOOL WAS OUT AND THE DAYS WERE LONG. JUNE TURNED INTO July, and July turned into a very hot month. Charlie and I spent as much time as we could outside because the house felt hot as an oven. We loved being in our front yard together. There was a huge oak tree that was so big it looked like it must have been living there forever. I figured it must be the wisest tree around. Grandpa had swung a rope around one of its biggest branches years ago and had tied a tire onto the end of the rope. He told me he had done it for his grandkids.

The tire swing must have been there a long time, too, because there was a deep groove in the branch where the rope swung across. I worried about it sometimes, wondering if it was causing the tree any pain and wondering when the tire swing might make that big old branch break, but it never did.

Charlie and I loved to play on the tire swing in the summer under the shade of that old tree. Most of the time we took turns on the swing, but sometimes we fought over who could go first. Charlie usually got to go first, but that was okay, I guess.

When it was really hot out, like it was in July, we would get the garden hose and turn it on and spray each other while we swung back and forth under the tree. I would always try to make my spray look like it was raining under the tree. Charlie just liked to spray the water right at me and make me scream.

Our front yard also had this old fireplace looking thing made out of bricks sitting off to the side of the big oak tree. I guess Grandpa had put it there, but I never knew why. Maybe it had something to do with the house that burned down, but I was never told. Charlie did not know what it was there for either, but we had fun crawling and climbing on it just the same. Sometimes Daddy used it to burn garbage in, and then it would stink up the whole front yard, and Charlie and I would have to find other places to play.

There was also a big tank in the front yard that looked like a big torpedo, Charlie said. Mama said the tank was for heating the house and that it had gas in it that we used during the winter to keep warm. Charlie and I loved to climb on top of it and slide down its curved sides. Whenever Mama caught us doing it, though, she would get very mad, make us go inside, and threaten us by saying she would tell Daddy when he got home. It was not long before it became more of a game of not getting caught by Mama than it was about sliding off the tank.

There were a lot of trees in our yard and a lot of land, but mostly, we stayed pretty close to the house. We would wander out to the big open field and jump on the boulders there or hide in the grass, but we were too afraid to go any further into the wooded areas that surrounded the house. Mama said there were bears around, and she was right.

One day, early in the morning, we could hear Mama outside screaming. Charlie and I ran to the window to see Mama in the yard wearing her nightgown with a bag of garbage in her hand. She was swinging it at a baby bear while running back to the house yelling at it to go away. We thought the baby bear was so cute and cuddly looking, and we wondered why Mama was so afraid of it. She explained that it was not the baby bear she was afraid of; rather, it was the baby bear's mama that scared her because she said that the mama had to be close by.

Mama did not let us out of the house for the next few days. She put together a bunch of things like a shovel, a bat, and cans of hair spray and Raid by the front door. I asked her what it was all for, and she said that if a bear came in the house she would be able to protect us with those things. She explained she would spray the hair spray and Raid in the bear's eyes to blind it so she could beat it with the bat or the shovel. Mama was very serious about this, and Charlie and I thought it could be a real possibility that somehow that mama bear was going to come back and get in the house. At least Charlie slept way in the back room. I was in the front room on the couch right next to the front door staring at Mama's collection of bear fighting tools trying to go to sleep. Finally, after about three days, Daddy called Mama an idiot and told her to put that stuff away and let us kids outside. I was simply impressed that Mama had gone to such extremes to protect us. Sometimes things just never made sense to me.

We were so glad to be back outside, out of the heat of the house. Mama cooked and baked no matter how hot it was, and the house would get so hot that I felt like I could barely move in it, let alone eat what she was cooking. I did not trust her cooking anyway. I never did get over the feeling that somehow she was trying to kill me or poison me, no matter how much time had passed. In the early afternoon, we saw a car pulling into the driveway. It was our older cousin, Margaret. She was nineteen years old, and she never talked to Charlie and me much. I guess she figured she was just too old to be hanging around us. She stopped by often, though, to visit with Mama. Mama called her a hippie but said she was family so she had to accept her.

Margaret was tall and thin with long, dark hair that hung straight down past her butt. She wore a red bandana around her head, and I do not remember ever seeing her without it. She was kind of pretty, but she had bad skin on her face. Charlie called her pizza face, and we would laugh behind her back. She wore faded blue jeans that had holes worn right through them on the knees. The jeans looked like she had drawn all over them. There were all kinds of shapes and symbols on her pants, even on the butt part. Her shirt was brightly colored with red, orange, purple, and blue. Mama said the shirt was tie-dyed. It had a fringe hanging down from the bottom of it that went all the way around. The fringe moved like it was dancing to a song whenever Margaret walked. I thought it was pretty, and I wished I had one. Margaret slung her purse, made out of the seat part of an old pair of blue jeans, over her shoulder as she got out of the car and headed for the house. She waved and said hi to us on her way in.

A few minutes later, Margaret and Mama both came back out of the house walking toward us. Margaret was carrying an old red high chair. The seat of it was made of red vinyl, but it was tattered and torn, and the stuffing was sticking out of it. It had been behind the house, sitting outside for as long as I could remember. Margaret must have gone back there to get it. I thought maybe she wanted the old rusty looking thing.

Margaret put the chair down in the yard under the oak tree and called for me to come over.

"Get up on this chair, Emily," Mama said. "Margaret is going to cut your hair."

Cut my hair! My hair was long and past the middle of my back. I loved my hair, and I loved playing with it and braiding it and putting it in pony tails.

"I don't want to cut my hair! No Mama!" I yelled and ran away.

"Get back here right now or I will call your Daddy at

work, and he can come home and cut your hair off, but it is coming off one way or the other," Mama yelled.

I believed every word she said, so I came back and sat down on the chair. My bottom felt wet from where the stuffing of the chair had gotten rain water soaked in it, but I didn't complain about it. The ragged edges from the torn vinyl bothered me more than the wetness because it dug into the back of my legs. I asked Mama if we could cover the chair with a pillow and she told me no because I was just the right height already on the chair for Margaret to cut my hair.

"How do you want me to cut her hair?" Margaret asked Mama.

"Short, like a Dorothy Hamill haircut," Mama said, and then she went back into the house.

Dorothy Hamill was a lady that liked to ice skate a lot, and Mama loved to read about her and watch her whenever she could find her on the television. Her hair cut was cute, but I still wanted to keep my long hair. Well, at least Mama didn't say to cut it short like Charlie's.

Margaret starting cutting my hair. I cried as I watched the long strands fall to the ground. Charlie stood by with a look of horror on his face; even he could not understand why Mama was making me lose all of my hair.

"Why are you cutting her hair off?" Charlie asked Margaret.

"Because it's so hot out this summer, and your Mama says she never takes care of it, and there are always snarls in it," Margaret quickly answered.

"I don't have snarls in my hair," I protested.

"Well, maybe not today, but your Mama says she is tired of your long hair and she wants it cut off, so I am cutting it off. Your Mama is paying me $2 to do it, too. I am in beauty school right now learning how to cut hair, so I kind of know what I am doing already," Margaret chattered.

I felt a little better hearing that Margaret kind of knew what she was doing because she was going to school to learn about it, but usually Margaret never made me feel good about anything. She was gruff in her speech and sounded like she was ready to be mean even if she did not have a reason to be.

"Quit your sniffling, Emily. I am almost done, and it's not like I can glue it back on anyway, so just get over it," Margaret commanded.

The ground around me was covered with my brown locks. Charlie sat close by watching, and I could tell just by the look on his face that it was not going to be good. When Margaret said she was done, Charlie's mouth dropped open, and he hung his head down, shaking it sadly from side to side. Then, he got up and left the area.

"Can I see it yet?" I asked.

"Yes, but remember, I am just learning and it will grow back anyway. It's just hair, and at least it is short like your Mama wanted. It's not like you are out to impress anybody," said Margaret.

Margaret handed me a mirror, and at first I did not even recognize the person staring back at me. That could not possibly be me in that reflection – could it? Oh, no! She did cut all my hair off! Margaret had cut my hair off above my ears, and it was choppy all the way around my head. My bangs were super short and crooked, and I had never had bangs before. It looked terrible. I looked so ugly.

"This is not what Dorothy Hamill's hair looks like!" I shouted.

"I know, Emily. I tried, but it kept being crooked, so I had to keep cutting it off to try to get it straight. It's all your fault anyway. If you had sat more still I would've been able to cut it much better," Margaret responded.

Mama came out of the house, and I heard Margaret saying she was sorry for how bad my hair had turned out.

She told Mama it was my fault for not sitting still. I thought I had sat still, except for maybe the crying.

"Don't worry about it, Margaret. Her hair looks fine. It's just what I wanted – very short," Mama said as she handed her some money. They both turned and went back to the house. When Mama got to the door, she yelled back at me to pick up my hair from the ground and get it thrown away.

I jumped off the chair and grabbed handfuls of my hair and sat there in it crying. "Why does Mama want me to look so ugly all the time? She makes me homemade clothes that are ugly and the kids at school tease me and now she has had my hair chopped off. It's not cut – it's chopped. Why Mama," I kept asking myself as I sat there crying holding my hair.

Charlie came back and told me it would be okay and not to worry because school was nearly two months away yet, and my hair would look great by then. He helped me pick up my hair and throw it away. Charlie said that as long as I avoided looking into a mirror it would be like it never happened because I wouldn't be able to see it. I told him I could feel it though, so he said not to touch my hair anymore, and I listened to him. Charlie was so wise.

Daddy came home late in the afternoon around suppertime. When it got close to his arrival, Charlie and I made ourselves scarce. We never knew what kind of mood Daddy would come home in and did not want to be the first ones to find out. Charlie and I were in the field lying in the weeds when Daddy came home the day I lost my hair.

After Daddy went into the house, Charlie and I crept up to the house quietly to see if we could hear anything. We always tried to figure out if they were fighting before we went in. As we got closer, we could hear Mama through the kitchen window telling Daddy that Margaret had come over and cut my hair and that she needed Daddy to give her back the $2 for the haircut because she had taken it out of her grocery money.

Daddy said, "You did what?"

"I had Margaret come over and cut Emily's hair. She never takes care of it, and it always looks like a rat's nest, and, besides, it's hot out. How would you like to have that long hair hanging down your back in this heat?" Mama said.

It seemed like Daddy did not even hear her explanation. Again, he said, "You did what!?"

We could hear Mama rattling pans around for cooking supper, but she did not answer Daddy this time. It was clear that Daddy was getting mad. I guess he did not know that Mama was having my hair cut off.

"How much did you have her cut off?" he asked.

Mama stayed quiet for a couple of seconds, and then said softly, "I asked Margaret to give her a Dorothy Hamill haircut."

"A who?"

"Dorothy Hamill. You know. She is that cute young girl that ice skates that I like so well," Mama said.

"She has short hair like a boy," Daddy yelled.

"Well, it's not like Margaret was able to make it look that way anyway, and it's not her fault. Emily refused to sit still, so her hair is shorter than what it was supposed to be. It's just hair. I don't know why you are getting so pissed off about it," Mama said gruffly.

Suddenly, we heard a slapping sound, and Mama cried out. Charlie and I both jumped. My heart started beating faster and harder in my chest. Daddy rarely struck Mama.

"Why did you hit me!" she sobbed.

"Girls are supposed to have long hair!" Daddy yelled, "Why didn't you ask me first? You knew I liked our little girl having long hair. You did this because you are jealous of your own daughter – you always have been. You are a sick, twisted bitch"

Mama did not answer him.

"Get the kids in the house. I have to see this for myself," Daddy instructed her.

My thoughts ran quickly, "I never knew that Daddy liked my long hair. Maybe Mama having it chopped off is a good thing! Maybe it is Mama's way of trying to protect me from Daddy. Maybe that's why she always dresses me in ugly clothes too. Maybe, just maybe, Mama is trying to make me look so ugly that Daddy will stop touching me. Oh, how I hope it works. If it does, I will never grow my hair out again."

Mama came to the door and yelled for us. We came around the back side of the house at her second yell and pretended to be out of breath from running.

"Your father wants to see you," Mama said to me.

Daddy was standing in the living room by the couch when I came in. I kept my head down, so afraid that I would be the next person he would slap. Charlie headed for the back room where he slept.

"Pick your head up so I can see your haircut," Daddy ordered.

I picked up my head but still avoided eye contact with Daddy. Daddy looked at me and then slowly sat down on the couch. I instinctively touched my hair as if to say I missed it too.

Mama was standing behind me, but when Daddy sat down on the couch, she hurried to the kitchen muttering that she had to finish cooking supper.

"Come over here, Emily," Daddy said.

I moved closer by Daddy, and he reached out and touched my hair. He had a look of real concern on his face and a gentleness that I had never seen before.

"I am sorry you lost your hair," Daddy said.

I didn't say a word.

"It will grow back, don't worry. You are still Daddy's pretty little brown-eyed girl – hair or no hair," Daddy said.

"Can I go back outside?" I asked.

"Yes," he responded.

I dashed out the door and ran for the safety and security of my pine trees. I let the branches surround me and take me away to my pretend castle where I was a princess and everyone was nice and nothing ever hurt or went wrong, but I had trouble staying there. I could not understand what had just happened.

I thought, "Why did Daddy say he was sorry for my hair being cut off? Why was he being so kind to me?" He still thought I was pretty though, and that made me worry. I guess all of Mama's scheming was for nothing. Daddy would never stop touching even if I were bald.

I pondered, "Maybe Mama is not trying to protect me by making me ugly. She never tells me I am pretty, but she never tells me I am ugly either – she just treats me like I am ugly. Maybe Daddy is right, and Mama did it just because she doesn't like me – because she is jealous of me – that feels more right to me. It's Daddy – it must be because of Daddy. Why can't she see it's not my fault! It can't be – I don't care what Daddy says...oh, but what if it is my fault? I hate this! I hate them!"

I went back to the house when Mama called me for supper. Later that night as I lay under my blanket on the couch, I prayed to God that Daddy would not come out to touch me just this once, but God must not have heard me because Daddy came out of his bedroom and stood by the couch.

He crouched down so that he was level with me. I turned my head away, bracing for whatever was to come. Daddy did not say a word to me. He picked up my blanket and pulled it over my head. I was thankful for the cover and the feeling of being able to hide under it. I heard his zipper go down, and he grabbed my hand out from under the blanket. I turned my body away from him as much as I could, but he yanked me back – hard. Daddy took my hand and wrapped it around his pee-pee like he had done so many times before. I just laid there and pretended I was dead and waited for it to be over. I was hoping it wouldn't take too long, especially since I was having trouble breathing with the blanket over my head.

Daddy moved my hand back and forth, back and forth very fast on his pee-pee. His body shuttered, and my hand was wet. He dropped my hand, zipped up his pants, and went into the room where we had the bucket for going to the bathroom. I didn't move a muscle. My hand felt like a foreign object to me. I didn't want it to belong to me anymore. I left it outside of the blanket all night by itself, cold and crusty from the stuff Daddy had left on it.

CHAPTER THIRTEEN

DADDY'S GONE

SUMMER PASSED AND SCHOOL STARTED AGAIN. CHARLIE WAS right; my hair did grow back, but it was still very short by the time we started school in the fall, and, of course, all the kids teased me and said I looked like a boy.

Mama had decided that she was going to get a job. She said Charlie was almost ten years old now, and I had turned eight over the summer, so we should be able to be home by ourselves for a little while at least. Mama said we were going to need extra money because Daddy had to go overseas for twelve months, and we wouldn't have as much money as we had before. All I heard was that Daddy was going to be gone for a year!

Daddy left on a Monday right before Christmas. We all went to the airport to see him off. I was so excited that he was going to be gone for a year that I had trouble concentrating on watching the airplanes flying in and out. Finally, it was time for Daddy to leave. Mama was crying and Charlie looked sad. I figured I had best look sad, too, if I knew what was good for me. Daddy hugged Mama and then Charlie and then there was me. I stayed in the background not wanting to hug him good-bye, but he grabbed me anyway.

"You be a good girl now, Emmy, for your Mama while Daddy is gone," he said.

"I will," I automatically responded.

"The time will go by fast, you will see, and Daddy will be home in no time," he assured me, and smiled as he stood straight and tall.

Daddy was wearing his dress blue uniform – that's what Mama called this particular disguise. He had another uniform called his khakis, but I rarely saw him wearing it. We looked like the best family in the world standing there with our sad faces saying good-bye to our Daddy all dressed in his Air Force uniform. How would anyone ever be able to believe the truth about us? We all wore disguises, even me, maybe me best of all.

Mama got a job at a frozen food factory. She worked during the night and slept during the day when Charlie and I were at school. She seemed very happy and said she was making a lot of new friends. It was scary at first being alone when Mama left for work at 10 p.m. but Charlie made me feel safe, and, besides, one of the monsters that lived in the house was gone.

Our telephone started ringing a lot more than it ever had before because of all of Mama's new friends. Charlie hated Mama's friends, and when they called he would answer the phone and yell to Mama that "Stupid" was on the phone for her. Mama would get so mad at Charlie! She would come running in the room, grab the phone from him, hit him over the head with it, and then talk very sweetly to whoever was on the phone waiting for her.

Mostly Mama had ladies calling the house. She said she met them at her work and at a place that grown-ups go to after work that she called a tavern. After Daddy was gone for a couple of months though, Mama had men and lady friends calling the house for her, and then Charlie got really mad. He hated the men that called for Mama, and, worse yet, he hated the men that Mama would have come over to visit her; so did I.

One day the phone rang and Charlie ran to answer it as usual. He said hello and then yelled right into the receiver, "Mama that filthy-pig man you like is on the phone," and then he threw the phone down and ran back to his room. He was going to be in trouble for sure.

Mama was in the kitchen fixing supper. She was cutting up a chicken with her big butcher knife. When Charlie went running by her to his room, Mama followed him. This time she didn't come to the phone right away. I ran from the living room to see what was happening. I was worried for Charlie. He was always pushing Mama's buttons, she said. I was never as brave as Charlie. I figured I could not chance making her dislike me more than she already did because I believed she would not hesitate to kill me. She liked Charlie a lot more than me though, so he could get away with so much more than I ever dared.

When I got to the kitchen I could see into the back room where Charlie was on his bed, lying on his back with his legs and arms up in the air in what Daddy called the "The Dying Cock-a-Roach" position. He was trying to cover his body and his head from the whacks that Mama was giving him. He was screaming at the top of his lungs. It sounded like she was killing him. Mama had hit Charlie many times before, so I couldn't figure out why he was acting so crazy this time; usually, he would just lie there and wait for her to tire herself out and then smile at her as though he were asking her if she were done yet.

I was scared to get any closer, but I was too worried about Charlie not to, so I moved into the room. Mama was so busy beating Charlie that she did not even see or hear me come in until I started yelling too: Mama was beating Charlie with the butcher knife! She was not hitting him with the sharp side, but still it was so scary seeing her throwing that big knife around. She was whacking him with the dull side of the blade and hitting him with the flat side of it. I had never heard Charlie scream so much or so loud in my life.

I started yelling at Mama to stop, but it was like she did not hear me. She was calling Charlie bad names and telling him he was rotten like his Daddy. I yelled again reminding Mama that someone was on the phone waiting for her. Still she kept hitting him, and he kept screaming. I felt helpless. If the knife slipped or if Charlie moved the wrong way, it looked like the knife could stab him. The knife looked bigger than it had ever looked to me before.

"Mama! Mama!" I yelled again. "Mama, the phone! Someone is on the phone for you!"

I grabbed the back of her shirt and tugged on it with all my might. I was afraid she was going to turn around and hit me with the knife, too, so I ducked as I pulled on her shirt. She was jerking around so much as she beat Charlie that I lost my grip and stumbled backwards. I fell and whacked my head hard against the wall. I heard a ringing in my ears and tried shaking my head to make it go away, but that did not work. I had to try again because Mama looked crazy and wild-eyed. She looked like she could kill Charlie any second. I grabbed the back of her shirt again and ducked. This time I held on tight as I continued to yell for her that someone was on the phone waiting for her.

Finally, she heard me and turned around. She stopped and took one last look at Charlie trembling on the bed, made a snorting sound, and said, "Too bad it wasn't the sharp side." Then she stomped out of the room. We could hear her pick up the phone and say hello in her sickening sweet voice that she reserved for her special friends.

I stood there looking at Charlie. I did not know what to do to help him. Charlie wasn't crying, and he wasn't screaming anymore. He was just sitting there staring at me as though I wasn't even there. Then he got up and ran out of the house. I tried to follow him, but I could not find him, and he could run so much faster than I could. Charlie didn't come home until after supper that night. I was so worried about him, but Mama didn't even mention his name the whole time he was gone.

Charlie walked into the house as though nothing had happened and looked Mama straight in the face. She stared back at him, but neither one said a word to the other. Charlie went back to his room and stayed there until the morning.

The next day Mama's friends were calling again, and again Charlie raced to answer the phone and scream names at the person on the phone, "Mama, pig-face is on the phone for you!" he yelled. I was amazed! He was fearless. I admired him, but I was afraid for him. Mama came into the room, whacked him on the head with the phone, and started talking sweetly to her friend. She apologized for Charlie, saying he was going through a bad time because our Daddy was gone. Mama never beat Charlie with a knife again, but Charlie never stopped calling Mama's friends names. I think she just gave up, and her friends probably got used to it.

There was one man Mama seemed to like best of all. Although she would often have men come over to the house, this one seemed to be her favorite. His name was Stan. Charlie and I hated Stan. Charlie looked like he had fire coming out of his eyes when he looked at Stan visiting in our house or sitting at the supper table with us. Stan liked to drink beer, so we always had beer in the house now. He tried to get me to drink it once, and I took one taste of it and spit it back out. I couldn't understand why anyone would want to drink something that tasted so icky.

Stan was a big, heavyset man. Mama said he was going to school at the technical college, so we had to be quiet when he was over at our house studying. Mama explained that going to school was his job right now, and it was really hard, and that's why Stan liked to drink beer because it made him feel less stressed. Charlie and I were at a loss to figure out what she was trying to tell us, but to us it all sounded like just a bunch of excuses for why Mama had him sitting in our house day after day.

Mama waited on Stan hand and foot. Charlie said he should have to do some chores around the house like everybody else, but Mama said "no" because he had too much school work to do. One day Mama told Charlie to go and empty the bucket we all went to the bathroom in. Poor Charlie. I felt bad for him, but at the same time I was so glad that that was not my chore. Charlie was extremely mad. He told Mama that Stan should have to empty it, too, because he went to the bathroom there and it was not his job to take out Stan's poop, but Charlie did not use the word poop; he used the bad word that begins with s and ends with t. Mama slapped Charlie so hard across the face that he nearly fell over. I was hoping he would just go and do it and get it over with so that Mama would not hit him anymore. I think she was as shocked as I was to hear Charlie use a cuss word.

Charlie glared at Mama with the look of death in his eyes, and then he turned and glared at Stan. Stan said nothing. He was sitting on the couch with a book in his hand. Charlie went to the room where the bucket was and took the toilet seat off the top of the bucket. It was just an ordinary five gallon pail that we used, but Mama had bought a toilet seat that she balanced on the top of it so that we had something to sit on when we used it. The bucket was so full that Charlie had a hard time moving it, and it sloshed out a bit as he carried it through the house. The smell was so strong and so bad that it lingered in the house after Charlie had taken it outside. Mama yelled to Charlie that when he got back he could clean up what he had spilled, which at least wasn't much. I would've cleaned it up for him, but Mama would've slapped me for it.

It was extremely cold outside, but Charlie didn't stop to put on his coat. I think he was so angry that he did not care if he froze while he was out there. He had to take the bucket out past the outhouse to dump it in the woods. It was quite a distance to go without a coat on, but at least a path had been formed by numerous trips to dump the bucket all winter long. The path was narrow and slick from a lot of use.

Charlie was only gone a few moments when he came bursting back into the house covered with the pee and poop that had been in the bucket. He had slipped and fallen on the path, and the bucket flew up, he said, and spilled all over him. His pant legs were soaked with pee, and there were hunks of poop hanging on him. Toilet paper and poop were all over his shoes inside and outside. His hair was even a little wet with pee, so it must have splashed a lot when he slipped and fell. He smelled just like the inside of that bucket, and as he stood there dripping the pee and the poop on the floor, Mama pointed at him, laughing so hard she snorted. Stan started laughing too. I didn't think it was funny.

"That's what you get for sassing your Mama," Mama said.

Charlie said nothing. He just stood there and looked so angry that I was afraid he was going to hurt someone or something. He had the empty bucket dangling in his hand and he threw it across the room at Mama.

Mama moved back so the bucket would not strike her. It landed on its side, and some of the leftover pee drained out of it on to the floor.

"What goes around comes around, Charlie," Mama said. This was one of her favorite sayings. She didn't say anything about Charlie throwing the bucket at her which kind of surprised me, but I think she must have realized how angry Charlie was, too. It sure didn't help with the two of them laughing at him.

Charlie walked back to his room, took his clothes off, and wiped his legs dry with a towel. We did not have a bathtub or a shower, and we were both too big now for the metal tubs that Grandma used to wash us in, so Charlie had no real way of getting clean. He would have to wait until Mama took us to our great-Aunt May's house, which would not be for at least two or three weeks.

Charlie put his clothes in a heap in the same room where we kept the bucket. Mama left them there for over a month and finally she picked them up and took them to the laundry mat. Charlie never did clean up the pee and poop that was spilled in the house. No one did. Mama just let it dry, and eventually the poop got swept up when she cleaned the floor. Our house smelled so bad.

The next time Mama told Charlie to empty the poop bucket, he had the same argument with her about how Stan should have to empty it, too. Stan got up off the couch and told Charlie to do what Mama told him to do or he was going to give him a beating.

Charlie looked him square in the face and snarled, "If you ever touch me or my sister, I will kill you!"

Charlie sounded pretty serious to me about it, although I wasn't quite sure how he would kill him, but I believed him when he said he would do it. Stan never bothered Charlie again. Charlie took the bucket out and emptied it.

Charlie's birthday was a few days after he spilled the poop bucket on himself, and Mama said she was going to take us out for his birthday, but she would not tell us where. It was a surprise, she said. We got in the car; Charlie sat in the front seat, and I sat in the back. We rode quietly downtown with Charlie watching closely to see where we were going. The radio was on, and Mama was singing along with the song "Crazy."

"Worry, why do I let myself worry? Wondering what in the world did I do?" Mama sang.

I smiled to myself, thinking, "What did I do?" Mama turned around quickly, looked at me, and told me I should be singing, too. So I started singing with her, although I could never sing as pretty as the lady on the radio and neither could Mama.

The lady singing the song was named Patsy Cline, and she had such a beautiful voice. Mama said that she died in an airplane crash. I felt bad for her. I felt bad for me, too, because it meant she would not be able to sing any more

174

songs, and then I felt guilty for thinking about myself when the poor lady had died such a horrible death. It scared me just thinking about an airplane crashing out of the sky.

The song was nearly over when Mama said we were almost there. She pulled the car over to the side of the road in front of a building that looked very old and run-down. The entire block on both sides had the same kind of old and run-down buildings on it. The buildings were made out of brick, and some had windows broken out of them on their second floors. The sidewalks were cracked and had garbage strewn along the edges of them next to the buildings. There were a few dirty people with matted hair and filthy old clothes walking in and out of the buildings, but not many. It didn't look like a place Charlie or I would want to go to celebrate a birthday.

Mama was smiling when she got out of the car. She bent down and told us to get out before she closed her door. We both got out and looked around. I buttoned up my coat quickly because it was so cold outside. Charlie was wearing his coat, too, but he left his zipper open. The cold did not bother him nearly as much as it did me.

"Where are we going, Mama?" I ventured to ask.

"Right there." She pointed to the building behind us. "It's the tavern that I've told you guys about where I go with my friends: the Crow's Nest."

Charlie and I looked at each other, and I thought to myself that this could not possibly turn out to be a good thing. Charlie did not look mad, but he did look hugely disappointed. I felt so bad for him that I just wanted to go up and hug him. He had been hoping Mama was taking us bowling and for pizza and soda.

We started walking towards the Crow's Nest, and before we could get to the door, Stan opened it and yelled out that it was about time we showed up. I guess he had been waiting for us. Once inside, it took a long time for our eyes to adjust to the darkness. It was dreary and dirty looking;

it looked liked nothing cheerful could ever exist within its walls. There was a bar on the left hand side that ran half way down the room with short, round stools in front of it that were nailed to the floor. The stools were covered with a brown vinyl, or maybe they were just brown from being so old. On the other side of the room there were four booths and beyond that two tables and the bathrooms. The place really was not that big. It felt crammed together.

There were about fifteen people inside, which made it seem even smaller. The room was cloudy from cigarette smoke that made Charlie and me cough. A couple of people got up from one of the booths and said we could sit there. Charlie and I sat down, but Mama went up to the bar. She said she would be right back; she was going to get us something to drink.

"Do you think you are going to get a birthday present?" I whispered to Charlie.

"I don't really care," he said.

"Yes, you do. She must have a present for you or a birthday cake," I responded.

"Where? Did you see her carry anything in? I didn't," Charlie noted.

He was right. She hadn't carried in anything but her purse. Maybe this was Mama's way of getting back at Charlie for calling her friends names and for yelling at her over emptying the bucket. I wouldn't be surprised. I wished I had a present for Charlie. I wanted to go home. It did not feel right there, and the people seemed strange, dirty, and odd.

Mama brought us each over a glass of soda with a narrow straw in it. The glasses were tall and thin with smudge marks all over the outside; at least I think the dirt was on the outside of the glass. She tossed an envelope down in front of Charlie and said happy birthday to him. Stan called her name from the bar, so she turned around and went back there.

"Are you going to open it?" I asked.

"No," he said.

"Why not?" I continued.

"I don't want anything from her. She's a bitch," Charlie said.

"I would still see what is inside the envelope though. Maybe it is something you can use, and you might as well take it," I reasoned.

Curiosity got the best of Charlie, and he opened the envelope. Inside was a $10 bill and nothing else. Charlie took it out and laid it on the table.

"That's a lot of money, Charlie," I said, "What are you going to buy with it?"

"I don't want her stinking money," he said.

"Take it, Charlie. You can get yourself whatever you want with it. Take it please," I begged him.

I wanted him to have something for his birthday because being at the Crow's Nest with no birthday cake and no friends, nothing except old people sitting at the bar with our Mama, was not the kind of birthday I wanted him to remember. At least if he took the money he could go and buy himself something. Maybe he would remember that more than he would remember being at the dirty Crow's Nest.

Charlie was thinking it over when Mama walked over with Stan. Mama saw the $10 on the table and asked Charlie if he liked his birthday present. Charlie did not answer her.

"Well, if you don't want it, I'll take it," said Stan as he reached for the money.

Charlie grabbed the money quickly and put it in his pocket.

"I guess that means he likes it," said Mama to Stan.

"How long are we going to be here?" Charlie asked Mama.

"Well, I thought I would give you two a couple of dimes, and you could go over and pick out some songs on the jukebox to listen to," she said.

"I want to go home," said Charlie.

"Me, too," I offered.

"You two are never grateful for a damn thing. I bring you out, buy you soda, give you money for your birthday and money to play the jukebox, and you can't just sit here for a while so I can visit with my friends and relax! I gave you $10! Do you think money grows on trees, Charlie?" Mama hissed.

I was afraid that Charlie was going to reach into his pocket and throw the money back in Mama's face, but he did not. He kept it. I was glad. Mama would have let Stan spend it anyway, so it was better that Charlie had it. Mama tossed two dimes on the table and told us to go and play music if we wanted, and if not, she didn't care. She and Stan turned around and went back up to the bar.

We sat in the booth playing with our straws and squirting soda at each other through them. We had nothing to do but watch the people in the bar, and the more we watched them, the more we disliked them. Mama seemed so different to us there. She was laughing and rubbing herself up against most of the men in the room, and they were putting their arms around her and kissing her neck. I could only watch so much, and then I had to turn away.

"Come on, Charlie. Let's go play the music. At least it's something to do," I said as I scooted out of the booth.

Charlie got up and went with me to the back of the room where the jukebox was located. As we were standing there picking out the music, I noticed Mama look back at us. For just a moment, she looked like she had a sad face, but then one of her friends touched her, and she was all smiles again.

After the songs were over and our soda was gone,

Mama said we could go. We were so thankful. We never wanted to go there again, and we told Mama so when we got in the car. She called us ungrateful again. Charlie leaned his head against the window all the way home and didn't say a word. Mama turned the radio off. I stared out the window wishing I could make Charlie feel better and hoping that tomorrow would be better since it would not be his birthday. When things go bad on your birthday, you feel worse than when they go bad on any other day.

When we got home the telephone rang, and it was Stan. Mama said she had to leave and go pick him up, but she would be back soon because she had to work later that night. She said Stan would be coming over to spend the night, which he did sometimes when Mama was at work in the evenings. He would drink a lot of beer when Mama was not around, and then he would start talking to Charlie and me. Often times when he was drinking and Mama was at work, he would try to sit on the couch next to me when I was watching television at night. He would move closer and closer to me until finally he could reach me, and he would start rubbing my back with his hand. I felt frozen in place. I think Charlie got mad at me because I didn't move away, but I felt like there was some weight on me keeping me on that couch: fear.

I was afraid to move away. I was afraid it was my fault again that someone was touching me. I was afraid that if I moved off the couch Stan would get angry and do even more to me or maybe even something to Charlie. I thought if I sat there and let him rub my back maybe that was all he would ever do. He never touched me when Mama was home, and he never touched me unless he was drinking, so I figured it was his drinking days when Mama was at work that I had to worry about.

Mama said it was only right that Stan sleep back in the same room as Charlie. Charlie was so mad! Mama got rid of his bed and put up a set of bunk beds for the two of them. While Daddy was gone, Mama sometimes made me sleep in her bed with her. I think it made her feel better just having another body in there with her at night. I did not like sleeping in there with Mama. Mama was so big and fat, and she sweated a lot, so at night it smelled like lots of dirty, sweaty armpits in the bedroom, and Mama snored so loudly that I had a hard time falling asleep. I tried very hard every night to fall asleep before Mama so that I did not have to hear or smell her.

One night I had gone to bed before Mama and had fallen asleep. In the middle of the night, something woke me up, and instinctively I lay still and listened. The bed was moving up and down, and I slowly turned my head to look at Mama, but when I did, all I saw was a pillow propped up between my head and Mama's, so I couldn't see her face.

I could see someone on top of Mama though, and it scared me. As I lay there listening, it did not take me long to figure out it was Stan on top of Mama.

"You feel so good. Oh, God, how I love being inside of you," he whispered to Mama.

I didn't hear Mama say anything, but she was making a moaning sound. I was lying so close to Mama that my leg was touching hers. I wanted to move away; I wanted to run out of the room, but I didn't dare to move. I didn't want them to know I was awake. The room smelled of Mama's sweat and beer from Stan's breath. It was putrid and made my stomach sick. Stan looked so grotesque up there on top of Mama humping up and down on her. His face looked all puffed up because he was holding his breath a lot. It made me think of the game where you had to rub your head and pat your stomach at the same time. Maybe Stan could not hump on top of Mama and keep breathing at the same time. I don't know. I just wished they would stop what they were doing, and Stan would go back to his bed where he belonged.

Suddenly, I felt Stan's hand touch my leg. Mama whispered to him to be careful where he put his hands because she was afraid he would wake me up. He told her he was being careful, but he did not move his hand off my leg. He started moving his hand up between my legs, while I lay there pretending to be sound asleep. He touched my pee-pee area in the same place that Daddy did. He started rubbing me between my legs and moving up and down on Mama even faster. Then he grunted really loud and stopped. He crumbled down on top of Mama breathing very hard.

Mama told him he had to get up now and go back to his bed before Charlie or I woke up and caught him there in bed with her. He got up and left the room. I still hadn't moved. Mama turned over and went to sleep, farting really loud after Stan left, which didn't help the smell in the room one bit. I couldn't fall back asleep. I kept wondering if Mama knew that Stan was touching me in my pee-pee while he was on top of her. I hated it; I hated her; I hated Stan; I hated that she brought another monster into the house; I hated not knowing if she knew he was touching me. I wanted to get up and go wash myself where he had touched me with his filthy, fat, grubby hands, but instead I lay there pretending to be asleep, knowing that I would have to do my best to never sleep in her bed with her again, but how could I get out of it?

Sometime during the night I had finally fallen back to sleep. I woke up before Mama, and I had to go the bathroom really badly. The minute I opened my eyes I remembered what had happened during the night, and I was already worried about how I was going to get out of sleeping in Mama's bed ever again. I did not want to wake Mama up. It was never a good thing to wake Mama up before she was ready to get up, yet I had to go to the bathroom so badly that I did not think I was going to be able to hold it much longer. I made a quick decision. I thought it was a great idea at the time, but I forgot to think about the trouble it was going to cause me in the long run. I peed in the bed.

Mama woke up immediately. She screamed at me, "You just pissed the bed!"

"I'm sorry," I tried to explain. "I had to go really

badly, and I didn't want to wake you up. I guess I had to go worse than I thought."

Mama slapped me hard across the face. "You are such a little pig, aren't you?" she said, "Get your ass up and clean up this bed and that means washing the sheets and scrubbing your piss off my mattress! You are such a pig! It will be a cold day in hell before I let you sleep in my bed again."

I felt triumphant. I did it! I might have gotten slapped for it, called names, and have to clean it up, but it sure was worth it. I got up immediately and started cleaning up the bed. I took the sheets off and put them in the laundry basket. We did not have a washing machine, so Mama would go to the laundry mat every two or three weeks.

"What the hell do you think you are doing?" Mama asked.

"I am cleaning up the room like you told to me to do," I answered.

"I told you to wash those sheets and I mean wash them!" Mama yelled.

"How?" I asked.

"Don't be so stupid, you dirty little pig. Get them in the sink, get some water and soap, and scrub the piss out of them with your hands. Then rinse them and hang them outside on the line," she instructed. "But go scrub the mattress first so your piss doesn't get soaked all up in it."

Still, I thought it was worth it. I didn't mind washing the sheets by hand. I made a game of it by pretending I was Cinderella, living with my evil step-mother who made me do all the work in the house, but someday Prince Charming would come to rescue me.

Mama told Stan I peed the bed the minute he got up. She told Charlie too, which kind of embarrassed me because I couldn't tell Charlie why I did it or that I did it on purpose. Mama didn't stop there though; she spent the day on the telephone with her friends and our relatives complaining about me and what a little pig I was for peeing in her bed. I was humiliated, but still, it was worth it.

That night and every night thereafter, I got to sleep on the couch away from the men that Mama brought to her bedroom.

Chapter Fourteen

Mama's Men

Mama's sister, Aunt Mabel, lived on the same road as we did but on the other end of it. There was nothing about the two of them that looked the same; you would not have even known they were sisters, except for the meanness in both of them. Aunt Mabel lived the same way we did, with no toilet or bath tub or shower. She had a bucket in her house, too, and an outhouse not too far from her front door. Aunt Mabel was taller than Mama, and she was thin. She had brown hair that was down to her shoulders, but she usually had it pinned up. It looked greasy and shiny on top of her head. She liked wearing clothes that were very colorful and super, super tight. The buttons on her shirts always looked like they were fighting to keep her clothes together. Mama hated the way Aunt Mabel dressed. She said if she wore her shirts any lower, she might as well flip her boobies out for everyone to see. Mama said she dressed like a street walker. I asked Mama what a street walker was, and she said it was Aunt Mabel.

Aunt Mabel had two girls — Susan, and Patty, but no husband. I guess he left right after Patty was born. Susan was 12 years old, and Mama said she was not fat, but she was "chubby." I thought she looked okay. She had very light blonde hair that was almost white. She didn't talk to me much because I was too little, but she did talk with Charlie once in a while. Patty was six months older than me, and she sure thought that made her the boss whenever we were together. We didn't like each other much. I think it was only because our Mamas fought all the time. I liked playing with Patty when she was being nice, but she had a meanness about her like her Mama and my Mama. She also liked to steal my things. Mama would invite Aunt Mabel and her two girls over so I could sneak down to their house and take back the things that Patty had stolen from me. I never took anything that wasn't mine. Patty never said anything about it, but she had to notice that the things she had stolen kept getting back to me somehow.

I tried to stay away from Aunt Mabel's house as much as possible because she was never nice to me. She didn't like me. She said she preferred boys to girls, and she meant it because she liked Charlie a lot more than she ever liked me, and she would tell us that, too. Her face would light up whenever she was around Charlie. If Charlie was at her house, she would try to get him to sit by her or be with her doing something. She would give him candy and treats that the rest of us were not allowed to eat. Charlie hated her.

Aunt Mabel would say mean things to me, and sometimes I did not understand why what she said was mean, but I could tell it was supposed to be mean – like when I was over there once and I had to use the bathroom. It was really cold outside, so I asked if I could go in the other room to use the bucket that they used inside. Aunt Mabel told me "no" and said that I could go outside and use the outhouse. Then she turned to Mama and said in a gruff voice, "I just shit in there last night, and the turd froze standing straight up through the toilet seat. Yeah, Emily will sure enjoy that when she sits on it."

Mama looked at her funny, but then they both

laughed together. Whatever they meant by that I knew it was supposed to be mean. I went outside like I was going to use her outhouse, and instead, I ran all the way home and used our bucket inside, and then I stayed home. When Mama got home, she was mad at me for leaving without telling her, but she didn't say too much about it.

About a month later Mama wanted me to go over to Aunt Mabel's with her, and I hated the thought of going because Aunt Mabel would just find some way to make fun of me or embarrass me again. Mama asked Charlie to go, too, and he said no, but Mama insisted and told Charlie she would give him a dollar if he went with her, so he decided to come with us. She did not offer me a dollar.

We took the car down to Aunt Mabel's house, although we could have walked because it was just down the road a ways, but Mama hated walking. Mama always got mad when we went to Aunt Mabel's house because she said that Grandma and Grandpa had given her the house and the ten acres of land she lived on, and she didn't have to pay one red penny for it. I think she was jealous of Aunt Mabel, and Aunt Mabel was jealous of Mama. I don't know why Aunt Mabel was jealous of Mama, maybe it was because Mama had a husband. I wondered if Mama knew that pennies were not really red.

Aunt Mabel's house was very dark on the inside because there was only one window in the main room and she had that covered with a heavy blanket. It was like she was allergic to the sunlight, or maybe she felt like she had to hide from something. Sometimes I felt like I had to hide, but that was usually when Daddy was coming after me. Mama said going into Aunt Mabel's house was like walking into a cave. She was right.

Aunt Mabel's favorite thing to do was to sit on the end of her couch, watch television, and smoke cigarettes. She must have dropped her cigarettes a lot because her couch had lots of burn holes all over it. She probably had a hard time finding the cigarette once she dropped it because it was so dark in there. I hated being the one who had to open her door first because the smell of the house was so strong that it would hit me like a wall. It smelled like there had not been fresh air through her house for at least one hundred years.

Aunt Mabel hardly ever left home because she said every time she went out some man would see her and instantly fall in love with her and cause her nothing but trouble. She thought she was beautiful, and she bragged about being the best cook in the world. She looked okay, except she was always dirty, but she wasn't beautiful like the ladies I would see on television. I don't know about her cooking though because I tried very hard never to eat it. I didn't trust her cooking any more than I trusted Mama's cooking.

It only took us a second to get to Aunt Mabel's in the car, and I walked as slowly as I could to the front door. Poor Charlie was the one who ended up opening the door first. We all went inside, and once our eyes adjusted to being in Aunt Mabel's living room, Charlie and I were surprised to see Stan sitting there on Aunt Mabel's couch looking all comfortable and like he had been there for some time. Mama must have already known about this because she did not seem surprised at all.

"The rest of your shit is in the back of my car," she said to him. "Get it out now or I'll burn it."

"Why do you have to be such a bitch?" Aunt Mabel asked, as she walked into the room.

"You are calling me a bitch! When you are the one who took Stan from me! Who's the bitch?" Mama yelled.

I wished I did not have to be there. I sat there very quietly on the couch as far away from Stan as I could get. Charlie sat next to me being quiet, too. Stan had not said a word either.

"I didn't take anything. He came on his own free will. I guess he got tired of rolling you around in flour to find your wet spot. You're nothing but a fat, sloppy pig!" Aunt Mabel yelled at Mama.

We didn't know what it meant to roll Mama in flour, nor did we know Stan had been doing that to her, but it must have been something bad because it made Mama so mad that her eyes looked like they were going to bulge out of her face, and she turned red. She got very close to Aunt Mabel, and I thought she might hit her.

"Well, you're nothing but a bag of bones held together by a piece of leather skin. You truly are the community bicycle. Everyone gets a ride. You whore," Mama yelled back at her.

Stan got up and went outside to get his things from Mama's car. It was mostly his books that he had left at our house. He never did bring much with him when he stayed over, and I rarely saw him change his clothes. Once Charlie and I figured out what was going on, we turned to each other and smiled. We were so happy. Now we understood why we had not seen Stan at the house for a couple of weeks.

Mama called Aunt Mabel a bitch one more time, then grabbed me by the arm, yelled for Charlie, and said we had to go. We didn't even get to see our cousins. Mama stormed out to the car where Stan was just closing the back door. He had his arms full of the books he had left at our house.

"I hope you are very happy, you bastard," Mama said as she got into the car and slammed her door.

I hurried up and got in the car before Mama yelled at me, too. I wanted to do everything I could to stay out of her way. Stan never looked up at Mama. He turned his back to her and slowly walked back to Aunt Mabel's house.

Mama made the car spit up rocks as we left Aunt Mabel's driveway. We made it back to our house in record time. During the next month Mama started having all kinds of men friends stopping by. When she wasn't working, she would call up DJs on the radio late at night and sit and talk with them. Sometimes she even made me ride in the car with her when she would take food to them. I could tell she was lonely.

One evening after supper, a car drove up into our driveway and a very, very large man got out. He was so big that when he got out of the car the car actually bounced back up on the side he had been sitting on. He wasn't very tall and he waddled when he walked. He had a big mustache and wore thick, black-rimmed glasses.

Mama looked out the window with Charlie and me and said, "Oh, that's Richard. You guys know Richard. He is the DJ from that radio station that I talk to all the time. He is a nice guy."

Mama hurried to the door to let him in, but she could have walked much slower because it took Richard quite a while to get to it; by the time he did he was all out of breath, saying he needed to sit down right away. Mama took him into her bedroom immediately and had him lie down in there. She closed the curtain that separated her bedroom from the living room, and she stayed in there with him for hours. Finally, she came out and said Richard was going to spend the night because he was too tired to go home. We were not surprised, especially since he had worn himself out just walking up to the house.

Mama said Richard was going to sleep in her room with her, but that it was alright because they were just friends. I didn't care where Richard slept as long as it was not anywhere near me. Charlie, however, was not happy about the arrangements, and he called Mama a "bitch" and ran out the door. I was shocked! I was even more shocked when all Mama did was sigh heavily and turn around and go back into her bedroom. She didn't come out again until the morning.

Richard was gone before we woke up in the morning, and we never saw him again, nor did we ever speak about him. Mama stopped listening to the radio channel that he was on. We do not know why they stopped being friends, but we did not care either. She started listening to other channels and calling the DJs on those channels.

Mama had other men friends over, too. It seemed every other day a different man was stopping by and spending the night. We did not even know some of their names. One man came over pulling a snowmobile behind his car. He looked surprised when Mama came out of the house to meet him. I don't think they had seen each other before, and Mama was a very, very big woman, so that probably shocked him a little bit. He seemed more interested in Charlie and me than he did Mama. He asked Mama if he could give us a ride on his snowmobile. I didn't want to go because I was afraid of him, but Charlie was not afraid of him one bit. He jumped on the back of it with him, and off they went through the yard and into the snow covered field. When they got back, Charlie told me I should try it, and he finally talked me into it. It was fun, except the man kept one of his hands on my leg the whole time and wanted me to hold onto him extra tight. Later Charlie asked me how I liked it, and I told him how the man had made me hold him tight and how he had touched my leg, and Charlie said he did the same thing to him. We weren't sure if it meant anything or not, but we were glad we never saw him again.

One day when it was starting to get warmer out because spring was coming again, my cousin Susan came running down the road toward our house screaming at the top of her lungs. It was about 7 a.m., and we were getting ready for school. Susan was dressed in her nightgown without a coat or shoes on, and although it was getting warmer out, it was still cold enough in the mornings that the puddles in our driveway were frozen. Susan shattered the ice, as she ran through the puddles, creating pretty designs on the top of them.

Running close behind her was Aunt Mabel, and behind her was Stan. Aunt Mabel had her nightgown on too, but she had a dirty, old blue robe tied around it. She also had some slippers on her feet. Stan was dressed in long underwear with his rubber boots on. All three of them looked frightful.

They were all shouting, screaming, and running. They looked like they had lost their minds. Susan didn't stop until she got up to our doorstep. Because of all the commotion they had caused, all three of us were already standing outside waiting for her.

"What in the hell is going on?" Mama asked through Susan's cries.

"My mama tore my hair out because of Stan!" Susan sobbed to Mama. Sure enough, there was a huge bald spot on the side of Susan's head that looked all red, sore, and a little bloody. I felt bad for her.

Mama turned Susan's head so she could see the bald spot. She looked shocked and upset. Mama ran back into the house and got a rag to put on Susan's head to catch the blood that was dripping down her face. As she was standing there helping Susan hold the rag to her head, Mama asked, "What do you mean because of Stan?"

Susan looked at Charlie and me; we were standing there with our mouths open horrified by the huge, bloody, bald spot on her head. She looked like she was trying to decide something for just a second, and then she turned back to mama and said, "Stan pushed me down on the bed and put his wiener in me, and mama came in and saw him doing it, and she blamed me, but there was nothing I could do about it – I couldn't get him off me. Mama thinks I wanted him to do it – I didn't want him to do it – he hurt me so badly – Mama pulled him off me; she started beating me and pulling my hair out! I didn't know where else to run to," Susan said in one long rambling sentence.

By this time Susan's mama had made it to the house, and so had Stan. Her mama started hitting her and yelling at her.

"You dirty rotten little bitch! I knew you were after him the day he came into the house!" Aunt Mabel yelled at Susan while she tried hitting her in the face, but Susan was pretty good at covering her face up with her arms.

"He made me, mama!" she sobbed, "He made me do it. He pushed me down on the bed and made me do it!"

"You stupid bitch! You have been prancing your ass around him every day! What in the hell did you think would happen? You knew exactly what in the hell you were doing. Now, you have gone and ruined a good thing that I had going. I hope you are happy, you stupid bitch," yelled Aunt Mabel.

Mama asked Aunt Mabel what she was talking about, and Aunt Mabel said that Susan would come out at night with her nightgown on and sit on the couch to watch television. The next thing she knew, Stan would be sitting right next to her rubbing her back. Aunt Mabel said Susan just sat there unless she was told to get up and go to bed, and she looked like she liked it.

"I told her and told her to knock it off, but does she listen to me? No. The stupid cow," said Aunt Mabel.

Susan was hunched over crying really hard and wailing when her mama spoke. I felt so bad for her. She kept trying to tell her mama that she did not want Stan to touch her and that he hurt her.

"He hurt me, mama," she kept saying over and over again. "I didn't do anything, mama! He hurt me!" she screamed, but Aunt Mabel was not listening to her.

"What did I do wrong, mama? I don't know what I did! I didn't want him to do this to me! Mama, he hurt me! I don't understand what I did wrong? Mama!" Susan yelled at her mama, but Aunt Mabel ignored what she was trying to explain to her.

I was so scared, and I wanted to run away, yet I wanted to stay and watch the whole horrifying scene. I thought,

"I bet this is exactly how Mama would treat me if she ever saw what Daddy does to me, except I am pretty sure she would kill me. I know she knows about it because I told her right to her face, but I think hearing it and seeing it are two different things. She will never listen to me that it isn't my fault, that I don't like it, that it hurts me, that I beg Daddy to stop. No, she will blame me the same way Aunt Mabel is blaming poor Susan." Mama and Aunt Mabel may not have looked alike, but they sure acted the same.

Mama had gone back into the house for just a minute, and when she came back out she had a cake pan in her hand, and she charged toward Stan. Stan just stood there while Mama beat him over the head with the cake pan. He must have a pretty hard head because the cake pan got all bent out of shape, but it didn't seem to really hurt him at all.

"You dirty bastard!" Mama screamed at Stan.

Stan didn't say a word, and I wondered why he was even there. Mama told Susan to get inside the house, and then she told Aunt Mabel and Stan to get off her property, and that they would figure all this out later. Mama was trying to sound mean and in charge, but I could also tell that she was happy that Aunt Mabel was having problems because of Stan. Aunt Mabel knew Mama was happy about it, too.

Aunt Mabel did not like the idea of Susan staying with us. She wasn't done beating her yet, but there wasn't much she could do, so she turned around and left with Stan. As she was walking down the driveway we heard her say to Stan, "When we get back to my house, you get your shit packed up and get the hell out."

Mama went inside to be with Susan and told us to stay outside and wait for the school bus. Susan was going to miss school for a couple of days, so I volunteered to go to her sixth grade teacher and tell her she was sick. I was hoping the teacher would not ask too many questions, though, because I had no idea what I would have said.

We never knew what Mama and Susan talked about, but Susan stayed at our house for a couple of days and slept with Mama in her room. Mama was much nicer to Susan than she ever was to Charlie or me, so Susan thought we had the best Mama in the world. I wish Mama would stick up for me just one time like she had for Susan.

A few days after Susan went home, Mama came home early in the morning from work with Stan in her car. He had his things with him, and he brought them into the house as though he were staying for a while. Charlie and I were both surprised: Charlie was angry; I was scared. Stan had rubbed my back, too, and I did not like it either. I didn't want him to do to me what he had done to Susan. I was petrified. He had already touched me once in my pee-pee with Mama right there! I thought, "Why does there always have to be a monster in our house! What is Mama thinking? Why is he here again?" We thought we had gotten rid of him for good.

Mama said to stop staring at him. Then she ordered us to go get a bowl of corn flakes for breakfast. She said there would be plenty of time to look at him later because he would be staying with us for a while. Charlie hung his head down and shook it in disbelief.

Charlie and I ate fast and went outside. Charlie was so mad that he started kicking the side of Mama's car. He was lucky that she did not come out and see him kicking it. Charlie was talking to himself, and I couldn't tell everything he was saying, but it sounded like he was saying something about killing Stan if he stayed in our house. I was worried. Charlie looked pretty serious to me.

Stan spent the night that night, but Charlie was so intensely angry that I think it made Mama change her mind about having him there, so in the morning she told Stan he had to leave. After Mama got back from taking Stan away, she came in the kitchen where Charlie and I were sitting. She started yelling at Charlie that she is allowed to have a life, too, and that Stan was not harming anyone by staying with us. Charlie sat there and smiled at Mama while she yelled at him, then Mama said he was just like Daddy, and she turned around and went to her bedroom.

Charlie was nothing like Daddy.

Charlie was my hero.

CHAPTER FIFTEEN

THE CARCASS

SUMMER ARRIVED, AND BEFORE I KNEW IT JULY WAS ALREADY here and soon it would be time to go back to school. It was a beautiful day, so I decided to take my Barbie dolls outside and play with them in the middle of my pine trees. I loved playing with my Barbie dolls. I had a couple of girl dolls and one Ken doll. I would play with them and pretend they were together like I thought a mama and daddy should be, but sometimes I would make the Ken doll hump on top of one of my Barbies like I had seen Stan doing to Mama.

Luckily, Stan never came back after he left the house the last time. Mama still had men over, but not quite as many as she did when Daddy first left. She was spending more time away from home after work now. She said she deserved time with her friends down at the Crow's Nest because soon she would not be able to do anything because Daddy would be home in just a few months. I hated that reminder. Charlie and I did not mind her being gone at night at all. For us, it was like being on vacation.

As I was playing with my Barbies, I could see my

cousin Patty coming down the road on her bicycle. It looked like she was going to stop at our house, so I got out from under my pine trees because I did not share that place with anyone, least of all Patty. Sometimes Patty wanted to be friends, and then other times she just wanted to be mean. I never knew what mood she might be in at any given time, and sometimes she was in the opposite mood to what I thought she was in. It was very hard to know how to be with her. It was not much fun.

She drove her bike up all the way to the oak tree where Charlie was swinging on the tree swing. She was talking to Charlie when I walked up next to her. She was trying to convince Charlie to go on a bike ride with her, but Charlie said he was not going on any bike ride with a girl, especially on such a hot day.

"How about you, Emily? Please, please, please!!!!! Mama gave me $5 for helping her do chores, and I want to go to the General Store and get something. Mama said I could ride my bike over there if someone would go with me. I will buy you a candy bar," she begged.

It sounded like fun to me, but Mama was asleep from working all night, and there was no way I was going to wake her up to ask her if I could go do something that sounded like fun. She would just say no anyway. I looked at Charlie and said, "Do you think it is okay?"

"Yeah, Mama will be asleep for hours yet. Just be careful and get back here before supper when she will be awake. You can take my transistor radio with you if you want to. I just put new batteries in it yesterday," said Charlie.

"If Mama finds out I took my bike to the General Store she will kill me," I said.

"She won't find out," said Charlie, "Trust me."

I did trust Charlie; it was Patty I did not trust. Something was telling me not to go, but it really sounded like fun at the same time, especially since Charlie said I could use his little transistor radio! I had to go.

I went in the house as quietly as I could because I had to get my sneakers. I had been barefoot outside, but I couldn't ride my bicycle like that because it would hurt my feet going that far. I only wore my sneakers when I had to because they were getting so small for me that my big toes had worn holes right through the top of them, but I would not be getting a new pair until school started. I had never ridden my bicycle as far away as the General Store before. I was starting to feel very excited.

I put my sneakers on outside and grabbed my bike. I loved my bike. Mama had bought it for me in June at a garage sale. I didn't care that it was used because it was perfect. It was just what I wanted. It was pink and had a banana seat and high handle bars and, best of all, my bike had a white basket hooked over the middle of the handlebars. It was so much fun to ride. Our road had a hill just a little ways down from our house, and I loved taking my bicycle there and riding down the hill as fast as I could go. I felt so free with the wind blowing through my hair as I raced down that hill. It made me giggle.

After I got my sneakers on, Patty and I jumped on our bikes and headed out. We turned Charlie's radio up as loud as we could and sang along to every song we knew. Some songs we did not understand, but we sang them anyway. We were going really fast down a hill when one of our favorite songs came on. We kind of goofed on the words, but we could sing it really well when it got to the chorus: "... Bye-bye, Miss American Pie, drove my Chevy to the levee, but the levee was dry, and them good old boys are drinking whiskey and rye, singin', this'll be the day that I die, this'll be the day that I die..."

We sang as loud as we possibly could as we rode down the road smiling, pedaling, glancing at one another, and enjoying the sound of our voices. The song was confusing to us because it sounded happy during the chorus, except for when it talked about dying. We couldn't figure out what the song was about, but we argued about it just the same; neither one of us even knew what a levee was supposed to be. I would have to look it up in the dictionary at school, if I remembered when I got there.

I felt so happy peddling fast and singing with my hair blowing around my face. I was still worried about Mama finding out, but there was nothing I could do about that now. I put my fear about Mama in its own little box and closed the lid. I needed to enjoy as many moments as I could because soon Daddy would be home.

It was a long bike ride. We had to stop several times to rest. It wasn't that far when Mama took us by car to get there, but by bike it was a lot longer, which surprised me. Once we got there, Patty looked around in the store and bought us each a Coca-Cola and a Butterfinger candy bar. She also bought herself some comic books, a jump rope, and some candy to take home for later. She still had lots of money left to come back again. She was trying to spend all of it, but there was not really anything that good to buy.

We rested just a little while and then started for home. I was beginning to get very worried about Mama waking up. The closer we got to home the harder it was for me to keep the lid on my fear of Mama. Neither one of us had a watch, but it seemed to me like we had been gone a very long time, but maybe not. We put the things that Patty purchased in my basket and started off for home drinking our soda pop and eating our candy. It was a glorious day: the freedom – the sweets – the warmth of the sun – the wind through my hair when I peddled fast – the music that seemed magical as it came out of Charlie's transistor radio.

We were riding single file because a car was coming. Patty was in front of me. We were almost ready to turn onto our road. I looked down for just a second or two, and Patty must have slammed on her brakes because all of a sudden I was sailing through the air and landed with a thud in the ditch. Everything in my basket was scattered including Charlie's radio. I quickly got up, yelled at Patty, because, of course, I blamed her for my own stupidity, and started to pick things up. Thank goodness Charlie's radio was okay. We got back on our bikes and headed for home.

When I got home, Mama was still sleeping. I had a couple of scrapes and cuts from the fall, but nothing too serious. My wrist was really bothering me, though, and Charlie said it looked like it was swollen. He said I had better tell Mama just in case I broke it. I didn't think it was broken, yet I trusted Charlie to know better than me since he was the older. We decided to tell Mama that Patty and I had been riding bikes in the driveway and I fell and hit my wrist on a rock. Charlie was going to tell her for me because I couldn't look at Mama and lie.

By the time Mama woke up, my wrist was really swollen. Mama had me put ice on it right away. She said that should make the swelling go down and help it to feel better. I didn't want to go to the doctor, but Charlie kept insisting to Mama that she take me to the hospital. Mama told Charlie I would be fine and I agreed.

"You don't care about us. All you care about is your pig-faced friends and going to the Crow's Nest with them," Charlie yelled at Mama.

Mama got mad and said "fine," she would take me in. I still didn't want to go, but I didn't say a word. I think Charlie was more upset about Mama going out with her friends than he was about my wrist, but he used my wrist to control Mama, and he acted like he had won. Charlie rode with us to the hospital. He had a smug smile on his face the entire way.

The hospital was on the military base. Everything there was neat and orderly and smelled so clean. I couldn't get my eyes to move around fast enough to take it all in. We had to wait for a few minutes, and then we saw a nurse. She was dressed in all white. She had on a white uniform, white stockings, white shoes, and even a white hat. She looked like an angel. She had blonde hair and sparkly blue eyes and the softest hands when she touched me. She was so pretty and thin. Mama hated her. I could tell by how rude Mama was talking to her. I felt dirt-dirty next to her white pureness. Mama had not taken us for our baths at our aunt's house in quite a while. It was summer time, so she did not worry about it as much as she did during the school year. I was hoping the nurse did not think I smelled bad. I looked up at her and smiled, hoping my face was clean at least.

The nurse checked me over, and then said kindly to me that the doctor would be in in a few minutes. When she left, Mama said, "Wasn't she a skinny little bitch."

The doctor came in. The doctor was older looking than Mama, much older in fact. He was a very large man with big hands and a gruff voice. He did not seem very nice, and he looked tired. He sat down on a stool in front of me and told me to show him my wrist, so I did. He told Mama it would be fine and that it was only a sprain and he would have the nurse wrap it.

"You hardly looked at it. You didn't even x-ray it," Mama said.

"Madame, I am a doctor and I get to do the deciding as to what is medically necessary," the doctor replied.

"Well, maybe I should just take that up with your commanding officer," Mama said.

The doctor signed heavily and said, "Madame, you are welcome to do as you please. Your daughter has sprained her wrist. Now, as far as any other ailments, I can include in her chart that she has a case of the creeping crud, and by all looks of it, so does her brother," the doctor snapped back, "Where is their father?"

"It's none of your business where their father is," Mama said.

"Fine. I will send in the nurse. You do as you please, but I suggest you get these children cleaned up on a more regular basis," the doctor commanded. He slammed the door behind him as he left.

I sat there wondering what kind of ailment was the creeping crud. Charlie had it, too, and he looked okay to me, so maybe it wasn't that bad. There was no way I was going to ask Mama what it was because she looked so mad that I was afraid she was going to yell at the nurse when she came back in to wrap my wrist, but she didn't. Mama just sat there steaming until the nurse was done, and then she grabbed my arm and yanked Charlie and me out of there.

The second we got in the car, Mama started yelling. I was glad to be in the back seat.

"If it weren't for you stupid little brats I wouldn't have to put up with this kind of crap!" yelled Mama.

We sat quietly. There was nothing we could say and we knew it.

"I work my ass off – I am all alone – no one helps me – and you two can't seem to stay out of trouble for one damn second! Then I have to run you to the hospital, and I knew you didn't need to go, where I get yelled at because you have the creeping crud. Well, by God, I would think by your age that you could wash your own damn face," Mama continued yelling, although we were not quite sure who she was talking to or if she were really talking to either one of us in particular.

So, that was it. The creeping crud referred to Charlie and me being dirty. Yes, we could wash our own faces, and I was rather embarrassed that I had not washed my face before we left the house because I felt so filthy in comparison to the nurse, but Charlie and I could never tell Mama when to take us for our baths. She always decided when we should go over to Aunt May's house.

The next day Patty was over. Mama was hanging laundry outside on the line when Patty rode up on her bicycle. She knew that neither Charlie nor I had told Mama about me going with her to the General Store, yet the first thing she said to Mama was, "I'm sorry Emily got hurt yesterday on our way back from the General Store."

I knew better than to trust Patty. I knew better than to trust anyone, except maybe Charlie; no, I guess not even Charlie, not really because I could not tell Charlie about Daddy. I was too afraid Charlie would hate me or be mad at me. I couldn't trust anyone with anything.

People hurt people all the time and it seemed like they did it because they thought it was fun to see someone else hurting; or they did it because they could; or they did it because they felt better by making someone else hurt. Patty certainly was smiling as she let Mama know I had gone to the General Store. Mama was mad but not as mad as I thought she might be. I think she was still thinking about the doctor saying we had the creeping crud, and maybe she was feeling guilty about it – at least I liked to think that might be true. She took my bike away for two weeks and then took us to Aunt May's for a bath. For the hundredth time, Charlie and I wondered together why we did not live in base housing where we could have had a nice home with a real bathroom with a bathtub and shower. We didn't understand why, and we never dared to ask.

Mama decided that she wanted to go to visit Grandma, Grandpa and her brother Melvin. They all lived close to each other. Grandpa had started a small five acre garden where Uncle Melvin lived, while Grandma stayed home taking care of the trailer that we used to live in. It sounded like she was lonely. I missed her so much. I was also excited to see my cousins, especially Mary. I had not seen her since the time she had spent a couple of weeks at my house.

The trip there took a few hours. Mama seemed happy all the way; she was even singing along to the radio and asking us to sing with her. Charlie refused because he said Mama sang girl songs, but I would sing along with her. Mama turned the radio up because Tammy Wynette was singing, and Mama loved her songs. She looked at me to make sure I was singing with her: "Sometimes it's hard to be a woman. Giving all your love to just one man. You'll have bad times, and he'll have good times doing things that you don't understand. But if you love him, you'll forgive him, even though he's hard to understand. And, if you love him, oh be proud of him, 'cause after all he's just a man. Stand by your man."

I loved it when Mama was in good moods like this. She loved the song by Tammy Wynette. I wondered if it was because Mama felt like she had to stand by Daddy? Regardless, I wanted to suck every last minute of joy out of Mama's good mood that I could.

We finally arrived to Uncle Melvin's house. It was a huge, old, two-story farmhouse that looked like it had seen better days. It was white, but the paint was so chipped and flaked off that it was more brown now than white. The roof looked in pretty rough shape, too. It had a big front porch that wrapped around half of the house with five steps leading up to it. There was a door on the side that opened into the kitchen and a door on the front that opened into the living room. The yard was very large with huge, old oak trees in it. The trees were beautiful and noble looking. They looked like old soldiers standing guard around the house protecting it. Their presence made everything seem more peaceful.

Off to the left hand side of the yard, there was a large, rundown barn that was sagging in the middle. The barn had a fenced pen attached to one side, and inside the pen there were a couple of pigs. I also saw several chickens roaming around the yard looking like they were lost and confused. In a field on the other side of the barn, there were old, rusty cars parked looking as though they had been left there to die.

Uncle Melvin was married to Aunt Jody. They had five children, and my cousin Mary, who was nearly eleven years old now, was the oldest. When we drove up, my Aunt, Uncle, Grandma, Grandpa, and all my cousins came running toward the car. It felt wonderful to feel so welcomed by so many people, but unfortunately that feeling did not last for long.

Mama told Charlie and me to go and play with our cousins while she talked with Grandma, Grandpa, and Uncle Melvin. We could hear them arguing before they even got to the front door of the farmhouse. Grandpa and Uncle Melvin were a lot like Mama and Aunt Mabel; they could be very mean and unkind. None of them seemed to be anything like Grandma who was always so gentle, sweet, and kind. I wondered how she stayed so nice living with such mean people.

I would have rather stayed and visited with Grandma, but I had to do what Mama said to do, especially in front of others, so I gave Grandma a big, long hug so she knew how much I loved her and missed her, and then I turned and ran toward the other kids.

With Charlie and me, there were seven of us standing there together. We were all dirty looking with stringy, greasy hair and wearing what Mama called "play clothes," but really there wasn't much difference between our play clothes and our regular clothes. Our cousins must have been wearing their play clothes, too, because they were dressed in dirty, torn, and shabby clothing just like Charlie and me. Our filth alone made us look like we were related.

Our cousins were Mary, almost 11; Beth, 9; Jack, 7; Tommy, 6; and Alice, 4 1/2. Mary and Charlie became the instant leaders because they were the oldest. Mary started to run toward a huge garden of tall, tall corn stalks. She turned her head back toward us and yelled for us to follow her. We all began to run and giggle. Soon it didn't matter how dirty we were or how tattered are clothing was because we were having such a good time chasing Mary through the cornfield that each one of us forgot how poor we looked. We felt like royalty playing and running through those corn fields. Who could see dirty faces, stringy hair, and tattered clothes through the laughter that twinkled in our eyes?

We ended up playing a game of tag in the corn field, which was more fun than any other game of tag I had ever played. I loved the feeling of the tall corn stalks surrounding us, protecting us, shielding us, and keeping us from the grown-ups. From the house they would not have been able to see us.

After we played for a while, I had to go to the bathroom. I could have squatted right there in the corn field, but I was too embarrassed in front of my boy cousins. So, I headed back toward the house. Mary said they had a regular bathroom inside the house. They were lucky.

I thought I was heading in the right direction, but I must have gotten turned around a little bit because I was lost. I decided to walk in one direction until I came out of the field and could see where I was located. It took a while, but when I came out of the corn stalks, I found myself staring down at the body of a dead horse. I screamed and screamed.

The horse was beautiful, or it had been when it was alive. It was brown with a white spot on its nose. The poor thing was left to rot behind the barn without even being buried. Its swollen belly and brokenhearted, maggot-filled, face was swarming with flies. The stench was unbelievable. This was horrific! I loved horses. I thought, "Did they know about this? How could anyone know about this and leave this poor horse to die and rot behind a barn? Uncle Melvin could do it; he was mean enough."

The grown-ups must have heard me screaming because they were coming outside as I cleared the side of the barn on my way up to the house. Mama stopped me as I came running up.

"What's the matter? Is someone hurt?" she asked.

"No, Mama. It's the horse – the horse – it's dead," I said. And then, against my better judgment, I started to cry.

Uncle Melvin was standing there and he started to laugh; in fact, he was laughing so hard at me that he was bent over grabbing his knees. Mama didn't like Uncle Melvin, and they rarely got along, so I was hoping this meant that Mama wouldn't like his laughing.

"What in the hell is so funny? What is she talking about? What horse?" Mama asked Uncle Melvin.

"Oh, it's just the damn farm horse we had here. I don't know what was wrong with it. I haven't got a f'n clue. There is no way I was going to pay some big vet bill for a damn horse. It just died a few days ago or so. It wandered out there, lay down, and just never got up again," Uncle Melvin answered after he stopped laughing.

"Why in the hell don't you bury it?" Mama asked.

"Bury it! What the hell! How in the hell am I supposed to lift the dead weight of a f'n horse to bury it? I figured I got lucky by it going behind the barn to die. You know, out of sight out of mind, although the smell of it is starting to pick up on the wind, but that will pass," he explained.

"You are a pig," Mama said as she turned and stormed back into the house without one word of comfort for me. I didn't expect any anyway. I thought I was lucky she had not yelled at me or laughed at me with Uncle Melvin for being stupid about the horse. I didn't know if Mama really was upset about the horse or if it was just something she could complain about when it came to Uncle Melvin.

I continued on to the house finally remembering why I had come up there in the first place. The door of the house opened into the kitchen, and the first thing I saw was the refrigerator that Mary had told me about when she was at my house. I couldn't believe it. It looked like someone had taken it hostage or something. I had never seen anything like it. The refrigerator was wrapped twice around with a heavy chain, and it had a padlock holding it locked. It might have been white once, but it looked kind of yellow now, probably from age. It was shorter than our newer refrigerator and squatty looking. It looked like there had once been some letters that went across the top of it, but if there were, they were long gone. I stood and stared at it. It didn't make any sense to me at all. Why would they chain up their refrigerator? Then I remembered Mary telling me it was so she and her brothers and sisters could not get in to it. I felt sad for them.

"Would you like a soda pop, Emmy?" asked Aunt Jody.

"Yes, please," I answered, mostly because I wanted to see how she went about opening that refrigerator.

Aunt Jody pulled a chain with a key on the end of it from around her neck and used the key to unlock the padlock. When she removed the padlock, the chains fell to the floor with a crash. I jumped. She opened the refrigerator, ignoring the chains as though this were an everyday event, and turned to ask me what kind of drink I would like to have.

"I don't know," I said quietly as I stared inside the refrigerator at row after row of soda pop. There must have been a hundred bottles of soda pop in the refrigerator. I wondered with that much soda pop why they thought they could not let the kids have any of it. It seemed pretty selfish to me. There was no other food in the refrigerator – just soda pop. I wondered where they kept their other food like milk, eggs, butter and such.

"Here, just have a coke. Everybody likes coke," Aunt Jody said.

I turned around to catch Mama's face before the refrigerator was closed. I wanted to see if she saw what I saw and if she thought it was strange. She was looking right into the refrigerator like I was, except her face registered nothing. She was not surprised or curious or anything, so I assumed she must have known about this before. I hoped she wasn't considering chaining up our refrigerator.

The bathroom was upstairs. I put my coke down on the kitchen table and left for the stairs, grateful to be away from the grownups. The stairs were old and the wood was well worn in the middle of each step where people had been walking for years and years. The rail was wobbly, and each step creaked loudly as though I was hurting it as I stepped on it. I made it to the bathroom to discover that next to the sink was a huge hole in the floor that looked down directly into the kitchen. No one could see me going the bathroom, but I was certain they could hear me because I could hear them.

I finished and went back downstairs.

"How'd you like the hole in the floor? Good thing you didn't fall in," Uncle Melvin said gruffly.

"Why is the hole there?" I asked.

"So's we can keep an eye on you kids in case you decide to mess around in there – that's why," he answered and laughed.

"Take your coke and go back outside, Emily," said Mama.

I quickly headed for the front porch. Uncle Melvin was not someone that I liked to be around. I don't think Uncle Melvin ever loved anything or anyone in his life, least of all his family.

I was afraid to be around Uncle Melvin, and I was especially afraid to be caught anywhere alone with him. Last summer he had stopped over at our house to visit Mama. Mama was not home. She was out at the grocery store with Charlie. I was home alone. Uncle Melvin smelled bad like the men Mama liked being around at the Crow's Nest. He was stumbling when he walked, and I could smell beer and cigarette smoke on him. I had a hard time understanding him because his words sounded funny when he tried to speak. He looked angry, but he always looked angry. I told him Mama was not at home, and he said that was okay because I would do just fine.

Uncle Melvin pushed me down in the living room on the couch and tried grabbing at my clothes. I fought back, but he was heavy. I thought for sure I was going to get badly hurt or killed, but then I heard Mama's car pulling up in the driveway. Uncle Melvin must have heard it, too, because he stopped, then stumbled to stand up. I quickly got up and ran out the door toward Charlie. Uncle Melvin left shortly after that. I never knew what he said to Mama, and I never told Mama what he did. I figured she would never believe me anyway. I would just make sure to never find myself alone again with Uncle Melvin if I could help it.

The kids had all returned to the yard when I got back outside. Mary asked me where I had gone, and the younger kids were asking me for a drink of my coke as though they had never had any before.

"I went to the bathroom. Why is there a hole in the floor in the bathroom?" I asked Mary as I handed off my coke to one of my younger cousins to share amongst them.

"I guess the heat doesn't work right, so it was getting so cold upstairs last winter that we kids couldn't sleep up there. Daddy got mad about that because he did not want us downstairs where he and Mama slept, so he went upstairs and cut a huge hole in the floor and said that heat could get up there to us through the hole and that should be good enough to keep us warm," she explained.

"Was it?" I asked.

"Not really, but we stayed upstairs anyway because no one wanted to get a beating. Being cold was better than a beating," she answered.

I nodded at her in understanding. I took Mary aside, in case the little kids didn't know, and I told her I had seen the dead horse. She got tears in her eyes right away and said they all knew about it, but there was nothing they could do. She said her Daddy had decided that he didn't really need the horse anymore, so he had stopped feeding it much of anything, and then it started to get sick, and her Daddy just laughed at it as it got weaker and weaker.

"I tried to keep the little kids from seeing it, but I couldn't do it. It made them cry, it made me cry, and it scared all of us," said Mary.

"It's behind the barn," I said sadly.

"I know," she said, "We don't ever go anywhere near there now."

"I'm sorry," I said.

"Thank you," Mary responded, and then she threw her arm around me and said we should go and play before the other kids noticed us being sad. Mary was always looking out for her brothers and sisters. I think she had learned how to use boxes with lids to put away bad thoughts and memories just like I had learned to do.

CHAPTER SIXTEEN

JUST 24 HOURS

AUGUST ARRIVED VERY HOT AND MUGGY. IT WAS HARD TO STAY inside the house because it seemed the hotter it got, the more it smelled. It smelled of garbage and animal poop and pee. The bucket that we used to go to the bathroom in didn't help either. The room it was in smelled just like the outhouse. I tried my best not to go inside the house as much as possible. Mama did not seem to mind the smell though; she stayed inside all the time, mostly cooking.

The bad stink in the house was probably because we had 48 cats and 9 dogs. It didn't start out that way, but the cats we had had babies, and then their babies had babies, and then their babies had babies and we just kept getting more and more cats. Lots of times Mama would bring home whole batches of stray kittens that people would leave on the end of our dirt road. It was the same thing with the dogs. We liked the cats and the kittens, but there was so many of them that we did not really know all of them. Some of them were pretty wild.

Mama still made us eat supper inside the house regardless of how hot it was in there. After supper, Mama told me it was my turn to feed the cats. She filled up a big cake pan with the leftovers we had from supper and then she mixed in some cat food. I took the pan outside and yelled, "Here kitty, kitty, kitty! Here kitty, kitty, kitty!"

Cats came running fast from everywhere! There were cats jumping down from the roof onto my head and back, and there were cats clawing up my legs. They were climbing up my body to get to the cake pan, hissing and fighting all the way. I was so busy trying to shake off the ones that had jumped on me from the roof that I forgot to drop the cake pan. Quickly, I remembered and I dropped the pan and got out of there. I could still hear the cats hissing, meowing, and fighting when I got back into the house.

The cats probably would not have been so anxious about eating if Mama would let us feed them everyday instead of every three or four days. Mama said that if the cats wanted to go out and "whore around" and make more kittens then that was their problem. She said she did not have enough money to feed them every day, and besides, she said, cats knew how to live off the land. Our cats must not have known about living off the land because they always acted like they were pretty hungry.

I was not really sure what a "whore" was, but the way Mama said it, it sounded like a "whore" was someone who had babies. I wondered if Mama was a whore because she had Charlie and me. I was not going to ask Mama though; that would not be a good idea, and besides the way she said the word "whore" made it sound like it was not a good thing to be, which might mean Mama thought it was not a good thing to have babies. I was confused by it. I asked Charlie, but he did not know either.

When the cats had cleaned up the cake pan, I took it back into the kitchen to get it washed. Mama was standing over the sink and moaning. She didn't look very good.

"Emily, Mama has to go and lie down. I want you to wash the dishes and clean up the kitchen for me," she instructed.

"Yes, Mama," I said. "Are you okay?"

"Just do as you are told and don't worry about me. I will be fine," she responded.

Mama had four pans on the stove heating, because, as usual, we had no hot water coming out of the faucet. She also had a crock-pot sitting in the middle of the stove between the pots of water. It was plugged into the back panel on the stovetop.

When the water started to boil, I turned off the burners. Looking at the hot water gave me the idea to bring Mama some tea. I went to the cupboard and got out my grandmother's teapot. It was Mama's favorite and mine, too. Just holding it made me miss Grandma. It was blue and white with windmills and fields on it. It was old and had a crackled look to it, but that made it prettier. It felt fragile, so I was always extra careful with it. I tried to imagine Grandma using the teapot when she was a younger girl, because that's when she said her mama had given it to her, but I had a hard time imagining Grandma in any other way except for the way I knew her. I gave the teapot one last hug and hoped that wherever Grandma was and whatever she was doing that at that moment she could feel the love I was sending to her.

I made the tea and took the teapot into Mama's room. I sat it on the nightstand. Mama's bedroom was the only room in the house that had brand new furniture in it. Mama and Daddy had gone to a big department store downtown and bought it "on time," Mama said, right before Daddy left. She got a big bed, a dresser, a nightstand, and an armoire. The armoire was her favorite piece, although I never quite understood what she was going to use it for. It was pretty though. I hoped that someday I would have a bedroom again with a bed in it. I didn't like sleeping on the couch.

Mama was lying with her back to me when I brought the teapot in, so I set it down quietly and tiptoed back to the kitchen to get her teacup and sugar cubes. When I got back into her room, she was moaning.

"Mama," I said softly, "I made you some tea. You like tea when you are not feeling good."

"Thank you, Emily. Pour Mama a cup with four sugar cubes," she said nicely.

I loved it when Mama spoke like this, but this time it kind of scared me because it made me worry more about her not feeling well. I started to become afraid that maybe she was really sick and would die. She couldn't die! If she died then we would be left with just Daddy. I could not even begin to imagine what that would be like, but it would be very bad. Even though Mama was not so good a lot of the time, and even though she did not protect me from Daddy, somehow I thought that the two of them together were better than the one. I felt guilty for thinking only of myself if Mama died, so I tried not to think about it anymore.

"Mama, are you okay?" I asked with the concern in my voice that I was feeling.

"I'm sick, Emily, and I need to rest. My stomach has some bad cramps that hurt, but I will be okay. Just let me rest," she said.

"Mama, are you sure you are okay? You look really sick. You are not going to die are you?" I asked.

"Damn it, Emily! How many times do I have to tell you that I am going to be fine!" she yelled at me.

That was more like the Mama I knew, so I knew then that she was going to be just fine and I didn't worry so much anymore.

"You are going to have to help a little bit more around the house for a couple of days. You will need to do some cleaning and cooking," Mama instructed.

"I don't know how to cook," I told Mama.

The only thing I knew how to make was peanut butter sandwiches, and Charlie hated peanut butter sandwiches. Mama liked them though, but then again, Mama liked most food.

"Oh, for God's sake, Emily, suck it up! I am sick! I don't give a crap what you do. Starve for all I care. Now get the hell out of here, and go and clean the kitchen," Mama yelled.

I walked back to the kitchen with absolute knowledge that Mama might be sick, but she was still her old self. Mama had piled most of the pans on the kitchen counter. I hated washing pans and silverware, and that night there was more of everything to wash because Mama had two of her men friends over: Bob and Phil.

Mama had Bob over all the time, and she tried to get Charlie and me to call him Uncle Bob, but we knew he was not our uncle. Whenever Mama had her men friends over, Charlie would disappear for a while, although that night he did eat supper, so he must have been pretty hungry to come in and sit at the table with Bob and Phil. Charlie was gone again now. I thought he went out riding his bicycle.

Bob and Phil were outside working on Mama's car. They were filthy, grimy, and greasy. They were both wearing some old blue bib overalls worn so thin that they had holes in them. The overalls were crusty with dirt from years of use and no washing. Mama had had the overalls from when Grandpa lived at the house, and she said they were too nasty to put into any washing machine, but it didn't seem like Bob or Phil cared about how dirty the bibs were because they wore them anyway. They really were not that much different from their normal dirty clothes that they wore all the time. Bob and Phil always looked dirty with greasy, crunchy looking hair.

When they came in for supper they did not even bother to wash their hands. They sat down at the supper table and started grabbing the food before Mama even had it all on the table. They ate a lot. The serving spoons had grime floating on them from Bob and Phil using them with their filthy hands. Charlie glared at them as they passed the food to him after they had taken what they wanted to eat.

I tried my best to be quiet as I started to move things around in the kitchen so I could clean it because Mama could hear everything I was doing, and I could still hear her because her bedroom was separated from the living room by the curtain that Daddy had strung across the room. Daddy had also put some wires in the ceiling and used them to hold up a wooden pole that Mama used to hang her clothes on. The pole was right next to the curtain in Mama's room. It bulged out the other side with the clothes into the living room, but at least it helped so Charlie and I could not see in her room. It was bad enough that we could hear what went on in there; we did not want to see anything.

I was very nervous about moving the hot pans of water. Mama usually moved them and rarely did she ever let me help with this part of the dish washing, which was fine with me because I hated getting burned.

A couple of summers ago Mama and Daddy had some friends over, and they were all outside sitting around a campfire that Daddy had made in the yard. They were laughing and talking about things that Charlie and I did not understand. I saw that one of the ladies had a bag of marshmallows sitting on the ground beside her. I walked up close to her, hoping Mama or Daddy would not make me go away before I was able to ask if I could roast a marshmallow.

I stood quietly behind the lady for a moment or two, and then finally I bent down and asked her if I could roast one marshmallow. She said certainly. I skipped off to the woods, feeling happy that I was going to get to roast a marshmallow and feeling happy simply because all of the grown-up people were happy.

I found my stick and went running back. One of the dogs was excited by my running, and he was running with me. I stood in front of the lady with my back to the fire as she handed me the marshmallow. The second I got the marshmallow in my hand, the dog jumped up on me trying to get it, and he knocked me down – right into the fire.

I sat there for what seemed like forever trying to decide if I was actually getting hurt and could complain about it, so someone would help me. Before I was done deciding, the lady had scooped me up out of the fire. I felt nothing. It was like my body was there physically moving, but I could not feel a thing, not emotionally or physically. This had happened to me many times before when Daddy would hurt me, but I had no control over it. Sometimes it happened when I did not want it to, and other times it would not happen when I wanted it to.

Mama and Daddy threw me in the back of their car and rushed me to the base hospital. I lay in the backseat, quiet, wondering if I was going to get a chance to cook a marshmallow when we got home. I doubted it – stupid dog.

The nurse took me in right away. I was very dirty this time. I could feel the dirt on me, but neither she nor the doctor seemed to pay any attention to that. The nurse had me lie on my tummy because my burns were all on my bottom and the top part of my legs. The doctor quickly sprayed me down with some foam from a large can. The shock of its coldness made me start to feel again, and boy, did it hurt! After a couple of minutes, the doctor wiped off some of the foam and said there was still charcoal stuck in my leg. He didn't seem too happy about it.

Once I got home, the burns hurt terribly, and they hurt for a long time. It was hard to walk, and it was very hard to sit down. Mama said it was my own fault for being so stupid. I suppose maybe I should not have been so excited about getting to roast a marshmallow. I never wanted to be burned ever again.

I figured the hot water on the stove could burn me just as badly as the campfire had, so I reminded myself to be very careful. I noticed that the crock-pot was still plugged in, so I figured the water from it would be the hottest to use.

Once I mixed it with the cold water, it should be enough to wash and rinse the dishes, and I wouldn't even need the other four pans of water. That sounded pretty good to me because then I would only have to move one pan instead of two or three.

The crock-pot was wedged between the other pans pretty tightly. I reached around to the back of it trying to find the plug so I could unplug it. I could feel the heat and steam from all the hot water in the other pans surrounding my face. I got it unplugged. I started to lift the crock-pot off the stove, but I didn't think about the cord that was dangling behind it. The cord got stuck in one of the grates on the stove as I was lifting it out and caused me to spill all of the hot water from it onto my right arm and hand. This time I felt everything immediately. I was screaming and didn't even realize it for a couple of seconds. I ran to the sink and started running as much cold water over it as I could get.

Mama arrived in the kitchen first, "What the hell is the matter with you, Emily! I told you that I don't feel good and that I need to rest," she yelled at me.

"I burned my arm, Mama," I cried while lifting up my already blistering arm for her to see.

"Good God, Emily. If it isn't one thing with you, it's another," she lamented. "Go and rub some butter on it, and I will see if the guys can run you into the base hospital."

Phil and Bob had heard me screaming, and they were standing right behind Mama. They told her they would take me to the hospital, so Mama went and lay back down on her bed. After Mama left the kitchen, I did not rub butter on my arm or my hand. I didn't want to go to the hospital looking like a roasted chicken all buttered up and ready to eat. What good would butter do it anyway?

I didn't want to go with Bob and Phil. Being close to them always gave me a creepy, scary kind of feeling deep in my stomach, but I had little choice. I was hoping they would clean up a little bit before we left, but they didn't even wash their hands or take off the filthy bib overalls they were wearing. On the way there, I kept my arm out the window so that the night air could cool it down. Every time I brought it back into the car, it heated up immediately again and burned badly.

We had a little bit of trouble getting on the Air Force Base because I was the only one with a military ID, and it was a kid's military ID. Bob had me show the military man at the gate my arm as he explained that I needed to be seen at the hospital and that he was bringing me in for my Mama who was sick at home. He finally believed us after seeing my arm and let us through. I doubt we would have had as much trouble as we did if Bob and Phil had not been so filthy and disgusting looking. I would not want to let them on my base either unless I absolutely had to.

The nurse took me in to see the doctor right away. She told Bob and Phil to wait in the waiting room for me. She did not say anything to them about how nasty and stinky they were, but I could tell by the look on her face that she thought they were disgusting.

The doctor came in and looked at my arm. Both he and the nurse were very kind to me. He told the nurse to clean my arm and hand and then to rub some salve on it and he would be back in a few minutes. The nurse was as gentle as she could be, but still, it hurt a lot. I couldn't help but cry. I could tell she felt bad for me.

Once the nurse put the salve on my arm it started to hurt even worse, but I did not tell her because I did not want her to feel bad. The doctor came in then and looked at my arm again and asked me how it felt, and I told him it hurt. He got up and got some bandages, and he wrapped my arm and hand in white gauze until my arm looked three times its normal size. The bandages kept all the heat from the burn inside, so it was hurting worse than before. I wanted to tear off the bandage, but the doctor said I had to keep it on.

On the way back home, I once again stuck my arm

out the window. It did not cool my arm as well as before, but at least it helped somewhat.

When we got home Mama was still lying in her bed and Charlie was watching TV. Phil left, but Bob was going to spend the night. I was tired, so I lay down on the couch but didn't cover with the blanket. It was much too hot in there for a blanket, and my blanket smelled so bad that I couldn't stand it getting by my nose. I think one of the cats went the bathroom on it. Finally, Charlie went to bed, too, and I was left in the living room listening to the sounds from Mama's room and struggling to get to sleep because my arm hurt so badly.

I could hear Mama and Bob talking in her room. Mama was telling Bob how bad she was hurting. She said she could not get the bleeding to stop and that she was bleeding a lot more than she ever had before. The thought of Mama bleeding a lot scared me, but I hadn't seen any blood on her when she was lying down in her room or when she got up and came to the kitchen because of my arm. I didn't see any bandages on her either that would cover a bleeding cut. I lay with my eyes closed, suffocating in the smell of cat pee with my arm on fire and wondering where Mama was bleeding from until I finally drifted off to sleep.

In the morning, Bob woke Charlie and me up. Mama was not there. He said that Mama had gone to the doctor during the night and she was in the hospital.

"Is she okay?" Charlie asked.

"Yes, she wants me to bring you kids into see her as soon as you wake up. Get dressed and grab your breakfast so we can go," Bob said.

Neither one of us felt all that hungry, so we threw on our clothes as fast as we could, thinking that with Mama in the hospital it had to be serious and our futures were at stake. Charlie and I both sat in the back seat. Neither one of us wanted to sit in the front seat with Bob. Bob always tried to act like our friend, but we could see through him.

He would need to get a better mask on if he thought he was going to fool me. I could tell that he only tried to be nice to us to get to Mama and a place to stay and food to eat. He probably did not like us at all. I am sure we were in his way.

When we got to the hospital, Charlie and I walked in slowly. It was very quiet in the hallways and my sandals clipped loudly on the tile floor as we made our way to Mama's room. I wished I could take them off. I felt like everyone could hear me and that I was bothering everybody in the hospital. Mama would be mad at me for making noise in there.

When we got to her room, Charlie and I stood at her door. Both of us kept our heads down staring at the floor, not wanting to look at her in a hospital bed. It was too scary.

"Well, don't just stand there. Get in here," Mama instructed.

"Hi, Mama," I said as I approached her bed still looking at the floor. Slowly, I lifted my head and could see there was a bag hanging from a pole with liquid in it. There was a tube coming from the bag that was attached to Mama's arm. I had never seen one of these before in real life, but I had seen things like it on TV on the Marcus Welby MD show. I was pretty sure that it was used to give Mama medicine.

Mama looked tired and weak. She was very white and looked cleaner than I had ever seen her before in my life. Her hair looked soft as angel feathers and her skin glowed. Her teeth even looked clean. The nurse must have bathed Mama before we got there. She looked good being clean but still sick.

Charlie sat down on a chair next to the wall. He refused to get any closer to Mama. He kept staring at the floor. He never did look at her or talk to her. I am not quite sure if he was mad or just plain scared like I was, and since he was a boy, he probably could not admit to being afraid.

"Mama is going to be in the hospital for a few more

days. I have cancer in my lady parts. The doctors are going to take it out of me and then I will be okay again, but I won't be home for a few days," Mama advised.

I stood there feeling concerned and thinking, "What did she mean by her lady parts? Is this something that all ladies get sooner or later? Does this mean I will have my lady parts cut out of me when I get older?" I decided not to worry about it for now and figured that would be something I could think about when the time came, although I wished I could ask someone the questions.

"Are you going to die, Mama?" I asked.

"Good gawd, Emily. I swear you never listen to a damn word I say. Didn't I just tell you that I would be home in a few days and that I will be fine? Quit asking me that! Now, Bob is going to stay with you for a couple of days before Daddy gets home to help me out with you two while I heal from my surgery," she said.

I felt the floor give way under me. My world suddenly caved in. I felt dizzy and light headed. I grabbed hold of the side rails on Mama's bed and asked, "Daddy is coming home? I thought Daddy was going to be gone until December." I was absolutely horrified that my time without the monster was cut so short.

"Daddy is coming home for just a month to help me out around the house while I heal. The people at the Red Cross are helping us to get him home. He should be here in just a couple of days now. I want you two to get the house picked up for when he gets here," Mama explained.

"Daddy is only staying a month and then leaving again until Christmas time?" I questioned, looking for confirmation.

"Yes, Emily – isn't that what I just said? You need to clean out those filthy ears of yours," she barked. "Now, go home and get some work done, and you had best be good for Bob. No fighting. Do you two understand me?" Mama said.

Charlie had already gotten up and left the room before Mama could finish what she had said, so I answered for the both us telling her that we would be good. I shuffled down the hallway after Charlie thinking Mama was not even going to die and still things were pretty bad for me. Daddy had been gone since Christmas of last year, and although living with Mama was not easy, it was much better when Daddy was gone – at least for me.

The next morning Bob reminded me that I was supposed to clean up the house. It was so hot in there, and I felt so discombobulated that the last thing I wanted to do was clean the house. I had no idea where to start anyway. Mama was something of a packrat. She kept everything and liked to pile it up in the corners of the house. Cleaning the house was like moving filth from one corner to the next, and no matter where you put things, it still smelled terrible in there. Besides, all I wanted to do was get out of there and run away somewhere and hide before Daddy got home.

Charlie was outside sitting on the tire swing. He was not swinging – he was just sitting there staring off into space. I decided not to go over and talk to him. He didn't look very happy. I wished I knew what he was thinking.

It was very cloudy and dark out, but still hot. It felt like it was going to rain with maybe a good old fashioned thunderstorm. That is what Mama called the storms that lit up the sky and boomed very loudly. I liked thunderstorms. They seemed to express everything I always felt on the inside but could not let escape to the outside.

I headed for my pine tree sanctuary. I crawled in on my hands and knees savoring the quietness and aloneness of being there. The ground smelled fresh and clean, and the trees surrounded me in their perfume. I breathed deeply and lay on my back in the middle of the biggest pine trees. I had nowhere else to go, and I really could not run away. I could stay inside my trees for as long as possible though, I supposed.

I must have fallen asleep because when I woke up it was raining and thundering and lightening. I was a little bit scared being in the trees with the lightening because Grandma had warned me that lightening looked for the tallest thing on the ground to strike, and I think my trees were the only tall things around. But I decided I still felt quite safe, and the branches being so close together kept me pretty dry. It was wonderful lying in there on my stomach peering out from under the branches watching the storm. I could feel the storm's anger and understood it. Beneath those trees, huddled close to the ground listening to the storm, I started to cry, and I cried and cried. I yelled with the thunder and screamed with the lightening until my throat hurt. No one could hear me because the storm was too loud. There was nobody around anyway, and I thought it was rather strange that no one had bothered to look for me all day. I wasn't sure if I should be glad about that or not.

It felt much cooler outside, probably because of the rain, and I could tell it was getting closer to supper time by the way my stomach was growling. There would be no supper tonight though because there was no one to cook it. I was supposed to cook it. I wondered if Bob or Charlie were mad at me or if they were worried about me. I dried my eyes and felt exhausted from all the crying, but somehow I felt less heavy, less sad than I had been before.

I ran all the way to the house, but still I was soaked by the time I got there. Charlie was inside in the kitchen eating a bowl of cereal, and Bob was nowhere to be seen.

"Where is Bob?" I asked Charlie.

"He went to the hospital to see Mama," he said.

"Oh, is there any cereal left?" I asked.

"Yes, there are some rice puffs in the bag on the counter,"

Charlie said, as he pointed to the half-eaten bag lying open on the counter.

I got a bowl and filled it with the rice puff cereal and doused it with sugar. Mama was not around so I could put all the sugar on it that I wanted to, and I did. The cereal was stale and turned mushy right away, but at least it was sweet, and there had been no one around to do anything to it to make me sick on purpose.

We ate together quietly. There wasn't much to say. We both knew it was bad.

"Bob said Daddy should be home late tomorrow around supper time," Charlie said, as he got up to put his cereal bowl in the sink.

"Oh," was all I could think of to say. Daddy was going to be home tomorrow around supper time. I had about 24 hours left before the monster came home – just 24 hours. I felt more afraid that night than I had any other night in my entire life. Daddy had been gone for about eight months. He had a lot of time to make up for, and as I lay on the couch trying to sleep that night I could feel myself running away – running, running, running, as fast as I could go.

Chapter Seventeen

1 - 2 Daddy's Coming For You

I was never afraid of the boogie-man. I lived with the boogie-man: Daddy. Daddy was going to be home in just a couple of hours. I had been outside all day wondering where I should go and what I should do. Everything felt so hopeless. Charlie had taken off to the woods early in the morning after he had eaten his cereal. I hoped he would be back before Daddy got home.

"Oh, dear God, please let Charlie be here with me when Daddy gets home. Please!" I prayed.

I was so afraid – so, so afraid. It felt like the world was spinning hopelessly out of control, and I had no way to stop it. Daddy would hurt me once he was home, of this I had no doubt; it was one of the certainties of my life; it was a governing rule of my life: Daddy will hurt me.

Bob had been gone all day. I figured he was probably at the hospital with Mama. I wondered if he was going to be staying in the house too once Daddy got home. There were so many questions and so much fear.

The day had started cloudy, and, by late afternoon,

the skies were dark and rolling once again with thunder. When the clouds opened up and started to pour out their rain, I saw Charlie running out of the woods. I thanked God for sending the rain and Charlie back to the house. Somehow I thought that if Charlie were with me when Daddy came home, then nothing too bad could happen to me. It was like Charlie was my invisible shield.

Charlie and I were sitting in the living room on the sofa watching television when we heard the rattle of the door knob. Instantly, we both sat up straighter and stiffer. Our awareness was at its highest. We did not say a word. I doubt if we had even been breathing. Whoever was on the other side of the door was having some trouble opening it. It must have swollen from the rain, that's what Mama said happened; "just like a sponge," she said. I did not understand how a wooden door could act like a sponge, but it did stick regularly during and after rain.

The clock showed that it was 6:15 p.m., so it had to be Daddy on the other side of the door. I quickly glanced over at Charlie. Our eyes met very briefly, but in that moment I felt Charlie surrounding me with compassion and love. I wished I could somehow protect Charlie from Mama and Daddy the way I felt he protected me a lot.

We both turned our heads back toward the door, watching and waiting. I couldn't really tell what I was thinking and feeling. It was as if everything in me and around me froze. Time stood still as we waited for that door to open. It was as if I had died for a moment because there was nothing, a vast space of nothingness.

The door popped open, and there he stood. He was wearing his uniform and had a big bag slung over his shoulder. He looked tired, annoyed, and angry. He stepped into the house and threw his bag against the wall. Charlie and I moved quickly to clear the couch. When Daddy was home we could not sit there. I moved to the recliner, and Charlie sat on the floor right in front of me. I would have burst into tears right at that moment, but I was too afraid.

Daddy tromped through the living room and went into his bedroom. He came back out a few minutes later with his regular clothes on. He walked over to the television and changed the channel. I had completely forgotten about what Charlie and I had been watching and besides, I hadn't been able to concentrate on it anyway, so it mattered little to me. I had something new to watch, and I had to watch it very closely.

From the television, Daddy went to the kitchen where we heard the refrigerator door open and the sound of soda pop bottles clanking together. Daddy was mumbling something to himself as he searched through the junk drawer for a bottle opener. He must have found it because we heard the pzzzzzt sound of a top being popped off a Coca-Cola bottle. Daddy came back into the living room with his cola. He put it on the coffee table, lit a cigarette, went to his bag, and started rummaging through it. The bag was sitting very close to Charlie and me, and Daddy's closeness made my skin bump and my breath go cold. He pulled out a coverless paperback book from his bag and sauntered back to the couch where he flopped down so hard that he grunted, and his stinky, black-socked feet flew up in the air and landed back down with a heavy thump. He opened his book and started to read. He had not said one word to Charlie or me. It was as if he had never left. Time had started up right where it had left off when he went away. Nothing ever seemed to change.

We had not had supper yet, but I was afraid to move. I did not want to draw any attention to myself, and, so far, I felt like Daddy did not even know we were there. Charlie was sitting very still, too, and looking down at the floor. I decided going without supper would not be a bad thing, and I would probably have thrown it up anyway because my stomach felt like it was curdling a gallon of buttermilk. Mama liked buttermilk. She drank it by the glassful. She tried to get Charlie and me to like it, but you only need to try something once to know how disgusting it was, and buttermilk was absolutely disgusting.

Everything in the house was still except for the smoke from Daddy's cigarette that twirled in the air. On the television was Harry Reasoner squawking out the 60 Minutes newscast. Daddy didn't seem to be paying any attention to what he had to say because he kept his face behind his book. I was having trouble sitting there because my insides felt like they were going to become my outsides if I did not get up and get out of the same room that Daddy was in. I was scared. I tried to pay attention to Mr. Reasoner, but he was talking about grown-up things that I could not understand. I nudged Charlie who looked up at me questioningly. I gave him the eye signal for let's get out of here. He understood me immediately.

Charlie moved slowly, and I followed him. I had just stepped into the kitchen heading for the room Charlie slept in when Daddy spoke for the first time.

"Emily, make me a sandwich. I'm hungry," he ordered.

"What kind," I automatically responded. I was surprised by the sound of my own voice and was amazed that I could answer him so quickly and so calmly.

"I don't care. Go look, and tell me what there is," he responded.

"Mama has some ham slices and cheese in the refrigerator, and we have peanut butter," I informed him.

"Never mind the sandwich. Bring me a tall glass, a loaf of bread, the milk, and a spoon," he commanded.

I did as he told me to do. When I delivered the requested items, I stood on the opposite side of the coffee table. I was afraid to get anywhere near him. I knew Daddy was going to hurt me, but every moment I could avoid it was one more moment that belonged to me. It was those treasured moments that no one could ever take away from me that I constantly longed for in my world.

Daddy opened the loaf of bread and took out a couple of slices. He tore them up and stuffed them in the glass. He picked up the gallon of milk and poured some over the bread in the glass.

"Go put this stuff away now," he ordered as he began to eat the milk soaked bread. It was a favorite treat of Daddy's, and he ate it often. It sickened me.

I put the bread and milk away and joined Charlie on his bed. He had some ham and cheese slices on a plate to share with me. He pulled out his checker board, and we started to play checkers while we ate our food. We played and ate in silence.

I could feel my heart beating rapidly the entire time we were playing. It seemed so loud to me that I was surprised that Charlie could not hear it. I was able to eat some of the ham and cheese, but it felt like it was stuck halfway down my throat. I tried to focus on the game, but I couldn't do it very well. I was waiting – waiting for the moment to arrive: it consumed me. I thought, "When would it happen? What was he going to do to me? I am sure he is already making plans in his head about how he will hurt me." My sense of dread and absolute terror were increasing very quickly.

We were almost done with our first game when I heard Paul Harvey on the television news channel say, "And that's the rest of the story," which signaled the end of the program. Daddy said he liked Paul Harvey because he called a "spade a spade and a jack a jack." I had not been paying very close attention to the checkers game with Charlie who was winning, and now I was paying even less attention. Since the news was over, I was pretty sure Daddy would be less occupied which made me worry even more.

"Emily, get your shoes on. I am almost out of cigarettes, and you can go to the store with me," he yelled back at us.

I looked up at Charlie with fear in my eyes.

"Can I go instead?" Charlie asked immediately.

"No, and you can't go with either. Someone has to be here to answer the telephone in case your Mama calls," he ordered.

I gave Charlie one last look that said thank you for trying. I moved slowly, but I did move. I didn't want to risk having Daddy come back to Charlie's room and beat us with his belt.

"Would you hurry your slow, sorry ass up? I don't have all frickin day! Let's go!" he screamed at me as I was trying to tie my sneakers.

We got in the car. Daddy had the windshield wipers on because it was still raining very hard outside. The thwack-thwack of the wipers echoed loudly in my head. The windows were fogged over but that didn't stop Daddy from leaving. As usual, I sat as close to the door as I could get. Daddy took a pack of cigarettes out of his shirt pocket, he pulled the tag around it that helped take the cellophane off, and reached in to get a cigarette. He lit the cigarette, inhaled deeply making a whistling sound between his teeth, and then blew the smoke out forcefully. I stared out my window and wondered why Daddy wanted to go to buy a pack of cigarettes when he had just opened a brand new pack. Then, to my dismay, I figured it out. Daddy didn't need cigarettes. He used that as an excuse to get me out of the house and into the car with him alone!

It didn't take long before the car was filled with smoke. I tried to roll my window down a little bit, but he yelled at me and told me to leave it up because he didn't want to get rain inside the car. It was hard to breathe, and I felt like my throat was burning. I started to cough, but that seemed to pull more of the smoke into me when I inhaled. I wondered if I was turning the color green because I sure felt green.

He drove us straight to the General Store, the same store that Patty and I had visited. I looked out the window the entire way there remembering each inch of ground as we drove by and missing the fun we had had that day, but most of all, missing the freedom I had felt.

As I sat huddled into the door of Daddy's car, I tried to make sense of things. I imagined I was the prisoner of an ogre and that my knight in shining armor would be coming around the corner any minute to save me, but he never showed up. I really had not expected him to anyway, but it was nice to think about. Someday though, I was certain, somehow I would be saved – somehow, someway. There was only one person in the whole world that could save me, and at least I trusted her: me. I would save myself just as soon as I was big enough to do it. Until then, I would keep making boxes in my head for bad memories and do my best to stay out of Daddy's path.

I tried not to think about what was going to happen, but that was very hard to do. I tried to imagine all kinds of different stories in my head to explain why I was in the car with a monster. It made it a little easier imagining the unimaginable than thinking about what was really happening. It made more sense to me that Daddy was an ogre and I was a prisoner than it did that Daddy was my Daddy and he was going to hurt me badly.

I felt fear like I had never felt it before. My stomach started to feel sick, and I needed to throw up. We were almost to the General Store, so I did my best to calm my stomach and wait until we stopped. I wondered if the fear I was feeling would still be this bad after Daddy hurt me. I hoped not. I prayed for it to be over quickly.

Daddy pulled into the parking lot and parked the car right up next to the store as close to the door as he could get. He jumped out without saying a word to me. That was my signal that I was not going in the store with him. After Daddy got inside the store, I opened my door and ran to the side of the building. I ignored the rain which was so thick it was hard to see through as it pelted down on me. I felt chilled as my feet splashed through puddles of water glistening with color from the slick of car oil. I stooped over and put my left hand on the side wall of the General Store. It was made from brick and felt cool and scratchy under my hand. It was wet from the rain, and it was solid as if it were trying to tell me it would be there forever. My stomach lurched, and I threw up. The rain coming down on my back felt good and helped to cool the anxiety I was suffering. It seemed like the rain was trying its hardest to clean me but couldn't figure out exactly where I was dirty. I couldn't figure that out either, but I sure felt dirty, ugly, afraid, alone, unwanted, unloved, and sad.

I stood there, wiped my mouth, looked around, and wondered how far I could run before Daddy came back out of the store. I decided it probably would not be far enough. He would find me, and then it would be worse for me. "Besides, where would I go anyway?" I thought. The only place that I could think of to run to, where it would be safe and I would have food, a place to sleep, and someone to love me was Grandma's house, and she lived too far away. I thought about running away into the woods behind the General Store for a minute or two, but the possibility of running into bears scared me too much, especially after finding out how fearful Mama was of them. I had thought there was nothing in the world that could truly scare Mama because, until the bear came along, Mama had always been the one doing the scaring, not the one being scared.

I hurried back to the car. I wanted to get back in it before Daddy came out of the store. My sneakers were squeaking and sloshing with each step I took. I was soaked from head to toe by the time I got back into my seat. My hair looked like I had washed it and had forgotten to towel dry it. It lay stringy and stuck to my face. The rain from my hair dribbled down to my eyes and mouth. It tasted salty from sliding through the sweat that had formed on my face when I was throwing up. I made it to the car before Daddy, but he was going to be angry because I had brought the rain inside on my body.

Daddy came out of the store, fell heavily into his seat,

turned the car on, and then turned on the radio. It was never a good sign for me when Daddy turned on the radio. For some reason, he liked having music on when he hurt me. I felt like the music was mocking me most of the time. It seemed surreal to me how the music could sound so normal and even sometimes happy when I was getting hurt so badly.

Daddy started to back up the car to get out of the parking lot. He didn't turn his head to look behind him; instead he looked in his mirrors to guide his way. He moved slowly until he got the car back out onto the main road, and then he started to drive much faster. I moved my feet because they had become uncomfortable with my socks being wet, and they were itching. The sound of my wet, squeaky sneakers caught Daddy's attention, and for the first time since he got back in the car, he glanced at me. I kept my head down so that I did not have to look at him. I never could look Daddy or Mama in the eyes. It was too frightening. It was too hollow.

"What in the hell happened to you!" he shouted. "Just look at what you are doing to my f'n car! You don't even have enough sense to stay out of the rain, do you? Jesus H. Christ! You best hope you don't cause any damage with your stupidity! I guess I just can't take my eyes off of you. What happened? Have you gotten dumber since I have been gone? What the hell!"

I didn't answer Daddy. Instead I leaned my wet head against the damp window and stared straight ahead of me. I didn't think he was really looking for an answer anyway.

"You are an idiot, a dumb little idiot," he said.

It was weird sometimes the things that I thought about, especially when I was feeling afraid, hurt, or unloved. It was better to try to think about anything, instead of feeling the pain that was deep in my stomach from Daddy calling me a dumb idiot. I wondered, "If I am an idiot, doesn't that automatically mean that I am dumb? Is a dumb little idiot the worse kind of idiot one could be?" I was never go-

237

ing to ask anybody these questions, but someday, I was certain, I would figure things out.

Daddy drove us toward our house, but when we got to our road, he kept going. My fears had been confirmed. My body stiffened in anticipation of the certain agony to come. My heart started to beat so fast that my chest was hurting. I could feel sweat coming down my face, and it stung my eyes a little bit when it rolled into them. I felt goose bumps rise on my arms, and I looked down to see all the little, tiny, almost invisible hairs standing straight up. They were scared, too. I wanted to cry, but there were no tears in me. I wanted to scream, but my voice had left me. It was like I had no breath left in me. I felt that old familiar feeling of nothingness as it crept upon me. I welcomed it and was hoping it would take me completely away from the ogre.

Suddenly, Daddy turned down a dirt road that looked more like a path than it did a road. I had never noticed this pathway before and wondered how Daddy knew about it. It was difficult to see from the main road, let alone know it was there. The path was very narrow, and there was tall grass growing down the middle of it. The grass was so long that I could hear it scraping underneath the car. The car bounced from side to side because of all the ruts Daddy was driving over as the path led us back into some thick woods. The trees crowded around us so closely that they scratched the car as we drove through them. I was stunned by Daddy's lack of concern for his car getting scratched, but then I figured he had other things on his mind that were more important to him than his car.

The further back Daddy drove, the more frightened I became. I thought he could kill me and no one would ever find me. The thought of death did not really scare me at all anymore. I felt ready for it, and I was certain God would take me to Heaven as long as he didn't blame me for what Daddy was doing to me. I asked God nearly every day to forgive my sins although I was not quite sure what my sins were, I trusted in God to know. I was very hopeful that I would be allowed in Heaven.

The pathway ended abruptly, and in front of me I saw a beautiful open meadow with tall grass and wild weeds growing everywhere. It was the kind of meadow that made me want to take my sneakers off and run through it just so I could feel it take me in. The meadow was longer than it was wide, and a family of trees holding each other arm in arm ran all around the edges of it. They called to me, assuring me I would be safe if only I could reach the security and tranquility of their branches. Once inside, they would close around me, hiding me from the evil ogre who had invaded the peaceful meadow. I heard the car turn off.

"Get out of the car, Emily," ordered the ogre.

I did not move.

"Get out of the car, now!" Daddy repeated, shattering my protective fantasy life, unbeknownst to him.

Still, I did not move.

"You really like to push your f'n luck with me, don't you?" Daddy asked.

I did not respond, nor did I move. I was having trouble hearing him. I felt myself slip away into my black hole of nothingness. The world looked dark around the edges, and I was dizzy. If I had been standing, I probably would have fallen down.

Daddy jumped out of the car and bounded over to my side. For a moment I considered jumping out myself, running straight out into the meadow, and never stopping until my heart burst from pumping too hard, but I felt so paralyzed that I wondered if I were still breathing.

Daddy yanked open my door, grabbed my arm, and pulled me out of the car so quickly that I did not have time to get my legs under me, so it hurt as my body thumped out of the car and onto the ground. I was ripped out of my black hole of nothingness and became acutely aware of everything around me.

Daddy pulled me up off the ground, which was muddy from the rain, and kept a tight grip on me. He stood in the rain for a moment, getting soaked, and looked around the meadow. Then he opened the back door of the car and shoved me in it. Daddy jumped in right after me, leaving the car door open. I found my voice and began screaming, but my screaming seemed to make Daddy hurt me worse.

"Knock it off, Emily! Shut-up!" Daddy commanded as he put his hand over my mouth.

"You are my Daddy!" I cried under the muffle of his hand. Daddy already had that faraway look of a stranger in his eyes that he would often get when he hurt me, so I doubted he could hear me at all; I wondered if he could even see it was me: me, Emily.

Daddy was on top of me with the rain water from his hair dripping onto my face and the smell of his cigarette breath in my nose, but I was kicking and squirming so much that he was having trouble controlling me. It had been eight months since Daddy had touched me, and my body was fighting with everything it had to keep it that way. I was thinking only of how to get away from him, how to become free from him. I didn't even think about where I would or could get away to; I just wanted to get away.

Daddy slapped me hard across the face and told me to settle down or I was going to get it worse. My face stung from the slap, but I couldn't rub it because Daddy had caught my hands and was holding them together above my head with one of his hands. Out of fear, I stopped moving, closed my eyes, and tried to go away in my mind, as I had done so many times before.

Daddy easily flipped me over on my stomach, let go of my hands, and brushed some mud off of the back of my legs before grabbing my wet skirt, and bunching it up over my bottom. He pulled down my underwear. I heard him loosen his belt buckle and unzip his pants. My tears had found me and were falling easily now. I rubbed my face against the fabric of the seat to wipe them away. It was prickly and rather worn because the car was so very old. I could feel Daddy's weight as he began to lie on me. I reached in front of me for the arm rest that I knew was on the car door. I found it and gripped it as hard as I could to brace myself for whatever was to come. I prayed to God begging him to make Daddy stop and begging him to help Daddy understand that he truly was my Daddy and not some ogre.

He pressed his wiener by my butt and pushed really hard. It hurt so badly! I screamed out, and Daddy slapped the back of my head to warn me again.

"It's just too damn dry," he said as he pulled himself back up.

I don't think he was really talking to me, and I had no idea what he was talking about. I was simply grateful that he had stopped. For a moment, I wondered if God had answered my prayers.

Daddy flipped me over onto my back and grabbed my hand. I closed my eyes tightly and turned my head away. He tried wrapping my hand around his wiener, but I held my fingers straight out as hard as I could. There was a strong odor of sweat and pee coming from between Daddy's legs. I stopped breathing through my nose, so I would not have to smell it, and I opened my mouth a little bit at the corner to get air. It seemed like everything about Daddy smelled bad; it also seemed like everything in my life smelled bad. It made sense to me that bad things would smell bad. Daddy was stronger than me, and it didn't take him long to have my fingers wrapped around his wiener and his hand around my hand making it go up and down stroking him.

"You have got the softest skin, Emily. It's so sweet," Daddy mumbled and then moaned.

I tried to ignore him, while at the same time I started to hate my soft skin. His hand started moving my hand faster and faster. Daddy was sitting with his legs straddled over me, and the weight of him was beginning to hurt me. I hoped he would be done soon.

With his free hand, Daddy turned my head toward him, but I still kept my eyes shut. He moaned deeply, and then I felt Daddy press his wiener against my lips. I clenched my teeth and lips. I felt something throb on his wiener and instantly felt a warm substance being squirted on my lips. The smell between his legs, with the smell of the wet stuff, was putrid. I started to gag, and some of the wet stuff got inside my mouth. My eyes flew open in response to the revolting taste in my mouth, and I spit it out immediately. I saw Daddy's face, and he was grinning wildly. I quickly closed my eyes again.

Daddy made me stroke him a couple of more times before he dropped my hand and backed himself out of the car. I lay there not moving, not ever wanting to move again.

"Get up, and get yourself together, Emily. I got to get back to the house. I am sure your damn Mama has called by now," he ordered.

Still I lay there. His voice sounded hollow in my ears. It echoed in my head like it had no soul behind it.

"Get the hell up! What the hell is wrong with you! Why do I have to tell you everything twice! Get up before I take off my belt. Get cleaned up," Daddy growled.

I scooted across the back seat on my butt until my legs were able to dangle down outside the car in front of me. I stood up, reached down, and pulled my underwear back up. I looked around trying to find something that would work to wipe the stench of Daddy's thick white stuff off my face, but there was nothing. I decided to use my shirt, although I really didn't want to because I did not want that stuff on my clothes either, but it was better than leaving it on my lips where its vile taste could still get in my mouth.

I heard Daddy strike a match, and I smelled the sulfur from it. He was in the front seat of the car when he turned around and looked at the back seat. The seat had a huge wet spot on it from where he had held me down because my clothes had been so wet from the rain.

"You had best hope that dries with no stain," Daddy said as he turned back around. "Get in, Emily."

I smoothed my clothes out as best I could and got back in the car. I was more worried about the mud on the back of my skirt and legs staining the fabric of the seat than I was the water staining it. Water dries clear, but the mud, I feared, might cause me a problem. Daddy smiled, and deeply inhaled his cigarette. I leaned against the door with my head down and listened to Daddy sing along with the radio. He seemed happy now. He grinned at me and sang like everything was normal as he drove us home. It was always so important to him to pretend everything was normal after he had hurt me. He expected me to pretend along with him, and if I chose not to, he could get very angry and upset with me. It was better to play along with him than risk being hurt more.

"Sing with me, Emily. You know this song. It's Ray Stevens. You like him, don't you, Emmy?" Daddy said trying to sound normal and cheerful.

I ignored him at first. I felt so agitated; my mind was tumbling uncontrollably. I thought, "How can he think I can sing about anything? My butt still hurts where he tried to push himself inside me! Oh, my God! I can still smell the stink of him on my face, and my stomach hurts from his weight straddled across me. Sing? How can I sing? I just want to die and go away forever and never, ever, ever come back! Dear God, please, please, save me and take me to heaven!"

"Emily, sing with Daddy. I know you know this song," Daddy requested again with a bit more snarl in his voice.

I started to move my lips to the words, but no sound could come out. Daddy seemed to be satisfied. His voice was deep, and it sounded strange to hear him sing such a nice happy song. The song did not belong anywhere in my world especially after what Daddy had just done to me, but there it was; it mocked me, and there was Daddy who looked strange as he sang loud and clear, "Everything is beautiful in its own way. Like a starry summer night or a snow covered winter's day. Everybody's beautiful in their own way. Under God's heaven the world's gonna find a way."

Daddy backed the car all the way to the road. The rain had settled down to a light sprinkle, and it looked like the clouds were finally clearing off in a distance. It was warm outside, but I was starting to shiver because I was so wet from the rain. We were close to the house so I did not ask Daddy to turn the heat on. I never wanted to ask him for anything. He wouldn't have done it for me anyway.

When we pulled up in the driveway, Daddy looked at me and told me to make sure I got the mud out of the car, and then he left, whistling the entire way up to the house. I didn't move until I saw the door of the house close behind Daddy as he went inside.

Finally, the air was mine again to breathe.

CHAPTER EIGHTEEN

RUSTY CARS & BABY DOLLS

MAMA WAS STILL IN THE HOSPITAL. CHARLIE AND I HAD BEEN told she was coming home soon. I hoped that meant Daddy wouldn't be able to touch me quite as much as he could with her away, but it would not stop altogether; it never had before. Now that Mama was coming home, Daddy should be leaving again soon. I would get almost four more months without him, and any time away from Daddy was good time.

Daddy had made supper. He had cooked some turkey HungryMan TV dinners in the oven. They were okay, and I had very little to clean up. After supper, I grabbed two of my baby dolls, and Charlie and I went outside to escape being Daddy's servant. If we stayed inside, Daddy constantly told one of us to do one thing or another – get coffee, turn up the TV, turn down the TV, turn the channel, get his book, get him something to eat – he never seemed to move for himself. Usually, Mama was home and acted as his servant, so we were not really used to this role, and we didn't like it one bit. Not once did Daddy ever say thank you.

Far behind the house, Grandpa had put several of his

old cars that had quit running. They were so far back that you couldn't see them from the house. Mama called the area they were in the "back forty." When I asked her what that meant, she called me stupid. Then she explained that the cars were on the edge of our property. We had fifty acres, not forty, so, I thought, "I am not the only stupid one." It made no sense why she said "back forty" instead of back fifty, but there was no way I was going to ask her to explain herself. Instead I said, "Oh," and smiled at her and thought, "Mama can be stupid sometimes, too."

The cars were all the same color of rust and had an old antique look about them. Charlie and I headed out to play in them. When we got up close to the field, it looked like a graveyard for old cars. The windows had long been broken out of them, and the seats had worn entirely away leaving the springs exposed. There were no tires on the cars, and they had settled far into the ground. It looked like the earth was slowly eating them. They were tired and worn, but to Charlie and me, they gleamed as though they were brand new. They were our ticket out of there, if only for a few moments.

I ran ahead to get into my favorite car, a huge one with four doors that would no longer open. I had to climb through the back window. The backseat was missing, and the front seat was nothing but a bunch of springs. I had to be careful how I sat on it. It was my favorite car because it was the biggest one, and I liked to pretend that I was driving my children to a park for a picnic. I put my dolls where the backseat would have been so I could keep an eye on them in case they needed me. I wanted five children, and someday, I was determined, I would have them.

Charlie took the car next to me and asked me if I wanted to race.

"I can't race. I have babies in the car," I told him.

"Oh, don't have babies right now, Emily. I want to race. We can play babies later," he pleaded.

It was always very hard for me not to do what Charlie asked because he rarely asked for anything.

"Okay, but I have to take my baby dolls out then," I said as I grabbed my dolls and placed them on the hood of yet another car. They could safely wait there for me. I wrapped them tightly in their blankets before I lay them down.

I climbed back into the car and looked over at Charlie who was intent on starting. His face was all scrunched up with a serious racing look. He stared straight ahead with his shoulders hunched up over the steering wheel. I smiled at him and said I was ready. I already knew Charlie would win the race, but I would give him a good run for it.

"Okay, ready, set, go!" Charlie yelled.

"Vroooom, vroom, vroom," I yelled back as I pretended to steer my wheel back and forth as fast as I could.

"You had better hurry up, Emmy! I am way ahead of you!" Charlie yelled.

"No you are not! I am right behind you! I am coming up beside you, Charlie. Move over and let me pass!" I yelled back.

"No way, Emmy! I am stepping on the gas even harder! Now, I am leaving you in my dust, but that was a good try," he said laughing at me. "You know you can't win. You're a girl, and girls don't race cars."

Charlie had all kinds of ideas of what girls were supposed to do and not supposed to do, and from everything I could tell so far, he was usually right. I had never heard of a girl racing cars, but I wondered, "Why not? Why can't a girl race a car?" I asked Charlie about this once, and he told me that girls couldn't race cars because they were girls. It still made no sense to me, but I smiled and nodded to Charlie as though I understood him completely.

"Charlie, wait up! You are going so fast that I can barely see you!" I yelled.

"I am crossing the finish line! I win! I win!" Charlie yelled throwing his hands up in the air and smiling from ear to ear.

"I lost again," I said trying to sound defeated.

Charlie laughed, turned his head, and started driving his car again. It was clear he was off on another adventure, but this time he was going without me. I got out of the car again and went to get my baby dolls. They had waited patiently for me. I picked them up, hugged them as hard as I could, kissed them on their foreheads, told them I loved them, and that I was sorry I had had to make them wait for me. I treated my baby dolls with the love I had always wanted. I couldn't remember ever being hugged by Mama or Daddy, nor had either one of them ever said they loved me. The only time I was ever touched was when Daddy hurt me. I promised myself I would be different with my babies when I had them.

I loved the long, long days of summer because I could stay outside away from Mama and Daddy much longer than I could in the winter. We played in the cars until we noticed the sun was going down.

"We better get back to the house before Daddy gets mad at us," Charlie said.

"Do you think he might be mad already? Maybe we shouldn't have come out here. I don't think we could hear him calling us from the house if he had wanted us. Maybe we should have told him where we were going," I said, suddenly concerned about the reality of my surroundings.

"I don't know, Emmy, but I will race you to the house," Charlie said.

Charlie was worried too. I could see the concern on his face, but he tried to hide it from me and be brave.

"Ready, set, go!" I yelled.

Charlie took off fast. He would win this race, too, because he was a faster runner than me. He had always been a faster runner than me. I was glad it made Charlie happy that he could win at something. We never really talked about how bad things were in our family. I could sense it between us though; it was like an unspoken language of understanding. So often when I would look at Charlie, his face looked like he was trying to say, "I understand, and I am sorry. I wish I could do something to change it." I loved Charlie, and I wished there was something I could have done to change things, too.

By the time we reached the front of the house, twilight had passed, and it was dark outside. We looked inside the front window where we saw Daddy lying on the couch with his book and the TV on. We headed for the big oak tree with the tire swing. I climbed inside the tire swing, and Charlie pushed me before he walked away and sat down on the propane tank. We looked out at the display of lights that danced in front of our eyes. It seemed like there were hundreds and hundreds of fireflies out. Charlie and I looked at each other and smiled.

"I am going to go and grab one of Grandma's old fruit jars so we can catch some of them, Emmy," Charlie said as he hoped off the tank, and headed for the shack that was used for storage. It didn't take long before he was back, and we were both running around trying to catch those elusive fireflies.

"You have to be quiet and real still," Charlie whispered.

"I can't catch one," I wailed.

"Shhhhh....I will get one for you," Charlie offered.

"Okay," I said, admiring my older brother and all of his many talents.

Charlie still had not caught any fireflies when we heard the screen door of the house squeak open. My heart sank. I felt like someone or something had sucked all the air out of my lungs at once. Our fun was over. There would be no fireflies to take with us.

"You two get inside here. It's dark out. You know you belong in the house when it is dark outside," Daddy ordered.

Charlie shrugged, told me he was sorry, said he would try again another night, put the jar down, and headed for the house. I stood still for a couple of more seconds, not wanting to give up the evening.

"Emily, can't you hear? Get your ass in here," Daddy repeated.

Charlie looked back at me as he walked past Daddy into the house. His look pleaded with me not to cause any trouble, so I started in. There would be other nights and like Mama said, "All good things must come to an end," although I could never figure out why it had to be that way.

Daddy came in the house after me and told us to get our pajamas on. We both did as we were told and came back to the living room. Daddy was no longer there. He had gone into his bedroom, which was strange because usually Daddy stayed up really late.

"Come in here you two. I want to show you something," Daddy yelled from his room.

Immediately I felt alarmed. Daddy in a bedroom could never be a good thing, but we had no choice. So we both entered his room uncomfortably. It felt foreign in the bedroom because Mama was not there. Daddy was stretched out on the bed. He was looking at a small, black and white TV that was sitting on his dresser.

"See what Daddy bought?" he said cheerfully.

We both just stared at it.

"Come on. Get up here on the bed, and we can watch TV together," Daddy offered.

I wish we could have said no but that was not an option, so we both gingerly stepped over by the bed and climbed up. I was extremely frightened. Daddy was being much too nice to us, and I feared every second that something truly evil was going to happen. Daddy was never nice just to be nice.

"You can lie next to me, Emily, and Charlie, you lay in front of her. That way we can all see the TV," Daddy instructed.

Daddy was on his side when he scooped me up in his arms and lay me on my side next to him with his arm under my head. I was petrified. Charlie avoided eye contact with me and lay down in front of me on his side, like he was told to do.

Daddy had some sort of war movie playing that neither Charlie nor I cared for, but Daddy told us to hush up and watch the show. All three of us lay there on our sides, packed close like sardines, covered in darkness, and watched the flickering black and white TV. I waited.

We lay like that for some time, and I was getting tired from holding my body so tense waiting for what I was sure was coming. Just when I started to think that maybe Daddy was not going to do anything, I felt him reach down and pull up my nightgown. My body tensed even tighter.

Charlie started to squirm a little bit in reaction to me tensing up, and Daddy told him to settle down and watch the movie, so he did. Daddy put his hand on my butt and squeezed me really hard. I thought maybe if I could concentrate on the movie I wouldn't feel a thing. In a way, it would be like I was not there at all. It would be like I was way far away, in the movie but regardless of how hard I concentrated on the movie, I couldn't wish myself away. All I could hear was Daddy's breath on the back of my neck. I couldn't believe he was doing this to me with Charlie right there in front of me! I thought, "What did this mean? Oh, dear, God, what did this mean?"

Daddy ran his finger down the middle of my butt and pushed his hand in between my legs. I held my legs straight out and tense. Daddy started to push his wiener up to my butt and rubbed on me with it. He took his hand away for a moment, and when he put it back down on my bottom, it felt slippery, as though it had oil on it. He pushed his finger inside my butt. It hurt! I sucked my breath in and held it as I sat as still as I possibly could and thought, "I can't risk having Charlie see what Daddy does to me. What will he think of me? Will he think it is my fault? Maybe it is my fault. Maybe I should just get up and run, but, if I run, he will catch me. There is nothing I can do." I prayed that Charlie would not see what was happening to me behind his back.

I watched Charlie closely for any movement, and I realized he had fallen asleep. I was certain that was what Daddy had been waiting for the whole time. I was not safe anywhere, but I was glad that in his sleep Charlie would be spared. I tried my best not to move or make a noise because I did not want to wake him.

"Watch the movie," Daddy said, as he continued to rub and push against me.

Daddy reached around me and covered my mouth. This meant real trouble! It was hard to breathe especially with the blanket and pillow so close to my nose. I felt like I was being suffocated. I started to suck air in as fast and as deep as I possibly could, as though it was the last time I would ever be able to do so, but Daddy didn't seem to notice how I struggled to breathe, although this did not surprise me; Daddy rarely noticed anything about me when he hurt me. He would get that far away look in his eyes, and if he did look at me, it was as though he looked right through me.

"Don't worry, Emmy, it won't be dry this time. That's the only reason it hurt so bad last time," Daddy whispered in my ear.

I screamed in my head, "What was dry? What was he talking about?"

Suddenly, I felt his wiener push hard against me like it was trying to find an opening. It felt big, hard, and angry once again. I felt Daddy grab it and move it toward my bottom. He pushed it inside my butt! I felt like I was being ripped apart! "Dear God," I prayed, "Please make me disappear! Please!" My thoughts scrambled fast and reached for something, anything, to distract me, "... Charlie and me playing with the cars – maybe, I actually win a race ... me having babies when I am all grown up ... five babies, boys and girls ... school is starting soon – who will be my teacher ... Mama is coming home ... I like my bike ... I should bike to the store again ... Oh, Charlie, please don't wake up." It didn't work. I couldn't think about anything for more than a second, except for the pain Daddy caused me.

Daddy took himself back out of me to my relief, but then he pushed himself right back in. I thought it would never stop. He rocked against me as he moved his wiener in and out – in and out. It hurt and it burned so terribly. I thought for sure I would explode. I just wanted it to stop. It hurt worse than anything Daddy had done to me before. I was certain something had been ripped apart in me because I felt torn open.

Daddy shuttered a little bit and then his wiener slid out of me. He took his hand off my mouth. I felt so weak from the pain and terror of it all. My insides trembled. I tried to force myself to disappear into nothingness. I was empty, alone, frightened, and I hurt so very, very much.

"Wake your brother up, and the two of you get out of here and get to bed," Daddy ordered.

I woke up Charlie, and he stumbled back to his bed in a haze of sleep, while I sluggishly went to the couch surprised I could even walk given how weak I felt. I lay on my side on the couch because my butt hurt too much to even sit on it. Although Daddy was no longer hurting me, I was petrified. I thought, "He likes to put his fingers around and in my butt, but why? Why would anyone want to touch you where your poop comes out? What was so wrong about me that made Daddy do this? Why does Mama let him do these things to me? Does he do the same things to Mama or Charlie?" I felt and dirty and ashamed.

I finally fell asleep crying. The next morning I was tired, and my face was puffy from crying. Charlie asked me what was wrong, and I told him I must have had a nightmare and cried in my sleep. I ate breakfast, cleaned up the dishes, and headed outside. I had not seen Daddy yet, and I did not want to.

I went to my pine trees and crawled into their comfort. They accepted me like a long lost child enveloping me in their purity. I allowed myself to feel safe. I made a bed with the needles on the ground and lay on my side. My butt hurt too much to lie on my back. I felt like I had to go to the bathroom, but I was very afraid to because I figured it would hurt too much, so I held it in and started to get a stomachache. I wished I could stay in the middle of my trees forever, but "wishing don't make it so," Mama always told me. I guess she was right. I closed my eyes and drifted back to sleep.

I was startled awake a while later by the roar of Daddy revving the engine on his car. He yelled out of his window to Charlie that he was going to pick up Mama and that Charlie needed to keep an eye on me. Charlie didn't even know where I was and neither did Daddy, but that didn't seem to bother him. Charlie said he would watch me.

After Daddy sped off down the road, I watched Charlie looking around for me. As much as I trusted Charlie, I could not come out from my trees as long as Charlie could see where I was coming from, so I waited and eventually, Charlie headed to the back of the house to look for me.

I sprang out from the pine trees and hurried to the tire swing. I waited there for Charlie to come back.

"There you are! Daddy said I had to watch you. Where were you?" Charlie asked.

"Nowhere," I responded.

Charlie accepted my answer and asked me if I wanted to ride my bicycle with him. I wanted to, but I did not dare sit on my banana seat, and I couldn't stand up the whole time, so I told him I didn't want to right then. He took off on his bike riding up and down the dirt road in front of our house.

I stayed in the yard thankful for the time alone. There was no one there to hurt me; there was no one there to love me either. It was better that way. I felt so lost inside, and nothing sounded like fun. I put my head through the tire swing and let my belly rest against it. I kicked it gently back and forth with my feet and felt the breeze on my face. It was peaceful. I wondered how long it would be before Mama and Daddy got home to shatter the tranquility of the day. I hoped they would take their time. We didn't need them.

My stomach started to hurt from lying in the tire swing, so I had to get out. I wanted something to take me away from there, far, far away. I thought of The Little Boxcar Children, a book I loved to read. The children lived in an old boxcar without any parents, and one way or another, they always figured out a way to survive without any grownups around to hurt them. I envied them so much. I went to the house and retrieved my book so I could join the children in the boxcar for a little while.

I loved to read. Reading was like going to other places, but no one ever knew you were gone. It helped me feel better, and it helped me forget, even for a few moments, who I really was and where I really lived. It was like going on a vacation without having to pack a suitcase.

Sometimes I read stories about people who had sad things happen to them, and it made me think that there were other people in the world that had a more painful life than me; yet, they also reminded me of how painful I thought my life was too. I had some favorite stories that made me feel happy, and I loved to read them over and over again. There was Mrs. Piggle Wiggle who always had something to teach kids, and she did it in such a nice way. She was funny, and I loved her. She reminded me of Grandma. My favorite stories, though, had to be The Little House on the Prairie. I wanted to be Laura Ingalls Wilder; I wanted her life. She was lucky. I wondered if her parents were really that good or if she was writing it like that so they would not get mad at her. It was so difficult to believe in anything anymore, but I chose to believe they were good because I needed them to be good. I needed to believe in them because, otherwise, it would've been hard for me to pretend I was Laura while I was reading her stories.

Mama said that Laura lived a very hard life and that we should be grateful that we live now instead of back then, which was like one hundred years ago. One hundred years was certainly a very long time. I couldn't even imagine it. To me, it seemed like summer lasted forever, let alone the thought of one hundred years, but, still, I couldn't agree with Mama because I thought Laura had a better life. Charlie said he wondered what they did all day long because they had no TV, but I didn't wonder about such things.

Laura wrote about her family and everything they did together. They spent a lot of time together, which is what I think they did to pass the time. They loved each other and liked being together. I wished our family was like her family. She never said her daddy hurt her. She never said her mama didn't love her. When I read her stories, I pretended I was her, but yet, it was very difficult for me to know what it was really like to have a mama and a daddy that showed how much they loved their kids. Oh, how I wished her story could be my story for more than just the few minutes I got to read her books.

I sat on the grass, leaned up against the tire swing tree, and had read about six chapters before Daddy drove back up the driveway. Mama was in the car, too, and she looked very crabby. They looked like they had been fighting on their way home. Mama and Daddy fought all the time, especially when they were in the car together.

When Daddy stopped the car, Mama got out and went to the house. She walked slowly doubled over. She groaned and moaned the entire way to the door. She didn't look like she was feeling very well at all, but with Mama it was always hard to tell for sure. I couldn't remember one day when Mama said she felt good. Mama complained about something every single day. Sometimes, she looked as sick as she said she felt, but other times, she looked and acted just fine, so Charlie and I never really knew for sure. I wanted to remind Mama about the story she liked to tell Charlie and me about the boy who cried wolf because Mama seemed to be just like him, except she cried that she was sick every day. Charlie warned me to never say this to Mama, and I knew he was right, but that didn't stop me from thinking it.

Charlie had come back up in the yard and dropped his bicycle by the tire swing. I had put my book down to watch Mama and Daddy.

"We better go in the house, too," whispered Charlie.

"Nooooo," I said automatically. "I don't want to go in there. Mama looks crabby."

"I know, but she is going to be even madder if she has to yell at us to get us to come in. You know she is going to want us in the house," Charlie explained to me.

I stared at Charlie trying to think of what would be the best thing for us to do.

"Come on, Emmy. I don't want to go in there without you. Come with me, please!" Charlie begged.

I decided it would probably be bad if I went in or stayed out, so it didn't really matter one way or the other, which was like it was most of the time.

"Okay," I said, as I got up, and tucked my book under my arm. I was always very careful about taking care of my books, particularly if they belonged to the library because I didn't want Mrs. Maki to get upset with me and not allow me to check them out anymore, especially after what had happened last year.

Last year I lost one of my library books. I told Mrs. Maki, and she said that it was okay but that I would have to pay for the book. I told her I had no money, and she said I would have to tell my Mama and Daddy to pay for it, so I asked Mama. She told me there was no way she was paying for a book because I had been stupid enough to borrow it from the library and bring it home. Mama said books belonged in the library, and I had no business bringing them home in the first place because they didn't belong to me. Mama never read books the way Daddy did. In fact, I never saw Mama read anything, not even the newspaper. She told me I caused the problem, so I could figure out how to take care of it myself.

I was very worried about what I would tell Mrs. Maki. I didn't want to lie to her, but how could I tell her what Mama had said, and where was I going to get money to pay for the missing book? The next time our class went to the library, I picked out two books, but when I went to check them out, Mrs. Maki said I couldn't check out any more books until I either brought back the book that was missing or my Mama and Daddy paid for it. I was devastated, but I told her I understood.

"You did tell your parents what I said, didn't you Emily," questioned Mrs. Maki.

"Yes, Mrs. Maki. I told my Mama," I answered.

"Good. Tell your Mama the book costs $3.95 to replace, and then let me know next week when she thinks she can get the money to us, but until that time, Emily, I am sorry, but I cannot let you check out any more books. Those are the rules."

"Okay," I muttered, as I turned around to go put the books I had wanted to borrow back on the shelf. On my way back to class I wondered where I was going to get $3.95 from, but then I remembered that Mama gave Charlie and me money every day to buy milk during our afternoon snack time. Not all the kids got to have milk in the afternoon because not all the parents could afford the 20 cents per day that it cost. Mama said Charlie and I were lucky to get the milk and that we had best drink all of it because money does not grow on trees. Mama constantly said this or that did not grow on trees.

If I saved my 20 cents a day I could pay for the book! It would take me awhile, but that was okay. It was better than nothing. Every week when it was library time I could give Mrs. Maki the $1.00 I had saved up. After about a month, I did get it paid for, and I never did find the missing book.

I tried to take good care of the few books that I owned – they were like secret treasures to me – so when we got inside the house, I quickly put my book up on a shelf that Mama had hung in the living room for such things. Mama was bent over the sink in the kitchen, while Daddy was in his usual spot on the couch with his book in his face while rubbing his stinking, black-socked feet together. Mama yelled at Daddy, and Daddy was doing his best to ignore her behind his book. Daddy was probably the reason Mama hated books so much.

"You are just going to ignore me, aren't you?" Mama yelled at Daddy from the kitchen. Daddy did not answer her. "What in the hell is the matter with you? You knew I was coming home, yet it didn't occur to you to maybe clean up the house just a little bit for me? Hell, you didn't even have to do it! All you had to do was tell your two little stinking brats right there to do something around here besides sit on their asses or go ride their bikes!" Mama said pointing at Charlie and me.

Daddy slowly put his book down on his chest and looked in Mama's direction. "It was a lot quieter here when you were gone," he said, and then he picked his book back up.

"Oh, I bet it was, you filthy pig! Your mother must have been a filthy pig, too. Is that where you learned to live like this! You are nothing more than a dirty, filthy animal! Look at this place. It smells like elephant shit in here!" Mama yelled.

Charlie and I stayed close to the door and looked at each other. We were both thinking the same thing: the house looked and smelled exactly the same way it did when Mama left. She must not be used to it anymore because she had spent too much time in the clean smelling hospital. The last time our cousin Margaret was over for a visit she told us that she would never come back because she could no longer stand the smell of the cat pee in the house. She said it made her nose burn. Charlie and I must've been accustomed to it. We could smell it, but it didn't make our noses burn anymore.

"This f'n place doesn't look or smell one bit different from what it did before you went to the hospital you stupid bitch! And, leave my mother out of it! She kept her house clean and didn't collect animals like they were f'n stamps! You want this place cleaner? Then, do it your f'n self! You created this mess, you clean it up," Daddy said.

"I didn't do this by myself, and I can't clean it up. The doctor said I couldn't do any type of serious housework for at least two more weeks and probably three," she said.

"Well, then, I guess your fat ass is just going to have to get used to living here again," Daddy said.

"What in the hell did you come home for? I thought maybe you would actually help me. I must've been out of my mind to think such a thing. What are you doing here? You are a total useless, piece of shit," Mama yelled at Daddy and started to cry. Mama always started to cry when she fought with Daddy. Daddy never cried.

"I'm a useless piece of shit? Who in the hell do you think pays for everything around her, you dumb bitch! I haven't seen one dollar from your big, supposed job pay for one damn bill. I am beginning to wonder if you really work, or are you out doing something else saying you are working?" Daddy accused.

"What in the hell are you talking about?" Mama asked showing immediate concern in her face.

"Why don't you ask your loving sister? She is the one who likes to talk about you behind your back. It sounds to me like the only job you have is being a whore. Who the hell would pay you for it, though? This I got to see. The bastard or bastards can have you. You are such a f'n treat!" Daddy fired back at Mama.

Charlie and I were paying even closer attention now because we knew all about Mama's men. Charlie looked smug and glad that Daddy knew, but he didn't say a word. Neither did I.

Mama looked over at us and said, "Nice of you to talk like this in front of my children."

"Oh, now they are your children? Before they were nothing but stinking brats. Do you really think these kids don't know what goes on around here? It's not like they are babies in diapers anymore," Daddy told her.

"There's nothing going on around here. Why don't you go back to your precious air base and get the hell out of here? We don't need you here," Mama yelled.

"I plan on it! And don't worry; you will still get your allowance check. I know that's all you worry about, you money hungry bitch. I will leave tomorrow if you don't mind. It's too late to leave today," Daddy said.

"Fine, but your dirty ass is not sleeping in my bed," Mama said.

Daddy laughed a very mean sounding laugh, and then he said, "You honestly think I would want to? Whenever I think I have seen you as dumb as you can be, you astound me by saying something that's even dumber than anything you have said before. Is there no end to your idiocy?"

Charlie and I were getting sore necks from changing directions back and forth between the two of them. They were arguing so fast that it was hard to keep up, but it was important that we did. We had to know where we stood in their fights especially if it looked like we were going to be blamed for their fight, which happened a lot. I thought it was going to happen during that fight too, but it seemed like they had kind of forgotten about us. I was relieved, and I was certain Charlie must have felt the same way.

They stopped fighting and did not say another word to each other. Charlie and I went to play checkers. About an hour later, Mama told me to sleep with Charlie because Daddy was sleeping on the couch. I was glad but worried that Daddy would come back there and hurt me, especially after what he had done the night before with Charlie right there in the bed next to me.

When I woke up in the morning, my first thought was that Daddy had not touched me all night long. I was glad. It was one more night that belonged only to me. I was surprised, though, because whenever Mama and Daddy had a fight, Daddy usually hurt me sometime during the middle of the night. To my horror, I wondered if maybe I had slept through it, but then I decided there was no way anybody could sleep through something like that.

Daddy was nowhere to be seen by the time I got out of bed. Charlie was sitting at the kitchen table eating cereal. I sat down next to him and whispered, "Where's Daddy?"

"He left already," Charlie answered.

"Where did he go?" I asked.

"I guess he went back overseas," Charlie said. "He said to say good-bye to you for him and that he would be back right before Christmas."

"Really? Oh. Well, where's Mama?" I asked.

"She drove Daddy to the air base and has not gotten back yet," Charlie explained.

"How long has she been gone?" I asked.

"I don't know...maybe a couple of hours. I was still in bed, but awake, when they left. You were snoring," Charlie said.

"I don't snore," I empathically stated.

"Yes, you do."

"No, I don't."

"Yes, you do."

"No, I don't."

Charlie smiled at me and asked, "Do I snore?"

"Yes," I honestly responded.

"So do you," he said smiling.

"No, I don't," I said smiling back at him.

We heard the dogs barking and looked out the front window to see Mama driving up the driveway. She had a very toothy smile. Bob sat next to her in the front seat. Charlie put his head down and shook it.

"Let's go play with the cars, Emmy," he said.

"Okay," I responded, as Charlie was already heading for the door. "Where are we going to go today?"

"Anywhere, anywhere, but here," he said with an angry tone.

"Okay. Do you want to race?" I asked.

Charlie quickly glanced back at me and grinned. Off he went, on his way to another victory.

About the Author

D R. RITA MAKELA HAS HER DOCTORATE DEGREE IN CLINICAL Psychology. She has spent several years specializing in work with the criminal population including those who are incarcerated. In addition, she has extensive experience working with the sex offender population. She is currently married, has 5 children, and 3 grandchildren. She lives in Northern Minnesota in the woods, and she spends her time loving her family and writing.